Resurrected

The Romani Realms Series

Book Two

by Mia Fox

Resurrected, Book 2, Romani Realms Series by Mia Fox
Published by Evatopia Press
http://www.evatopia.com
8447 Wilshire Blvd., Ste. 401, Beverly Hills, CA 90211
a division of Evatopia, Inc.

ISBN: 978-1-63099-007-7

Cover design by Eden Crane Design
http://www.edencranedesign.com/

Interior book design by Bob Houston eBook Formatting
Bob_Houston@hotmail.com

See other titles by Mia Fox at www.miafox.net.

Stay in touch with Mia Fox
Twitter @MiaFoxBooks
Facebook www.facebook.com/MiaFoxBooks

Dedication

For my parents - Johanna and Bernie

Acknowledgements

I may be "indie," but I'm fortunate to have a small team of people who so kindly offer their help, guidance, and friendship.

Many thanks to...

Jessica Molina Ramirez for being the best P.A. ever. How lucky I am to have found you.

Ginelle Blanch and Gabby Warner, my beta girls. Thank you for your eagle eyes and online promotion.

Lizzy Ford, for your friendship and advice.

Lisa Markson and Leanne Jacobson, FB mavens without a doubt.

Hugs to all of you!

Prologue

*I*t is with much difficulty that I write this note and leave it tucked safely away in my bottle. It awaits the next person who will release me. I suspect that they would want to get to know me and hear about those who I have served. Yet, I'm afraid that my departure from my current Releasors will leave me with a terrible sadness that is sure to permeate my entire being, and result in my not being able to speak about my past for some time to come.

It's apropos that as I write this, the morning fog still settles over Los Angeles, waiting for the sun to break through. It's not unlike my disposition at the moment -- cloudy and tormented, and yet hopeful that the coming days will bring brighter news. It is with a heavy heart that I begin my story...

I had spent centuries avoiding the Romani Realms and yet here I was...willingly about to enter its chasm. I knew what I would find there -- trapped souls and the mysticism that fooled one into believing that evil was actually innocent. Still, I couldn't let those thoughts overwhelm the task at hand. I had to risk everything or I would have nothing.

Just a few short months ago I was released by two seemingly ordinary high school girls, Charlotte and Samantha. Yet, ordinary was never an apt description for them. If the two of them had not possessed hidden talents, then Raven and Phineas, the demon gypsies who had plagued me for centuries, would never have orchestrated such atrocities against them, leading to this moment.

Although Phineas claims he never intended for Samantha to die, he is, after all, aligned with Raven, and therefore his intentions are circumspect. Yet even though I cannot fully trust him, I would be blind to not see the despair in his eyes at discovering that Charlotte succeeded in her quest to enter the Romani Realms to try and resurrect her best friend.

My requirement as a Genie was to serve both of my Releasors until either the third of their unselfish wishes was uttered, or the unthinkable occurred -- their death. The natural bravado of teenagers compelled Charlotte and Samantha to use up their first wish by making me prove myself. It was wasteful on their part and insulting to me, but nonetheless, I did as I was commanded.

We escaped using up the second wish when the girls prayed for each other's safety. If only the outcome had been different. Even James, my Shade who has protected me through the ages, although we only recently became acquainted and... ahem...got to *know each other on a more personal level...couldn't know which girl was in greater danger.*

Perhaps Raven orchestrated the confusion so that the inevitable would occur. Samantha's death. Charlotte's demise. Both gone. Both trapped in another realm.

With our attention divided between the two girls, it was as if we flipped a coin and later discovered that we chose incorrectly. So now, I'm forced to enter the Romani Realms with Raven by my side as the most unlikely of escorts. Each of us leaves someone behind -- for me it's James and for her, Phineas, although whether his loyalties remain with her or have moved on to Charlotte remains to be seen.

Both Raven and I have something to gain by entering the Realms. I am determined to bring Charlotte and Samantha back. She is after the Amulet of Pollox, the source of power that allowed Charlotte to enter the Romani Realms in search of Samantha.

One thing is for certain...whether it is I or Raven who succeeds, one triumph will equal the other's despair. This is the story of our journey.

Yours Truly,
Suki

Chapter One

I looked toward the bed, an iron, four-poster design with ornate scrolls and swirls at the headboard, beautiful by anyone's standards, and yet it didn't compare with the sight of James, more man than any I've known in over three centuries. He was without a doubt, the cherry on top of the sundae. Even though he was a Shade, my protector who watched over me, could read my thoughts, and move throughout time always escaping death, ironically, he still succumbed to slumber after our lovemaking. The melancholy that always hit me afterward struck me stronger than usual. I never liked saying goodbye, when his duties inevitably called him, but this time was different. I would be the one to depart.

I wandered aimlessly through my condo, a high rise in Beverly Hills with a view of the entire city, trying to stay busy by dusting photos and straightening knick-knacks. A picture of Charlotte and Samantha during happier times, their arms wrapped around each other's necks threatened to bring a tear to my eye, but I needed to stay strong and focus on the task at hand. I wouldn't let emotions bring me down because that's what Raven expected of me. She was the demon gypsy who had chased after me for centuries and now, she hoped that I would fail the challenge ahead of me and remain in the Romani Realms for eternity, along with my Releasors.

I shook my head and reached for my bottle. "It's just not going to happen. No siree, not even when cats fly." I said aloud.

"What? No round two?" James' honey smooth voice sounded behind me. I felt the strength of his biceps as his arms wrapped around my waist, and an involuntary chill as his warm breath tickled the back of my neck.

James had a way of making me smile in spite of my darkened mood. "I was giving myself a pep talk," I said still staring at my bottle. "Just reminding myself that I'm not going back into my bottle until I make things right as rain."

He turned me around to face him, and twirled a long brown tendril of my hair around his finger before gently placing it behind my ear. I rested my head against his strong chest and because he was still shirtless, I could easily hear his heartbeat. Any other time, the proximity of him in this state of undress would have led to suggestive banter, but given the circumstances I just inhaled deeply, willing the tears not to fall.

"Come on, Suki," he coaxed. "Be strong."

I straightened up and with resolve, smiled. "Here," I said handing him my azure blue bottle. "I want you to look after this for me."

He took it and traced his finger over the butterfly design, inlaid with colorful, sparkling stones that glistened in the light. "Okay, but it doesn't mean anything other than it will look nice with my decor. You're ready for this, you hear me? You've trained for it and you'll be successful. Nothing to worry about."

I gave him a feeble smile. "I know. It's just a walk in the park."

"That's right. And I'll be waiting on the other side in case you need me, but you won't."

He lifted my chin up, forcing me to stare into his clear, blue eyes. In addition to the fact that James was physical perfection, an air-brushed version of man if there ever was one, there were advantages to being with him beyond running my hands through his mane of wavy brown hair, feeling the hardness of sinewed muscles under my fingertips, and being brought to the height of pleasure. With every intimate moment we spent together our bond to each other grew, making our telepathic connection stronger.

So...about round two? His voice sounded softly and seductively in my head.

I didn't answer, but smiled so he would know that he was heard.

Or are you worried that I'll have you pinned again?

The comment was a reference to the training that I was so fiercely undergoing. In the Romani Realms my powers were likely to be impaired and being physically on top of my game was imperative. Ha, worried! I'll show him what worried means.

With one swift motion I spun around and wrapped my leg around the back of his knee and gave a hard tug. He went down immediately. Score one for me. But James was strong and after all, he was the teacher, so he didn't go down without bringing me toppling on top of him. In spite of my intentions and early victory, round two would be a tie.

He immediately spun me over, pinning me to the ground with his legs straddling me and his hands holding my wrists in place on the floor. As his words had threatened, he had me pinned, his face staring into mine, his mouth close enough to reach with my own and yet, he kept it irritatingly away. I wiggled underneath him to no avail.

"Now what? Little minx?"

I focused my thoughts and ignored James' proximity, putting the fact that he had one leg pressed between mine out of my mind. As if he knew what I planned, he inched his thigh upward, applying light pressure to tempt me even more. Desire started to fill me, but I had my pride.

Nice try. My thoughts reached out to him.

I'm not finished.

Closing my eyes, I inhaled deeply. A slight moan of pleasure escaped my lips as I pressed my hips against him. As James was being led to believe that I was falling for his misguided attempt at a seduction, I unleashed a powerful blast of wind, calling upon the element to distract him. The walls shook and with it, a framed picture fell. Items on my shelf sailed toward us, attempting to assault James into moving off me.

Only it didn't work. I was forgetting that few things concerning me got past James and faking arousal was no exception.

"Uh-uh, no magic. You're fighting like a girl."

"Fine, I've got one last trick up my sleeve," and in one swift motion, I did as I had been trained to do. Although James still had a hand on each of my wrists, I spread my arms wide, forcing his center of gravity to come forward, and then thrust my hips up hard and flipped over on top of him. Now who had the upper hand?

He could easily flip me over again, but with me seated on top of him as if James was my own stead, what would be the point? "So you do remember some Krav Maga moves," he noted appreciatively.

"Oh, I've got moves, Sugar." I ran my hand down James' chest, reveling in the tanned, toned muscles.

In response, his hands gripped my hips and maneuvered them back and forth, just as he liked. This was a time when I didn't mind that James took the round. My worry over the upcoming days' events had dissipated and I leaned forward to kiss him. His hands left my hips to hold my face. Our kiss became more passionate and this time, the sound that escaped my lips was in no means fabricated. Pure desire scorched through me, and as always, James knew just what I needed.

"You're feeling better?" he asked throwing me a top that had landed behind the sofa, and sadly covering his torso with one of his own.

"Much. Thank you. You have a remarkable talent for getting my mind off my troubles."

He wrapped his arms around my waist, easily encircling it, and pulled me in for a quick kiss. "I aim to please."

"Enough of that. A girl can't survive on kisses alone. Aren't you going to feed me?"

"I've already instructed the chef to have your favorite soupe à l'oignon ready."

"Such a light meal...are you trying to tell me something?"

James let his eyes roam over me. "You should know by now that you are perfection. The light meal is only the prelude to café gourmand."

"Coffee? That's it? I'm starving."

"You are the doubting Thomas today. I thought I took care of that," he said nuzzling my neck. "It's what goes with the coffee. I'm referring to an array of bite-sized desserts. In your case, the chef has prepared three miniature puddings: a mini triangle of flourless chocolate cake, an eggcup-sized crème brûlée, and a clafoutis. So, shall we head downstairs?"

I nodded and followed James out of my condo and into the waiting elevator that would take us to my building's lobby where a discreet door leading to the bar and restaurant that James owned was located. Maison 360 was designed like a 1920s speakeasy with dark paneling, plenty of cozy corners, and best yet, delicacies from around the world that weren't easy to come by and yet, James always managed to locate them as evidence by the description of what awaited me. Time travel had its advantages.

But as we walked into the bar, my appetite was suddenly stunted with the sight of Phineas sitting in my favorite seat with two leggy blondes on either side of him. They looked to be about twenty-one with the sexual confidence of cougars as evidence by the fact that one had her hand on Phineas' upper thigh and the other had a arm around his neck. He whispered into each of their ears, and they immediately left.

I thought about turning and leaving as well, but without even a glance in our direction, he spoke. "It's about time."

"I see that you're not suffering from loneliness with Charlotte gone," I seethed.

"I don't even know them. They just...made themselves at home," Phineas shrugged.

He was as handsome as ever so it was easy to see why he wouldn't be alone at a bar, but still the sight of him with a girl other than sweet, seventeen-year-old Charlotte, when I knew how she had fallen for him and what the result of that infatuation had been for her, made me shake with anger.

"And you just couldn't bring yourself to ask them to leave?"

"Suzette, everyone has their own ways of handling grief."

My mouth dropped open with the implication of his words. Samantha had lost her life and Charlotte may have thrown hers away and for what? The mistake of falling for the wrong guy.

"What are you doing here?" I didn't attempt to hide the hostility in my voice. "I've been waiting for over an hour. You two sure go at it."

"Eww, you were listening to us? Wait a minute, you weren't perched outside the window watching?" I said suddenly lunging for him.

Running a hand, from his head to toe, he indicated his human form with a flourish. "I'm all man."

James shook his head, looking disgusted at the comment. Although truth be told, Phineas was gorgeous by any girl's standards. His looks were more pretty boy than James' rugged manly appeal. Phineas never seemed to have a hair out of place. His light brown locks had highlights of blond and dipped just over his green eyes. His jaw line was strong, but smooth unlike the stubble that graced James' sexy features, and his high cheek bones gave him a model's good looks. In fact, he looked like he belonged on the beaches of Malibu, posing for the latest Volcom or Quick Silver ad. Although he was a definite looker, he wasn't James, who coursed with testosterone, but I was biased. It was impossible for me to overlook Phineas' past treachery, even if he swore it was at the insistence of Raven.

James held me back, yet still shot Phineas a warning look. "You didn't answer Suki's question."

"What you see is what you get. I haven't shifted into bird form for a week. That doesn't mean I'm immune to your thoughts. You're connected to Charlotte and Samantha, and whether you believe it or not, I still love Charlotte and she was in love with me. It means that our mutual connection to her, gives each of us insight to each other. You see, Suzette, we're practically relatives. Besides, you guys are loud."

"Oh don't be gross." I had forgotten all semblance of Southern gentility and tried to wring my hands around his neck, but James reached an arm around my waist and held me in place by his side.

"Come on now," James spoke in a soothing voice. "He can't help that he's an untrustworthy ass. He's an abomination that is neither human nor supernatural. What can you expect of something that is created with dark magic? He's not worth your energy."

"That's ripe coming from you, James. You're king of the reincarnations. Been down to Atlanta lately to see Maebeline? I expect that she's always willing to bring you back to life with a quick spell or potion. What I can't wrap my head around is why you would be willing for Suzette to go into the Romani Realms alone."

"Phineas, you don't know anything about it."

"And you don't know what Raven is capable of down there. You think what she does here is bad? In the Romani Realms she can harness the power of any demon gypsy who has gone before her. You won't survive it, Suzette."

"Don't you think I want to go with her?" James spouted back. It was the first time I had seen his anger take hold. "She will survive, but not if you put those negative thoughts into her head."

"Ahh, right. Positive affirmations are going to save the genie from a gang of gypsy demons gunning for her."

James looked ready to tear Phineas' head off and I knew it was time for me to remember the manner in which I was brought up.

"Please, you two...we're in a public place. Let's put aside our differences...for Charlotte's sake. If what you say about your feelings for her is true, then certainly you can agree to that, Phineas."

He ran a hand through his hair and paced to the other side of the room, calming himself. James went behind his bar and poured himself a drink. By the time he had put one back, Phineas had returned and extended his hand to James.

"I want her back safely. That's all I want."

James looked to me and I nodded my assent. With that, James accepted Phineas' hand and the two shook. A customer at the other end of the bar flagged James down and even though he hadn't meant to work, he took the opportunity to further cool down.

Phineas turned his attention to me then. "I didn't mean to upset you, Suzette, but surely you must know how dangerous it's going to be for you. Why doesn't James go with you?"

"He can't, and it's my decision."

"But why?"

"Samantha is dead and Charlotte has gone to bring her back. And from where? I don't even know if one can come back from the Romani Realms. Certainly Charlotte should never have entered them and I can't have James going there too. It's too much on my conscience."

Phineas grew quiet and looked across the bar into the massive mirror that hung behind it. I met his gaze in the mirror and instantly regretted what I had said.

"It was supposed to be me," he said quietly.

"Phineas..."

I couldn't pretend that I liked the guy. I wasn't even sure that I trusted him or knew for sure that he hadn't contributed to Samantha's death, but I couldn't deny that Charlotte had loved him and he did seem torn up over her.

"I meant to go into the Realms the day of Samantha's funeral, but Charlotte was so impulsive...and so smart. I never would have thought a human could pull something like that off."

I smiled, a feeling of pride over Charlotte coming to me. "She's amazing. And maybe, just maybe she'll pull it off."

"But you're still going to try this alone?"

"My best chance of returning with them is by having James remain here to pull me back. He and Maebeline have brought each other back from the dead more times than should be possible for even a supernatural. If I'm going to gamble with my life, I'm betting on him to save me."

Phineas just nodded to himself, appearing deep in thought. Finally, he spoke. "You know why I'm here?"

"I'm assuming because this is the only place in the city where Raven can't hear our thoughts. Dating a Shade has its advantages. James has extended the protective field that surrounds my condo to the whole building." I leaned back in my chair and noticed James eyeing me from down the bar where he was mixing a cocktail. "Besides, the food here is to die for."

"I didn't come for the food," Phineas said, taking a long drink from a short glass, downing the clear liquid and then grimacing before continuing. "I want to go into the Romani Realms as well. I know she loves me and I can convince her to come back."

I laughed aloud. The thought was preposterous. "You are even more delusional than Raven if you think I'm going to willingly go into the Realms with both of you. You might say that you have Charlotte's best interests at heart, which by the way, I'm not totally convinced of yet, but sending you in there is craziness. Even if you wanted to bring Charlotte back, the chances of Raven convincing you to do otherwise and then using your powers against her are too tempting down there."

"I've convinced Raven that I was devoted to her before, even when my heart belonged to Charlotte."

"And she fooled you," I said simply. "Raven's powers far exceed yours and she can manipulate and control you. It's too much of a risk. Besides, you're assuming that Charlotte would choose a life with you over her friendship with Samantha? She already established her loyalties when she left after the funeral."

With that stinging comment, Phineas waved to a bartender on duty, indicating his desire for another round. James, always with a watchful eye where I'm concerned, came over instead. "Haven't you had enough?"

"Just give me another, James."

James rolled his eyes and seemed to weigh out the advantages of having Phineas where he could keep an eye on him versus sending him back to Raven where he could end up plotting against me. James' eyes met mine and I merely shrugged my shoulders, an acceptance that Phineas had become our drinking partner for the time being, although it was barely even lunch time.

"The same?" James asked.

"Nah, tequila shot."

"You're not going get sick in my bar by switching from vodka to tequila."

"Of course not. It's physically impossible for me."

"You can still feel some affects of it," James pointed out.

"Just fill the glass...dad," Phineas said with annoyance.

"You're older than I am, you crazy demon," James said as he filled a shot glass with amber liquid, and muttered under his breath, "even if you don't look it, jerk."

Phineas immediately downed it. "Being older and looking older are two different things. Going supernatural at a young age has certain advantages."

James rolled his eyes and seemed relieved to be summoned to the other end of the bar. "You don't mind if I leave you alone with your asinine thoughts?"

But upon returning James seemed more annoyed than when he left. He poured another shot and lined it up next to the existing one. "Courtesy of the young ladies at the end of the bar."

"Ha! Told you old man," Phineas beamed, and toasted a thank you to the girls who had sent over the drink.

Given the choice between Phineas' youthful appearance, for all intents and purposes, a 20-something year old with a sexy arrogance or James' rugged appearance, the strong jawline that seemed to always have a perpetual bit of scruff, his physique broader than Phineas', I'd choose James. Yet, throughout the hour that we had been seated at the bar, more than one young woman had sidled up to Phineas, his looks more eye-catching because of his supernatural turning, and I might add *superficial* beauty bestowed upon demon gypsies. Phineas may have been drool-worthy, but James, whose blue eyes could undress my every thought, was all man. More than one young woman had given me dirty looks because of my proximity to both. If they only knew that this was hardly a social gathering.

Phineas nodded toward his empty shot glass indicating he wanted another.

"So are we going to drink all afternoon?" I asked, addressing Phineas for the first time in half an hour.

He quickly drained his last shot, and turned on his barstool to face me. "What if I went back to 1850s England while you went into the Romani Realms?"

"I thought you said you couldn't get drunk."

"I'm serious, Suzette...as well as sober."

"You're not going anywhere near that office with its time travel formulas. That's what caused this situation. If you hadn't taken Charlotte there in the first place..." James' voice rose slightly.

"Wait," I interrupted. "He might have a point."

You can't trust him. James said in my head, his voice sounding angry.

"Maybe we have to try?" I tested my ability to answer back, but my response came out aloud.

"Looky there," Phineas said with amusement. "The love birds have a new trick. You can hear him whisper sweet nothings to you?"

"Watch it," James warned.

Phineas put up his hands in mock submission, and imitated talking back with a silent gesture of his mouth and eyes rolling.

"That's real mature," James noted with annoyance. "You see?" he said in my direction.

"James, we can use all the help we can get."

James walked in the opposite direction and no sooner turned back around, frustrated with the situation as well as with me. "How can you even consider trusting him after...after Samantha died and Charlotte...jeez, the whole mess?"

In spite of being warned against Phineas' allegiance to Raven, Charlotte fell hard for him and even traveled back in time with him. Talk about an extravagant first date. Unfortunately, this one didn't end well. Raven distorted the reality of their return into this realm. Whether Phineas knew what Raven was doing was unclear, but one thing was for certain, Charlotte should never have gone back with him. It gave her access to the Amulet of Pollox, the stone that holds the memories of the greatest minds that I have had the privilege of serving.

Phineas seemed equally distraught and as angry as James. "Charlotte was an emotional wreck after Samantha died. You saw her, Suzette. She was capable of...you know."

I nodded, knowing what Phineas was implying. Charlotte lost her best friend and blamed herself for the accident. She would have taken her own life as retribution, but found what she considered a solution, albeit an extremely dangerous one.

While Charlotte and Phineas were returning from the past realm, Samantha was also prone to Raven's influence. It was child's play for Raven. She simply allowed Samantha to see Phineas and Charlotte returning from 1850s London, and while no harm was coming to Charlotte, in order to return to the present she and Phineas had to run through the wormhole, throughout time, appearing as if they were running for their very lives.

The image Samantha saw seemed desperate and I responded to her totally unselfish prayer. Although she never uttered a wish, I ensured Charlotte's safety over her own. This unselfish plea would be her dying request for it allowed Raven to distort Samantha's reality to the degree that she didn't see the traffic of Pacific Coast Highway careening toward her, or herself about to plummet over the massive bluffs to her death.

"James," I said gently placing my hand over his, "I'm going into the Romani Realms -- tonight. I don't want to remember our last hours together as having had an argument."

James stared intently at me, and without warning placed his hand on the bar and catapulted himself over it as if it were the height of a child's step stool. His look was dangerous, direct and yet, I was frozen in place. But when he reached me, he simply took me in his arms and I melted into them. "You mean the world to me."

He took his hand and lifted my chin so my head tilted upwards and then his lips were on mine. Tender at first, with just soft kisses around my mouth, but the passion immediately overtook us and his tongue found mine. My hands weaved into his wavy brown hair and stayed in place so that his kiss wouldn't end. James didn't disappoint. His mouth left mine only to trace kisses down my neck, until his head reached my collarbone and he got a hold of himself.

He pulled himself up to his full six feet, pressed his forehead to mine and whispered into my hair, so only I could hear. "You just focus on coming back."

I nodded silently, afraid that if I opened my mouth to respond, the tears would flow and although, I wanted to trust Phineas, I sure as anything wasn't going to let him see me get emotional -- vulnerable.

James released his hold on me. When we stepped away from each other, we noticed a bit awkwardly that Phineas was staring at us, more bored than interested.

"You guys should really get a room."

James jumped to attention and once again tried to grab Phineas, but I put myself between the two of them. "Not now, you two...Let's focus on what we do know about how Charlotte got into the Romani Realms."

Overcome with grief about Samantha's death and the guilt that she was inadvertently the cause due to having gone to the past willingly with Phineas, Charlotte harnessed her new powers accumulated from the Amulet of Pollox and figured out a way to get into the Romani Realms, much in the way that Phineas had taken her into the past.

"I think she knows about a logarithm created by Charles Babbage," Phineas spoke up.

"Why him?" James asked.

"I worked for him and we were in my old office before Samantha's death."

"Oh now he tells us," James rolled his eyes, and then turned to me, "He's unbelievable."

"Thank you, I've been told that before."

I elbowed Phineas, "It wasn't a compliment!"

"Hey, that hurt," Phineas looked at me surprised, but James put a protective arm around me and smirked.

"Spill it," I said.

Phineas took a moment, but then told us about Charles Babbage, his former boss and the man who created the first computer, along with a logarithm that would later be used for time travel. Reaching for a cocktail napkin, he wrote down some formulas that looked more like chicken scratch than algebra, but then he explained the complex formula.

"When I worked for Charles Babbage the world was on the cusp of so many discoveries. The industrial revolution poured money into the city and he was at the heart of it. His logarithmic differentiation...these complicated formulas," he said tapping the paper, "were used to determine and analyze different functions. When applied to time travel, they made it easier to differentiate the logarithm of a function rather than the function itself."

"What does that mean in English?" I asked staring at his writings.

"In simple terms, this meant that Charlotte was able to break down a formula and see its separate parts, thus letting her figure out exactly what was necessary to do for her to physically jump dimensions."

"How would a seventeen-year-old human figure this out?" James asked indicating the napkin and Phineas' drawings.

I spoke up, both proud and wistful. "Charlotte has an eidetic memory. Anything she saw or heard -- both images and sounds -- was implanted in her brain."

Phineas continued, "I can go back to my old office and see how the logarithm works in reverse."

"But wouldn't Charlotte be able to figure that out?" James asked.

"It wasn't written in reverse so she never saw it. Are you willing to leave it up to chance that she can just 'figure it out'?"

I looked away from both of them, realizing that Phineas was right, but certainly not wanting to take his side in front of James. It wouldn't bid well with him for numerous reasons, least of all being the fact that women, including Charlotte, found Phineas irresistible. I wouldn't want to outright agree and have James' feathers get ruffled. Although his argument certainly had merits.

"I never thought she would use the information...to do this," Phineas said grimly. "I need to get her."

"Like hell you do." The edge in James' voice was as sharp as his words. "We told you, if you think we're going to allow you and Raven to be down there...with Charlotte, Suki, and God willing, Samantha, you're a crazier bastard than I ever thought you were."

"Easy," I said placing a hand on James' arm, before turning to Phineas. "What he means is that if you're in the Romani Realms with Raven, your bond to her will take precedence over everything else. Your perceptions will be altered and you may not even want to help Charlotte." I paused, finding the strength to say what had to be noted. "You might try to keep her there indefinitely with Samantha, which is what Raven hoped when she orchestrated this."

Phineas ran a hand through his sandy-colored hair, his green eyes taking on a worried look. "Then let me help by way of the past. While Suki is in the Romani Realms, I'll go back to the Industrial Revolution. If I know Raven, she'll try anything to stop her from returning to the present, including going to the past to destroy any of the data created by Charles."

For the first time, James seemed to approve of Phineas. "It's not a bad idea," he said putting a protective arm around me. "And you've got Maebeline and I to make sure nothing goes wrong."

A wry smile crossed my lips. "So with you as my Shade and Phineas as our honorary, demon gypsy friend, nothing can go wrong?"

Phineas put out his hand first. James took it and I placed mine on top of both.

"We work together and get Charlotte out," Phineas said.

"And Samantha...if she's alive," I added. "Once I'm there, at least my connection to them will allow me to see what's happening...even if I'm not physically near them."

James left us to retrieve three shot glasses from the bar, which he filled with amber liquid. He passed one to each of us, "To Charlotte and Samantha" he said raising his glass.

Phineas and I clinked our glasses together and repeated the sentiment: "To Charlotte and Samantha."

Chapter Two

Charlotte arrived in the Romani Realms as if she were meant for time travel. She found herself lying on her side in an open pasture. Taking just a moment to look up at the clear blue sky, she took a deep breath and like a baby fawn taking its first steps, adjusted to the changes her body had just gone through in a matter of moments. Passing through time with Phineas had taught her that the wind would be knocked out of her, but it was temporary and she had no time to baby herself.

Rising to her feet, Charlotte started across the meadow, surprised by the utter beauty of her surroundings. The expanse of grass was a green blanket that covered as far as she could see. The soft blades were evenly cut, perfectly manicured although not a person was in sight. Surrounding the outer edges of the meadow, for what seemed like acres into the distance, was a wall of Sycamore trees. The weather was pleasant with a light breeze in the air and the sun provided just enough warmth to feel like a comforting hug. Charlotte actually smiled to herself, enjoying her surroundings as she took her time crossing the expansive meadow, following a trail of monarchs that flitted to and fro.

The breeze grew slightly more forceful, but not enough to lead Charlotte to believe that she should turn back the way she had come. She still walked as if enjoying a Sunday outing, stopping to pluck a wild flower from the ground, staring with wonder at a deer standing just a few feet away, daring to meet her gaze before bounding off toward the trees. Her eyes followed the direction in which it departed and she was delighted to see cotton-tailed rabbits nibbling on yellow flowers and then scattering as she neared. Only the breeze hinted that the beauty around her was fleeting as darkened clouds rose up in the distance.

Be careful. I could sense her. I knew she was alive. But fear still gripped me and would continue to do so until I could be by her side. *Please, Charlotte. Take care.*

As she continued to cross the wide expanse of the meadow, the rustling of the wind sounded vaguely like children's laughter, normally a pleasant sound, but as there was nobody around, it was disconcerting. She was alone, but the desire to find the children that she was so positive she could hear became so suddenly overwhelming that Charlotte began to run toward the trees with all memory of enjoying a casual afternoon stroll now forgotten.

"Why are you running?"

The voice came out of nowhere and surprised Charlotte so much that she stumbled and fell, the blades of grass suddenly longer and nearly completely hiding her frame from view. Charlotte recovered and looked around, but saw nobody.

The laughter, now distinctly mischievous, returned on the wind.

"I'm right here," a child's voice sounded.

Charlotte sat very still, instinctively on guard. It seemed silly to worry. After all, she merely tumbled while running across a beautiful meadow, enjoying the beauty of nature on a spring day. Nonetheless, she sat with her knees pulled up to her chest, her arms hugging her legs, her eyes darting around to see if what she heard was real or imagined.

"Over heeere," the voice came to her, now tinged with annoyance. And then, just a matter of a few feet away from where Charlotte sat, a small girl of perhaps eight or maybe nine, suddenly sat up.

Charlotte's breath caught at now seeing the girl sitting nearly within reach of herself. The grass must have hidden her small frame from view just seconds earlier.

"It's fun to watch people from in here." The girl opened her arms to the meadow, and although she smiled sweetly, there was something in her eyes that reminded Charlotte of a naughty child she once babysat. She remembered how her ward would smile at her mother, promising to be good for Charlotte and the second her mother would leave the house, the girl would make Charlotte's evening a living hell with non-stop demands and spoiled antics.

"Ha, that's a good idea," the girl said.

"What?" Charlotte asked, finding her voice for the first time.

"That story you just told. About the girl? Duh."

The child suddenly turned her dark eyes away from Charlotte to stare at something in the distance -- something Charlotte couldn't see.

They sat in silence. Charlotte cautiously watching the girl, whose eyes were now a pale blue, continued to stare at the trees that lined the meadow with a foreboding look. Suddenly, she whipped her head back toward Charlotte, her blonde hair, which was the same shade as Charlotte's only it hung in curls as opposed to Charlotte's stick straight locks, swinging around her face. "You won't be able to see what I see unless you come closer."

"That's okay. I'm good here."

Good girl. Relief washed over me.

Charlotte averted her eyes and tried to busy herself by attempting to weave small blades of grass together, picking the ones with miniature daisies and telling herself that nothing was amiss. She was just enjoying nature, letting the gentle breeze blow through her hair. Everything was fine.

"Ick, why are you playing with those things? Charlotte, put those down!"

Charlotte met the girl's eyes, shocked at hearing her own name. Even more frightening to her was that the voice of the girl had suddenly sounded much like that of Charlotte's mother. How she missed her parents, long ago having died in a car accident. But why did her mother's voice sound angry?

The girl's demeanor changed with the wind and now she simply delivered Charlotte a sweet smile and pointed to the daisies that Charlotte had collected and dropped in the folds of her skirt. When Charlotte glanced down, she saw a pile of worms, long and skinny, red bodies wriggling on top of each other. She jumped up immediately with a scream, shaking out her skirt.

The girl jumped as well and came to Charlotte, placing her arms around her and staring up into Charlotte's horrified face. "What's wrong? You look so scared. Here, have a pretty flower. You seem to like them," she said and bent down to where Charlotte had dumped the worms on the ground.

"No!" Charlotte shouted.

The girl held out her hands, indicating that Charlotte should calm down and pointed to the ground. Charlotte followed her gaze and saw only a bunch of fragrant flowers by her feet. She looked back to the girl, who held out what she had picked up off the ground -- a daisy, which the girl now placed behind one ear. "Pretty, aren't they?"

Charlotte didn't answer, but instead turned the opposite direction and started to walk away. Until she heard the girl start to sob. "Please don't go. Look, I'm hurt."

She lies, Charlotte! But my thoughts were only unto myself.

The voice had manipulated back into that of a small girl and it did indeed sound sad. In spite of wanting to run, Charlotte turned back toward the girl, who was sitting in the same position Charlotte had been when she first happened upon her. The girl's knees were pulled up to her chest. She stared forlornly down at her legs. "See? It really hurts."

For the first time, Charlotte noticed the scratches and welts across the girl's legs. Angry red lines like the worms, Charlotte thought to herself. "There are no worms," the girl called out, again able to read her thoughts. Please help me get to *the other side*," she indicated the trees at the opposite end of the meadow, and then looked up at the sky now distinctly darker than when Charlotte had arrived.

Charlotte continued to stand over the girl, not saying a word, not moving a muscle, until the girl started to really sob.

"Alright, it's okay," Charlotte spoke in a quiet voice and leaned down. She awkwardly pet the girl's head and then gently stroked her hair until the child stopped crying.

"Thank you, Charlotte."

"How do you know my name?"

The girl cocked her head to the side, rolled her eyes skyward, and gave Charlotte a look that could only be read as 'you've got to be kidding me' when the sound of other children laughing erupted in the air around them. The girl held her hands up like a conductor readying a band. The laughter stopped and only the sound of leaves rustling through the distant trees could be heard.

"I don't know how I know. But it's a pretty name." The girl put her arms around Charlotte's waist and rested her head against Charlotte's stomach.

Awkwardly, Charlotte placed her own arms around the girl and they stood in this mock hug for a moment until the girl finally broke free, now full of smiles again. "I don't know my name, but you can call me Shadow."

A chill ran up Charlotte's body as she looked in the girl's face, taking in her features -- ice blue eyes, fair skin, blonde hair so light it was practically white -- characteristics very much akin to Charlotte's own.

"Do you want to hear a story?"

Before any sort of answer could be uttered, Shadow took Charlotte's hand and just as suddenly, all feeling of dread and worry within Charlotte dissipated. She saw Phineas in her mind, smiling at her. She felt his strong arms around her and remembered that she felt surprisingly safe while she traveled through time with him. *Trust him.* The words assaulted Charlotte's mind, jarring her out of the daydream. They were not my thoughts...they came from the Romani Realms. She had trusted Phineas. Not only with her life, but with Samantha's as well. Falling for him resulted in her forsaking any warning that Samantha had uttered against him. And now, this entire trip into the Romani Realms, the place created by demon gypsies to hold souls captive, was due to Raven's treachery and it was entirely possible that Phineas was involved.

"Did you like it?"

"What?" Charlotte asked in a daze.

"The story! Didn't you see it? About that man and your friend?"

Charlotte nodded mechanically. Her eyes slightly glazed over, her breathing shallow.

"You must be tired now." Shadow pulled on Charlotte's hand, indicating she should sit.

Charlotte laid down and stared up at the sky, not taking any notice that it was now dark and threatening. "How old are you, Shadow?"

The girl paused for a moment as if trying to weigh up the correct answer. She furrowed her brow and performed calculations on her fingers, and then replied simply, "Eight."

Charlotte smiled. Just as the beautiful daisies turned to worms and then back again to flowers, Charlotte's emotions vacillated from fear of this little girl to a fierce desire to care for her. She felt incredible peace as she closed her eyes.

Shadow sat down next to Charlotte and kept watch. The edges of the grassy meadow were starting to shift, the grass turning from vibrant green to a dry brown. As the breeze turned cold and stronger, the grass continued to dry up until the edges of the meadow were receding into a black, charred brush as if a forest fire was working its way from the outside in, moving closer to where Charlotte rested.

"It's time to go, Charlotte." Shadow stood up and pulled on Charlotte's arm.

"Just a few more minutes, please."

As much as I hated to admit it, the girl was right. *Listen to her, Charlotte.*

Looking out into the distance, Shadow could now see at least a quarter mile circumference of the meadow was now barren wasteland, the grass either dead or dying. Large pools of blackness, like pits of tar, started to spread closer to where Charlotte lay...oblivious to the changes around her.

The most disturbing of these was the emergence of mud covered hands and arms reaching out from the tar. The grass continued to die causing the meadow to recede at an accelerated pace. Black twigs now replaced every blade of grass with Charlotte and Shadow positioned on the only bit that still remained green.

A clawed hand reached up out of the tarry mud and grabbed around Shadow's ankle, scratching a trail up her leg. The little girl stared impassively at the soul that was desperately trying to catch its breath, its face contorted in anguish as it tried to pull itself out of the abyss. The little girl merely shook her leg free as if kicking away a sand flea.

"Charlotte, I'd like to leave this place now. Let's go for a walk."

Charlotte stretched her arms over her head, narrowly missing being grabbed by another one of the lost souls.

"Okay," she answered sleepily and pulled herself up to standing. "This place really is beautiful." She looked out at the distant forest, not seeing any of the changes that had occurred to her surroundings.

Shadow followed Charlotte's gaze, only her vision showed that the acres of meadow were covered by pools of tar, hands and arms protruding up around them at every step.

The little girl nodded in agreement.

Charlotte held out her hand, and when the little girl placed her own hand inside hers, Charlotte felt peace and walked with her toward the darkened forest.

Chapter Three

The most direct route to a destination is a straight line; and therefore, as I prepared to enter the Romani Realms, James and Phineas waited with me at the place where we last saw Charlotte -- Samantha's gravestone. That is, before she surprised all of us and entered the Realms alone, armed only with the knowledge she gained from her possession of the Amulet of Pollox, the stone that gave her knowledge of the greatest minds from the past. Even I couldn't simply enter the Romani Realms. I would need a guide, someone who had been there before and knew how to manipulate time to get there again. There was only one person who could get into the Romani Realms and still have the freedom to leave at will. Ironically, it was the same person who caused us so much strife. Raven.

"I felt the danger approaching Charlotte. She needs me. I'll find her and bring her back," I said more to calm my own nerves than to explain an obvious situation.

James reached out to touch my arm. "When you do find her...she may be different. The time travel, the opposing realms..."

I nodded, understanding his message. I had taken Charlotte and Samantha into another realm dimension once before. Without ever leaving the safety of my penthouse, the images of the past became so real that even our clothing seemed to change. The grinding of the time gears surrounded us and although we remained physically planted in the present, our minds traveled far back in time. We had seemingly gone back to London of the 19th century to meet a soothsayer. Madame Ruby showed Charlotte and Samantha the truth that their minds were closed off to, allowing Charlotte to see the destruction that Raven had wielded against innocents, while Phineas looked the other way and stood by her side. In my book, that meant he was equal in blame.

But the Romani Realms were different. There, nothing was as it appeared to be.

Sensing my growing nerves and resentment toward him, Phineas spoke, although his voice was barely above a whisper. "Maybe she won't show. It's not like she wants to help you. She's got both Charlotte and Samantha."

"But she doesn't have Suki," James said gravely.

"Yeah, somehow I doubt she'd give up the chance to get rid of me once and for all."

James wrapped his arms around my waist and turned me toward him. I rested my head against his chest, inhaled his scent, and felt myself relax. I closed my eyes and reveled in the safety I felt while in his arms, knowing that I would need to recall these sensory pleasures when under distress.

"Come on, now," James said suddenly as if knowing that my emotions were threatening to come tumbling out of me. "Tell me the most extraordinary thing about Charlotte and Samantha."

I chuckled lightly, knowing that there wasn't just one tale to tell. "They are extraordinary...exceptional. Appearing like ordinary high school girls, more interested in boys than school, and full of teenage bravado. But it didn't take long to realize that they were meant to release me because each one possessed a special trait -- something far beyond the ordinary."

The three of us stood silent as if each offering tribute to Charlotte and Samantha. Samantha had developed the rare talent for being able to sense a person's true nature, to innately recognize whether someone is of pure intention. The power doesn't come into play often, but when it does, it's a force not to be toyed with for it becomes all-consuming. Samantha's loyalty to Charlotte and her unselfish nature made her a perfect Releasor.

"Samantha never wished for anything to benefit solely herself. Instead, her last thought was to bring Charlotte to safety."

"I didn't mean for this to happen to Charlotte," Phineas said to me.

"I didn't say that," I answered a bit more coldly than I had intended. In my heart I knew that Raven would have kept attacking the girls until she achieved their demise, and yet having Charlotte fall for Phineas seemed to make it that much easier for her. I couldn't help wondering and wishing what would have been had he never shown up.

Samantha didn't trust him and I tended to agree. After all, Phineas had been given second life and turned into a demon gypsy from Raven's powers. I knew that trusting him was a precarious state to be in, as it was unlikely his loyalties would shift away from Raven, and yet, here we were.

"Go on," James urged, silently, speaking directly into my mind. In the last few days, he was speaking into my mind more frequently, insisting that we practice our non-verbal communication so that I could hear him once in the other realms. As my Shade, he was the only one able to get inside my head. At first it was a bit disconcerting, especially when he teased me, but now it offered comfort. *"Talk about Charlotte...the happier times,"* I heard him, although his voice was barely above a whisper on the wind. It worried me because I knew that if it were this quiet while I was right next to him, I may not be able to hear him at all once in the Romani Realms.

I shook my head, berating myself for my proper Southern values that had kept me from becoming intimate with James sooner. Eventually I succumbed to his charms, and I wasn't the least bit disappointed, but I had fought the urge for so long that it didn't give us much time together before we were to be forced apart and the only way for a Shade to really get inside a Genie's head was to get into her heart first. There was still a part of me that was closed up to that sort of intimacy because I knew that my time with him was fleeting. Eventually, something would cause Charlotte and Samantha to use up their last wish and I would be returned to my bottle.

With both of them trapped inside the Romani Realms there was a high likelihood that they would need their remaining wishes. Samantha was basically dead in this present realm, while Charlotte would perhaps be caught in between forever. I couldn't fault either if they were to use their wishes. Regardless of how much James meant to me, I loved the girls as well and without a second thought, I would go back to being locked within my bottle if it meant giving them the life they had lived before.

"Talk to us," James said, this time aloud, as if sensing that I was pulling away before even leaving. "Tell us about Charlotte."

I thought of Charlotte's striking Nordic looks. "You know what is the most remarkable thing about Charlotte? It's not anything as superficial as her beauty. It's her nature -- so sweet and trusting. And that memory of hers doesn't miss a thing...any comment, observation, smell or sound -- she was special even before she got a hold of the Amulet of Pollox. It makes sense that she was the one to find it. I can't think of anyone else who could put it to better use than someone with eidetic memory."

Phineas shifted uneasily. It was that damned stone that had inadvertently been at the center of this debacle. Raven had been after the source of the power that would be gifted to one very special Releasor. Although she searched for it for centuries, it wasn't until Charlotte had gone back in time with none other than Phineas when it was discovered. Waiting patiently as if it had a life of its own, the stone beckoned to her and when she came into possession of it, her already remarkable memory grew tenfold for now she held the memories of every Releasor of my past.

I smiled, thinking of Charlotte's modesty. She used to think her gift was evidence of her being a nerd, complaining that she would rather have perfect fashion sense than a perfect memory of school lectures. In reality, her trademark jeans and tees made her beauty shine even more because the simplicity with how she dressed made one take notice of her amazing features. And as for that remarkable mind of hers, she only discovered her gift quite by accident having never made a connection between her perfect grades and her special talent. She had chalked up her exemplary school record to a slow social life, but when traveling to the past with Phineas, she stumbled upon the logarithms and remarkably remembered them, allowing her to transport herself to the Romani Realms in the hopes of bringing back Samantha.

"Mourning a loved one's death can bring about dramatic changes in a person. In Charlotte's case, she became a young woman with a solitary mission: to right a wrong that she felt responsible for," I said looking directly at Phineas.

He nodded, feeling the sting behind my words.

"In the end, she left me too," Phineas pointed out.

As if punctuating his sentiment, an enormous black bird circled close to Phineas, nearly dive bombing his head, but choosing to land just behind us instead. Given its erratic flight just seconds earlier, we turned to stare at it and then watched as it shifted into the form of Raven.

"Feeling sorry for ourselves? You'll have a lot more time for that."

She wore her familiar gloat, along with black and tan riding pants, boots, and a black fitted top. The form-fitting outfit accentuated her lean frame, more muscular than thin. She tossed her hair over her shoulder, the shiny black locks looking like melted tar. Her dark eyes were framed with caterpillar lashes and shined with the knowledge that she had the upper hand.

Raven ran a hand over the top of Samantha's headstone and although it was just stone, her action somehow felt like an invasion, particularly since she was responsible for her death.

She stretched her arms out widely and emulated the movement she took while in bird form. Smiling up to the heavens she menacingly spoke, "Ahh, two birds killed with one stone. Gosh, don't you love the analogy?"

"Stop it, Raven," Phineas spoke up, although it was in a hushed tone for he wasn't accustomed to crossing her.

She turned and walked just inches in front of him and caressed his cheek with the same hand that had been toying with Samantha's grave. "Don't worry, dear Phin. Everything will be back to normal soon."

He shook his head. "Charlotte going into the Romani Realms should never have happened. Even you can't be that cruel to send someone who is alive and vibrant....there."

"He's right," I spoke up. "You've cut off your nose to spite your face -- with Charlotte gone, you've lost the Amulet of Pollox." In spite of the bravado of my words, Raven managed to make me feel insignificant with just one glance in my direction.

I compared my own outfit with hers. I was wearing a spaghetti-strapped, white summer dress that fell just above my knees with a pair of brown cowboy boots. I suddenly worried about its impracticality and realized that now was not the best time to be a slave to fashion. I reasoned that nobody had advised me on the preferred dress-code for entering a demon infested realm.

"Cute dress, Suki," Raven said, while casually twirling a riding crop.

I nervously tugged at the bodice, which suddenly felt in danger of falling downward, exposing me to the girl who was once my best friend, but now my rival. A self-consciousness crept over me, flushing my cheeks and making me feel out of my element.

James' arm protectively went around my waist and his hand rubbed my back, reassuring me and making me feel his protective presence like a shield surrounding me. It brought me the confidence that I knew I would need for dealing with Raven. I stood up a bit straighter, lifted my chin, and pushed my shoulders back. Meeting Raven's confident glance with my own, as if to say 'it's on' I answered back. "White is such a timeless classic look...if one can pull it off."

"Let's go already," she shot back. "Phin, you coming?"

Phineas had tried his best to look inconspicuous, trying to avoid appearing aligned with either Raven or myself, but now he was placed on the spot. I watched and waited to see his true colors emerge.

He glanced between myself and Raven before hesitantly answering. "I thought we talked about this," he said to Raven, although he glanced at me quickly and I saw the nerves that threatened him. He hadn't expected this from Raven. "It just seems that I would be of more use if I stayed here."

"Plans change," Raven said simply.

Plans. One word and yet, coming from Raven it carried the weight of immense threat. Raven had been planning and plotting how to get her hands on my Amulet of Pollox for centuries. Patience allowed her to wait through the passing of umpteen Releasors until the time came when the right ones, those gifted with unforeseen talents would come to possess it. Only it didn't go quite as planned as Charlotte managed to take it into the Romani Realms with her before Raven could inflict harm upon her.

"Well, I wasn't expecting to go on a trip today; I haven't even packed my toothbrush," Phineas said at an attempt at levity.

Raven's voice took on an ominous tone. "Everything you need is waiting for you." She held out her hand to him, and as he in turn took it, my heart sank. I know he had little choice and what I was hoping for, I didn't know. Realistically, it's not like he could have insisted on staying and having a boys weekend with James, but still, seeing Raven holding Phineas' hand, the man whom Charlotte had professed her love to, made my own heart ache with sadness.

Once again, Phineas caught my eye and I know he was trying to tell me that we had our own plan and it would be carried out, but suddenly the game had changed.

James stepped forward, purposefully placing his tall, strong frame in front of Raven. With his back turned to her, she couldn't see the exchange between us. His eyes bore into mine and then he closed them and nodded, a silent message that I should do the same. I no sooner followed suit when I heard his voice inside my head. For the first time, it rang out clearly and I was immediately filled with joy and more importantly, hope.

"You remember this feeling," he said directly into my mind. *"Take it with you and recall it whenever you need it. If you need me to pull you back, you reach out to me. I'll always be here for you."*

A sudden feeling of elation tore through my being. My heart pounded with exhilaration like an endorphin rush. With my eyes still closed, I inhaled deeply and relished the feeling.

James continued to speak to me silently. *"You are strong, Suki. Although I wish I had met you sooner...had more nights to hold you in my arms...but, the truth is, you survived three hundred years before the need for me to turn up arose."*

I felt James' strong hands reach for my own, his thumb lightly caressing the inside of my wrist, sending shivers of pleasure along with it. I don't think I would ever get used to this one special talent of his -- the ability to heal me mentally and physically with a magical touch -- but I was willing to spend the next century or so exploring it. I relaxed and listened to his smooth voice, sounding inside my head. *"Suki, you know that I can only move through time, but not other realms. Like you, I would need a guide. You need to be self-reliant in the Romani Realms. You will need to focus all of your power and energy on the task at hand."*

I nodded, feeling like an athlete receiving a pep talk from a coach.

I could vaguely make out Phineas arguing with Raven, but I did what James said and focused only on his words, echoing peacefully in my mind. *"Being your Shade is my greatest pleasure...but, you need to forget me."* A sudden flash of coldness shot through my body.

"No!" my eyes shot open, but the look he gave me told me that his mind was made up.

"Listen to me," he leaned in to whisper in my ear, our connection to communicate silently now broken. "When you enter the Romani Realms, you won't remember me as your Shade, just as the guy who tends bar in your building. I'll be insignificant to you."

"That's not true," I said vehemently.

"It's necessary, Suki...at least until you get acclimated. You have no idea what you'll be up against, none of us do and therefore, you don't need the distraction of a lover waiting in the wings. I'll still be watching for you and with Maebeline's help, we can pull you back."

"Ahh, lovers' quarrel?" Raven spoke with mock concern. "So tragic. It takes you three centuries to finally realize that he's always been with you, and what do you do? Decide to take a road trip in search of two pointless teenage girls."

Raven circled both of us as she spoke, and then sidled up to James, literally coming between us and pressing her chest up against his. "Well James, I guess we all make our own...bed."

"Enough," I said and grabbed James by the arm, pulling him away from her. I hated appearing weak, but I threw my arms around his body, burying my head in his chest and allowed the tears to flow.

He kissed the top of my head, and when he spoke, I could hear his voice choked. "Suki, it's for your own safety. And it's only temporary. I promise you."

I sniffed hard and wiped my eyes. It was as if James was trying to tell me something, but it made no sense. Forget him...only temporary? When would everything be as it should? My brain vacillated back and forth like Newton balls bouncing against each other. One thing was for certain; I needed to pull myself together for this show of raw emotion only gave Raven more ammunition against me. I could hear her caustic words as she spoke with Phineas about how pathetic I was, and even more upsetting, I heard him murmur his agreement.

"When will it happen?" I asked James.

He knew immediately what I referred to. "Memory of us being together like this will vanish once you enter the Romani Realms. When you gain control of the elements again, you'll be able to take back your memories as well."

I nodded, accepting the fate and understanding it better. "At least Raven won't be able to manipulate my thoughts for you. I may not remember what we had, but at least she can't destroy it."

"You're going to be fine."

"And you?"

James let go of a small chuckle and shook his head. "I'll be watching, but just as before you actually met me, you'll never know."

Raven left Phineas' side to invade our privacy again. "Sounds creepy, if you ask me. Kinda stalker like."

I rolled my eyes in response, doing my best not to betray my Southern roots with an unladylike comment, although plenty went through my mind.

"Phineas!" she called out and like a lapdog, he appeared at her side. She took his hand and then held the other one out to me. "Are we going to do this?"

"Like I have a choice?"

Raven looked at me and smirked. "Well, if you leave Charlotte to her own devices, she may never find Samantha." Raven tssked and shook her head in mock concern, "She could really get eaten alive there. Lost souls have a tendency to prey upon the innocent. Oh Suki, the guilt of this situation must really be eating you up."

"Your concern for my well-being is overwhelming."

"Well I was your friend once, let's not forget that. And, in the spirit of our past, I want to help you."

I looked at Raven, wishing I didn't have to say it, but of course, I did. "What do you want?"

"It's simple. I'll help navigate you to the Romani Realms, due to my gypsy heritage and dark magic teachings. And when you get there safely and find sweet Charlotte, you get her to turn over the Amulet to me."

"And then what? How do we get back? How do I trust you?"

"Maybe you can't, but you'll never find them alone."

I was rapidly growing a backbone. "You're not getting that Amulet unless Charlotte and Samantha get out safely."

"Whatev. Let's roll, Bitch."

With one last, longing look at James, I begrudgingly took Raven's hand. She no sooner met eyes with Phineas, who was holding her other hand. The look that passed between them gave me a sinking feeling in my stomach. It was a look of familiarity that lovers share. Raven turned to face me and with a knowing look she smiled a cheshire grin, the cat who ate the canary. And then, no sooner did her fingers wrap around mine, did the wind begin to blow, the ticking of clocks and grinding of gears sounded along with something else I had never heard when traveling to other realms...the horrifying squeals and screams of trapped and tormented souls.

Chapter Four

66 **P**hin, wake up...open your eyes." Raven stared down at Phineas' body and wistfully thought of the way it used to be between them. She knew that his allegiance to her was waning...if there at all. She gently stroked his hair away from his temple, taking care to brush it away from a gash that dripped with his blood.

The sight would have made me nauseous if I had actually been alert enough to witness her adoration. I could only see them in my dreams as the trip into the Romani Realms had left me incapacitated as well. I could just barely make out what was happening...

Their relationship was complicated. Raven had given Phineas ever-lasting life by instilling gypsy magic into him when he died at his own father's hands. The attraction between them was born out of Phineas' gratitude, but soon grew into the relationship of true lovers, if only because of their mutual need to connect with someone who wasn't going to die anytime soon. They had been together since the 1400s, although neither appeared a day older than twenty. They were more than attractive. As demon gypsies, their sexuality was heightened, making them irresistible and beguiling to the opposite sex as well as to each other. Staying together was easy. That is, until he met Charlotte.

"I just want things to be the way they were," Raven whispered softly to Phineas' motionless form. Still he didn't move. Raven wiped a wayward tear from her cheek, and was made aware of how the trip into the Romani Realms had affected her. She scowled at the wave of human emotions that suddenly flooded her psyche. She had long ago tuned them out and believed feelings directed at another person, at least feelings stemming from the heart, were a weakness.

"God my head is killing me," Phineas said more to himself than Raven. He looked around disoriented and Raven rushed to cradle his head. "What's wrong with me?"

"You're okay," she said with obvious relief.

Phineas looked at Raven curiously and sat up to dislodge her arms from around his neck. "My head is killing me. Can you give me some space?"

"Yeah sure," she replied. It was unlike her to allow anyone to snap at her, but she was feeling a bit vulnerable herself. "I'm just...it's good that you're back."

Still Phineas continued to hold his head in his hands. "How long was I out?" Phineas took in his surroundings -- the tall pines, expansive meadow, a light breeze and the sun-kissed day. It was idyllic, certainly not the realms that he had heard of, nor expected. "Wow, this isn't what I expected."

"You woke up at a good time. The surroundings change rapidly here and you've been out awhile. The first trip affects everyone differently. Some pass out; some feel like a hangover has hit them."

"More like a two-ton truck ran over my brain."

Raven reached out to try and caress Phineas' cheek, but she noticed how he flinched at her touch. She felt another wave of sadness hit her as he leaned back out of her reach. Even that slight rejection left Raven's emotions reeling and she gladly lowered her own head to gaze at the ground and swallow back the tears that were forming.

"You don't seem to have a scratch on you." Phineas regarded Raven, who let a wave of her shining black hair dip low over her eye, hiding any remaining sign that she had been crying. He dabbed his hand over a cut on his forehead that still bled.

"I'm used to it here," she said trying to hide the fact that the effects for her were emotional rather than physical. To her, this was far more disorienting and she took a deep breath hoping to recover sooner rather than later.

"Where's Suki?" Phineas asked, now remembering the journey more clearly.

It's about time. I may have been unconscious, but I was still able to decipher whether Phineas' thoughts went to me.

"Just beyond that rock formation," Raven jutted her chin out to indicate three large boulders that rose out of the ground in the distance.

Phineas looked in the direction that Raven pointed and then suddenly rose to his feet and started off in a hurry.

With annoyance, Raven shouted, "She's fine."

There's a word for women like Raven. Come on, Phineas. Show some spine.

"How do you know?" he called over his shoulder. "She's just lying here. She might have hit the rocks when she landed. Look at my head," he indicated the cut that was now bleeding more profusely.

"You need to slow down," Raven said more sternly as she grabbed Phineas' arm, pulling him back. "Your head is bleeding more because you're moving about too much. The air is thinner here. You need to conserve your energy and get used to the environment before you start running laps. As for Suki, helping her can actually harm her."

"What do you mean?" Phineas said staring off in the direction of the boulders.

"As much as I wanted to immediately hold you when I woke up, I didn't. Seeing you lying on the ground unconscious just about killed me, Phin. You were so still, I just...I just thought about what it would be like without you."

The tears started to flow freely from Raven as her words came tumbling out faster. She raked her fingers through her hair as she paced and continued to shake her head as if just verbalizing her fears would bring them to life. Phineas noticed that her breathing had grown as erratic as her behavior.

"I thought about never being able to talk with you, never having you hold me, never inhaling your scent!"

"I get it. Raven calm down."

"No, you don't get it," she said grabbing onto his arm. "Had I disturbed you, the transition would have been even worse. When you land, your body is still, but your brain is processing the transition. Waking someone up too early can result in their mind being left behind."

Phineas tried to pry Raven's hands off his arm to no avail. She held onto him with one hand, her grip unflinching, and wiped the endless parade of tears from her eyes with the other. Finally, he did his best to ignore her histrionics and stared off in the distance where I lay, as if weighing out whether to believe her or not.

"You see how your head isn't bleeding as much since you've been standing still? Come on. Let's stay here for awhile," Raven said while sitting back down and offering her hand up to Phineas. "There's nothing to do until she wakes up...she'll be fine. You don't want to do anything now...except be right here...with me."

He looked down at Raven, who still gripped his arm and realized that the Romani Realms had certainly affected her. He was used to her intensity and desires -- for control, for power, and even for his love, but this was different. Everything about her was magnified. Not only were her emotions heightened to a degree that he had never seen, he was all too aware of the pheromones that surrounded her. She had always had a way of making men swoon with the slightest glance and smile, but now in spite of her unattractive show of emotions, he suddenly couldn't help but feel their connection.

The day of Samantha's funeral he had vowed that he was going to find Charlotte and right their wrong. He was finished with Raven, although he didn't let on to this plan for fear of not being able to rescue Charlotte from the Romani Realms, but right now in this moment, he felt a renewed desire for Raven.

Don't fall for her. The dreams that accosted my mind were too painful. I remained incapacitated and for his part, Phineas seemed equally disturbed.

He shook his head, knowing that what he was feeling was an ocean larger than crazy. A desperate woman was never attractive in any man's book, but in spite of himself, he couldn't turn away from Raven. It was damned impossible to ignore the assault on his mind and body that she was throwing at him. He could feel his own heart beat faster, marking time with Raven's as if they were one. The attack of pheromones made it impossible not to feel her desire...and respond to it.

Realizing he had no choice, but to wait it out until everyone in his odd traveling party was physically able to continue the journey, he accepted that he had no control of the situation. He met Raven's wild gaze, and to her immense relief, sat down next to her.

Phineas' acquiescence was just what Raven needed to get her emotions in check. Once she allowed herself to feel, it was as if a floodgate opened up and there had been no stopping the irritating humanity that ruptured through her thoughts. She had been reduced to a hyperventilating, sniveling school girl and that just wouldn't do -- even if the wave of human emotions had served to bring Phineas back to her.

But that would be a temporary condition, lasting only as long as the effects of the journey, unless she took control of the situation. Phineas had barely sat next to her when she pressed her mouth onto his and although she could sense his wavering thoughts, he gave into the pheromones that were no longer an unseen and unproven force of connectivity between people. It was as if an invisible web had been thrown over the two of them, wrapping itself around them and working to bond them back together.

Raven wrapped her arms around Phineas' neck and relished in his kiss. The more he gave, the more she felt like her old self. Conniving. Resourceful. Deliberate. Gone were the effects of moving throughout the different realms and in its place was desire. A desire for the life she used to have with Phineas. A desire to collect the thoughts of the greatest minds throughout time. And to accomplish both of those goals meant regaining her control over Phineas and obtaining the coveted Amulet of Pollox, but not before she destroyed Charlotte and Samantha once and for all.

Charlotte. Only a day ago Phineas had told himself that nothing was more important than getting her back. He knew that going into the Romani Realms with Raven as a guide was the only way, and he was willing to do anything to help Charlotte, but this? His mouth pressed down on Raven's lips. This wasn't supposed to happen.

In spite of himself, Phineas found himself responding to Raven's advances. His head told him to untangle himself from her hold, to pull away from her body, but then he couldn't help but feel the curves of her breasts pressing against him, the way she allowed her hips to seductively melt against his, and being weak from the journey, both in spirit and physicality, his resolve also melted and he returned her kisses. This wasn't just a matter of her being incredibly seductive and him being a guy, even if he wasn't a completely human one. There was more at play here he realized as he allowed his arms to wrap around her waist. He should have willpower to resist, but as much as tried, he failed.

He didn't want to be with Raven, but the more he kissed her, the more he wanted from her. It was as if he were standing on the edge of a cliff and dared to step a bit too close to the edge. Like loose ground in danger of a landslide, his intention plummeted.

Memories of the time he took Charlotte into London of the 1850s swirled in his mind. He desperately tried to hold onto the image of how beautiful she looked, what it felt like to kiss *her*, but it was futile. He was powerless against the pull of Raven in these realms.

Raven opened her eyes mid-kiss and was pleased with what she saw. God-like Phineas with his golden complexion, blond hair dipping over one eye, his cheekbones strong and prominent -- that much hadn't changed. But what was different was how his brow was furrowed with such intensity as if his very life depended upon kissing her. He may have wanted to ignore any feelings of being turned on, but it was a fruitless battle that fueled Raven.

"I missed you," she said against his lips.

"Raven, I can't forgive what you did."

She may have power associated with three hundred years of extended life, but Phineas' developing love for Charlotte had rocked her confidence. Now was the time when she could take back what was rightfully hers. Her entry into the Romani Realms was complete and she intended to get the upper hand over Phineas.

"Shh, don't talk...just feel." As she spoke, she layered kisses down Phineas' neck and felt his reaction. His pulse pounded wildly against his carotid artery, bringing fresh oxygenated blood flow to his body. "That's better. You can't tell me this doesn't feel right. We can't turn our back on our history."

With every kiss, he felt his mind becoming more engaged to Raven's. The connection they shared as demon gypsies not only gave them power to communicate telepathically and shift into the form of a black bird, it also solidified their loyalty bonding. Phineas had dared break that bond, but Raven was determined that it wouldn't happen again. Although she cared for him, she hadn't felt true human emotions such as loss and regret in years. This trip into the Romani Realms had put her in touch with those feelings and it was an inconvenience she didn't relish reliving again.

She pulled back from Phineas carefully to test whether she really was gaining a foothold into controlling him once again. "Of course I love your spark of independence, but I much prefer you to be...pliable," she said running her tongue along his neck. The act made him shudder and she could feel his hardness press against her.

"Mmm, it's good to have you back. But I don't just want your *body* to want me...tell me *you* want me."

Phineas' brow wrinkled as if in pain rather than pleasure. His lips tightened into a thin line willing Raven to stop her seduction. He moved his hands from around her waist and instead took hold of her wrists and moved her offending hands away from where they rested around his neck. He remained holding her hands, but unable to pull his mouth from hers. He was still adjusting to his arrival in the Romani Realms and his resolve would only take him so far, unlike Raven who was quickly becoming acclimated to the thinner air and powerful magic of the lost souls who made the realms their home.

"Come on now, don't be like that," she said curling her fingers around his and gently placing his hands back around her waist. This time, he didn't resist.

"That's better. Admit it, this feels right."

With all his might, Phineas pulled away and looked at Raven. "It may feel good, but it isn't right."

"I'd say we're making progress."

Using her powers before becoming fully adjusted to the surroundings would only cause a set back, so Raven employed baby steps, gingerly testing her skills. She could tell that Phineas wanted to move away from her, but she maintained contact with him and concentrated on stirring the wind. Within seconds a light breeze brushed against their bodies forming a small whirlwind around them to block out any unwanted distractions. She moved her mouth over his once again and this time, felt his mouth relax against hers, accepting her kisses and within seconds, his tongue found its way into her mouth, lightly weaving around hers. His instincts took over his mind.

Their kisses grew more passionate giving Raven an edge and letting her focus her mind on Phineas' thoughts. Though once again careful not to tax her own powers, she tested them just enough to see how far she could influence his and saw that he was quickly succumbing to her seduction and control.

Raven let her hand travel down Phineas' chest and then lower to the front of his thigh where she teased him by staying put. She let the pressure of her palm increase and then ever so slightly moved slowly upward. "I'm getting close to the yummy part," she whispered in his ear.

"Raven..."

"Tell me. Tell me that you forgive me for Samantha."

She tilted her head upward, exposing her neck for Phineas to run kisses down its side. "I forgive you. It was...," he stopped mid-sentence taking in the scent of her perfume, the long lines of her graceful neck. "It was an accident, right?"

"Of course it was. I just wanted to scare her."

Her hand moved against the hardness of his manhood and their kisses instantly became more intense.

"But you took it a bit far," Phineas said, his breathing was heavy with the effort of resisting his desire.

"Hey, I didn't push her off that cliff. Phin, let me explain things in no uncertain terms," Raven said, suddenly thrusting her hand down the front of his jeans and manipulating him until he closed his eyes in rapture. "We are good together."

Phineas reached a hand onto Raven's shoulders to steady himself from the waves of temptation that were flooding his system. "I don't feel like myself. Raven, what's going on?"

"You're not used to these realms. You may be a demon gypsy, like myself, but you do not have my experience. Imagine how delicate Charlotte is fairing here?"

Phineas' eyes shot open. His hand went to Raven's and he forced her touch away, although he was brimming with desire for her.

That's it. Fight her!

Her eyes flashed with anger. "I'm impressed. You're more man than I give you credit for, and that's not a compliment. More human. You need to vanquish those silly emotions."

"What if I don't want to?" Phineas took a step back, only to have Raven immediately close the distance between them and wrap her arms around his neck.

"Then, you will experience extreme heartache because I will ensure that you watch Charlotte suffer before dying."

Phineas was taken aback quite literally. Raven's words filled him with dread and as she released her arms from him, a sudden wind forced him backwards and sent him stumbling onto the ground. Raven stood above him and Phineas waited for whatever else her temper planned. Instead, she wriggled out of her tight riding pants and lifted her t-shirt above her head before throwing it to Phineas. The wind died down to a gentle breeze and Raven's black hair blew behind her in a captivating fan. She smiled a mischievous smile, knowing that even though she wasn't in physical contact with Phineas, the bond between them had been reestablished. She held his gaze without blinking, willing his mind to release its loyalty to Charlotte and return to her. And just as she knew he would, Phineas couldn't take his eyes from her.

She extended her hand down to him, and he readily took it in his own as Raven lowered herself next to him. The sun beat down on their shoulders and Phineas whipped off the light weight shirt he was wearing and placed it on the ground for Raven to rest her head. Lying on her side, she crooked her finger at him and coquettishly requested that he come closer.

Phineas closed what little distance remained between them, taking Raven in his arms. She allowed one leg to drape over Phineas' thigh, letting him press against her. She was careful to slow down her advances at this point, instead hoping that Phineas would come to the conclusion that he wanted this as much as she did.

And he did.

He stared down at Raven, who looked more beautiful than even he believed possible. Men had always found Raven irresistible, not only due to her demon gypsy powers, but quite simply because she was a stunner. As Phineas looked at her, she smiled broadly, her teeth shiny and white against her tanned skin and black hair. Her brown eyes glistening in the sunlight. She lowered her impossibly long lashes, which gave her a feminine air that he didn't often see.

It fueled him to be the man she wanted and without further hesitation, he slid his arm around her waist and threw his body over her, pressing against her and relishing how she demurely gave away to his physicality. She no longer needed to call the shots or influence Phineas to behave toward her the way she craved.

He brushed her hair aside to gain access to her neck, where he layered his kisses downward and lifted up her top to reveal a lacy black bra that barely covered her ample breasts. She gently placed her hands around his head, encouraging him. Unlike before when she had to use more manipulative techniques, now it was all Phineas' doing -- his fingers deftly unfastened her bra and as he pulled each strap from her shoulders, he tipped his mouth down to each breast and gently traced his fingers around each bud.

"You're beautiful. You always have been," he said with more regret than Raven liked. He was falling, but not quite there.

"We're meant to be," she said placing her hand underneath his chin and turning his head so their eyes met. "I just need that Amulet, and then, we can have a child together and the Triad will be complete. Imagine the power we can harness...just for our use."

Before Phineas could respond, Raven arched her back and pulled his body back down toward her once again. His hands roamed over her breasts; her hands traced the muscles of his back. Raven felt him press himself against her and as he did, she opened her legs, allowing him to lie between them. His heartbeat grew rapid as she squeezed her legs around his waist and rocked gently against him. Their tongues intertwined and their bodies moved against each other in a hungry dance of need and desire. Just a few more minutes and he would be hers again, but an angry clap of thunder and the immediate downpour of rain made them jump and break free of each other's embrace.

I woke up alone. The sun shining down on me didn't help the pounding of my temples. I wanted desperately to close my eyes again, but it was too quiet. There was no sign of Raven or Phineas, and given the nasty gash that dripped a river of blood down my forehead, I assumed that I had been out quite awhile giving them reason to investigate our surroundings. I only hoped that my unconscious thoughts had been just a fabrication -- the aftermath of a difficult journey.

I stumbled to my feet, steadying myself against a boulder that was smeared with blood, no doubt my own. Given the fact that a bruise was already displayed on my shoulder and that my head was tender, I assumed the giant rock had served as my own welcome committee into these new realms.

I steadied myself and remembered the mantra spoken by Gautama Siddartha, who was born in what is now Nepal some 2,500 years ago. I had insisted that James introduce me to one of his descendants before this little vacay into the realms. James thought it more important to focus on physical training, but I felt I needed some mental preparation. Still he worried that we were wasting precious time so I had to employ time honored Southern social skills of persuasion. They don't say that you attract more flies with honey for nothing. I simply explained to James that no amount of fighting skills would save me from the battle my mind would wage against me when I landed here without my love.

He quickly realized the truth of that statement and introduced me to a Tibetan Buddhist who he served as Shade to and protected before taking on that role for moi. His prior ward had nearly lost his perspective about peace and enlightenment when human suffering seemed all around him. Siddartha was better known as Shakyamuni. Although he was born a prince, he turned his back on his privileged upbringing in search of how to help others. He spent a lifetime perfecting his practice and now, with the sight that greeted me, I realized I still had a lot of learning about how to achieve inner peace.

When I wandered off to get my bearings and locate Raven and Phineas never did I expect to find them the way I did. I nearly exploded with rage at the sight of them making out. The only thing that kept me from all out craziness was my throbbing head and the reality that my suffering would be nothing compared to what Charlotte and Samantha may be experiencing. I tried to keep my emotions in check as it became obvious from the sudden burst of rain that I didn't have complete control over my powers yet. It also stemmed to reason that if I couldn't quite control my powers, I may not be able to fully protect myself either. Still, my fury unleashed a nasty thunder storm, which although accidental, was also welcome.

"How could you?" I stared down at Phineas, who at least had the decency to jump away from Raven's arms at my approach.

"Suzette, it's not what you think...Suki wait," he called after me, when I immediately turned to leave.

"Oh, let her go," Raven's voice reached me. "She won't get far alone, and we'll have so much more fun without her."

Taking a deep breath, I looked skyward and concentrated on the mantra of enlightenment: Muni Muni Maha Muniye Soha, which loosely translated into seeking advice of a great and wise sage. I had to be pragmatic about my situation. If I thought about it, I wasn't angry at Phineas, but myself. After all, he was only doing what I had expected all along. One couldn't be disappointed in a dog left alone with a bone. On the other hand, I was angry at myself for so many reasons -- believing Phineas' fairytales about being in love with Charlotte, discounting James' words and warnings about him, and thinking that Raven would ever be of help to me on this suicide mission.

"I have no intention of leaving," I said evenly to Raven.

She smirked and baited me. "That's why you turned away at the sight of real love and passion? You haven't actually experienced that yourself, have you? I mean, I assume that's why James isn't here with you."

It would take a lot more than words to affect me. I wouldn't give her the satisfaction of hurting me in that manner. "Bust my buttons, I was never gonna to leave you here alone, certainly not with your bosoms exposed for all to see. I just wanted to shield my own eyes from such an unladylike exhibition. By the way, it's good to know that this trip hasn't caused you a loss of appetite. I see you've been tucking into the desserts lately."

"Screw you, Suki."

I smiled sweetly while she adjusted her jeans and smoothed down her top. In truth, she had a remarkable figure, more curvaceous than my slight frame, but I wasn't about to let her know that I harbored the eensiest bit of admiration for any part of her. We began our walk across the meadow, toward the wall of Sycamore trees -- an unlikely trio forging a trek into unknown and volatile territory.

Raven easily walked ahead while Phineas and I ended up next to each other a few steps behind. It wasn't that I had any desire to be near him, given what I had just witnessed, but the thin air made breathing difficult even with the slightest amount of exertion. Phineas seemed to struggle with the same problem as his words came out slowly and barely above a whisper, which may have been his intention.

"Please Suki, let me explain."

"I have nothing to say to you and I'm not your girlfriend, thankfully. You don't owe me an explanation."

"I want you to hear me out. All the things I said...," his voice grew even quieter and I could tell he feared Raven would hear him. "...what I said in the bar...it was the truth."

"You're just worried that I'm going to tell Charlotte that you're slimier than the backside of a lily pad."

"But I'm not. I don't know even know what that was...she just...you have to believe me."

"Believe what?" Raven was a good distance ahead of us, but suddenly she turned on her heel and I saw an exchange between the two of them that I hadn't ever noticed before. I had seen admiration cross Raven's face when Phineas had perfected shapeshifting. It was no secret that both of them had a mutual attraction. But for the first time, I saw something else in Phineas' eyes as he looked at Raven -- fear.

As sudden as a heart attack strikes, my own heart started to beat wildly in my chest. The palpitations were erratic and fast, making me gasp from both the sheer shock as well as a sudden and gripping pain that seized me. I dropped to my knees and struggled to breathe.

"Suki? What's wrong?"

I looked up at Phineas and upon seeing the surprise in his face I knew that he had nothing to do with the attack plaguing me. I could no longer even remain on my knees. The pain in my chest was so intense that I doubled over onto my side, pulling my legs up and desperately trying to get any air into my lungs.

"Talk to me!" Phineas yelled, but only the slightest whimper escaped my lips. "Raven, is it the realms? What's happening to her?"

Raven approached my side and leaned down to look into my eyes, which were open wide with fear. "Yeah, she doesn't look too well."

"Can you do something?"

"Yes Phin, I can. But why are you so concerned with her? It makes me sick."

Phineas caught my eye and we both came to the conclusion together. This attack did not come from within my own system; it was set into motion by Raven and although I had witnessed her ability to influence one's mind, never had I known her to be able to command such power over another person's body.

"Raven," I cried out weakly. "Please stop. You're going to need me to approach Charlotte."

"Really?"

"She's clever and resourceful. The Amulet gives her powers unto herself." But even with the Amulet, Charlotte was no match for Raven. Pairing them against each other would be like sending a kitten into the lion's den, but it was all I could muster in the moment.

"I have nothing to do with this, Suki."

Phineas grabbed a hold of Raven's shoulders. "What do you mean?"

She looked at his hands, aggressively placed on her arms, and then stared a deathly look into his eyes. "If you touch me, it better be with the hands of a lover for I swear if I ever see such disloyalty from you again, you will be sorry."

Phineas released his hold and ran his hands through his hair in frustration as I continued to cry out in pain. "What are you doing?"

My heart was now pounding with such force that one could see it flailing against my chest, turning a fist-sized portion of the skin that covered the organ black and blue.

"That?" she said, pointing to my writhing body on the ground. "I can make her good as new in a heartbeat...forgive the pun."

"Then why don't you?"

"I'll do one better, but first come here," she said tapping a finger against her lips. Phineas took a moment to assess the situation and knowing it was dire, he approached Raven, albeit not quite willingly. She, on the other hand, wasted no time in throwing herself into an embrace.

To Phineas' credit, their kiss was tentative at best. Raven's hands wove into Phineas' hair, keeping him in place so that she could grow his passion, but to her annoyance Phineas kept an eye on my collapsed form.

"I can see that you're a bit distracted." She lowered herself next to me and took in my condition.

My eyes were now closed, the effort of keeping them open being too difficult. She pulled back one eyelid and then dropped her hand as if repulsed with the imminence of my death.

Phineas watched as Raven stood up and closed her eyes, her hands were raised skyward: "The death of my enemy will not come; harness the spell and heal her suffering." As Raven repeated her chanting, the pressure eased from my chest and my heart no longer pulsated with a force that threatened to explode from my chest cavity. Slowly, the bruising of my chest dissipated and my breathing returned to normal. I was exhausted from the experience, but I would live.

"You see? I do have a heart. I spared poor Suki's life, now you can do something for me."

Phineas glanced at me quickly to ensure that I was okay before answering. "What do you want?"

"It's easy. Just put any feelings for Charlotte aside."

Knowing full well that Raven could read his thoughts and feel his emotions, he answered cautiously. "I...care about you, Raven. I mean, isn't that obvious from what happened between us before Suki got here?"

"Mmm, not so much," she answered and then turned her attention to me. "Suki, you have such miserable timing. You always have. If I had just five more minutes alone with Phin, we would have consummated our relationship and once again been one. It could have been the way it was with us."

I stood up slowly, willing myself to stand tall against her. "Maybe he still has a bit of free will left in him."

"No, he's always had free will. The difference in him occurred when I restored his humanity. That was obviously a big mistake."

"Raven, no," Phineas interjected, knowing how this could end for him. "You said yourself that we were better when I felt more for you. My humanity intensified things, don't you think?"

"Until your stupid heart betrayed me. So...this is how the rest of this little expedition is going to go. I spared Suki's life, but I'm taking back your humanity as payment."

"And Charlotte?" I asked, now knowing full well that Raven's powers were not only strong, but as volatile as her personality.

"Once that Amulet is mine, Charlotte is free to go home with you. She can go back to one of the dumb jocks at high school, and Phineas...you can watch her live happily ever after."

Neither Phineas nor I spoke. I needed to regain my strength and I wasn't about to foolishly say anything to set Raven off. As for Phineas, he knew that it was only a matter of seconds before he didn't care about anything that brought him to the Romani Realms in the first place. Raven had managed to get both of us here to help her find the Amulet of Pollox.

I knew now that the scene that I stumbled upon with Phineas and Raven was manufactured through her powers, but his love for Charlotte would wane as she took away his ability to feel. Even if Phineas did love her once, he wouldn't for much longer. Seeing the extent of Raven's abilities, it was now even less of a question of whether I would get Charlotte and hopefully, Samantha out of here alive. We now had to consider whether Phineas and I would be around to join them.

Chapter Five

Charlotte held onto Shadow's hand as they walked deeper into the forest, oblivious to the fact that the further they walked the less daylight appeared through the thick tree branches.

"Don't stop for anything, Charlotte."

"I don't like it here," Charlotte said as much to herself as to the little girl who accompanied her.

"It's the only way. You'll have to trust me."

With those words, memories of Phineas came rushing back to her. They were the same words he spoke when he took her back in time. Too many things happened that day. She had fallen in love with him, found the Amulet of Pollox, but instinctively kept it a secret; and she experienced loss. It was the day of Samantha's death and with the loss of her friend, Charlotte relinquished her trust of Phineas.

"Trust me," Shadow's words whispered around her, but she could no longer see the girl in the dark forest.

"Shadow? Don't leave me."

Charlotte started to run although she had no idea why. She also couldn't understand why she even wanted the creepy little girl with her, except that any companionship was better than the solitude and unknown experiences that kept occurring to her in these strange surroundings.

Although she hadn't been aware of the tarry puddles in the meadow, she noticed them now, along with what looked like bones jutting out from the black depths. Charlotte slowed down her pace to gingerly hop over the puddles. There was light in the distance, perhaps just a quarter mile farther. She hurried toward it, but felt something grab at her ankle and tug her toward the ground.

She went down hard, landing in one of the tar puddles that splattered into her eyes. As she wiped the murky liquid from her face, she stared as the small puddle in which she sat, mesmerized by its sudden expansion in every direction. With lightening speed it spread until the forest had completely disappeared and in its place, Charlotte found herself treading the black water of a swampy lake.

Vines underneath the surface of the water wrapped around her legs. The more she kicked, the more tangled she became until she was forced underneath.

"Take my hand," a voice called to her.

Instinctively, Charlotte extended her arm and was grateful when someone pulled on it, dragging her forward. The force in which she traveled caused the dirty water to splash in waves around her. It found its way into her mouth and she spluttered and coughed it out until thankfully landing in a heap on the shore.

"I love you, Charlotte."

Charlotte looked up to see Shadow standing over her in a white dress that was not only dry, but as clean and bright as the now sunlit sky.

"What is this place?"

Shadow smoothed the dirty hair from Charlotte's face. "Come on. I know where you can get cleaned up."

"I'm not going anywhere with you. Look where I ended up the last time I followed you."

Shadow's eyes suddenly changed from their icy, pale blue to a black so dark one couldn't even see her pupils. "Then you won't see your friend."

"Samantha? You know where she is? Take me," Charlotte's voice rose with the desperation of a girl tormented. "Please, take me to her."

The little girl held her arms out for a hug. Charlotte stared at her and started to cry from the stress and strain of the last few hours. The girl's blackened eyes continued to stare through her, making Charlotte's fear grow to an irrational height. She was now standing in the midst of a green grassy field with the smell of wildflowers filling her senses, and yet she shook with uncontrollable fear.

"Love me, Charlotte."

"I...I don't want to get you dirty," she said taking a step backwards.

"It'll be fine. You want to see your friend, don't you?"

Charlotte slowly took a step toward Shadow and placed her hands on the girl's arms at an attempt to hold her at a distance. But the girl wrapped herself in Charlotte's embrace. "Hold me tighter," Shadow instructed. Charlotte moved her hands to the girls' waist, but she screamed and released her at the sight of blood-stained handprints covering the girl's arms where her hands used to be.

Charlotte looked down at her own hands, but only saw the black mud from the swamp. She stared with horror at Shadow whose eyes now shined brightly, once again a beautiful hue of light blue.

"What's wrong, Charlotte?"

As Charlotte continued to stare at the little girl, the bloody handprints dissipated in the glowing sunlight leaving no trace whatsoever. "What's going on?" Charlotte asked, pacing in circles.

Shadow pointed to the far end of the field. "Over there. She's inside."

A few moments ago the field was a massive expanse of green grass, nothing else in sight. But now, a beautiful, octagon-shaped structure stood just a few meters away, it's walls made entirely of glass, shining in the sun like a beacon. Charlotte shielded her eyes from the sunlight, which reflected off the glass with intensity in spite of the distance. Shadow held out her hand, and this time, Charlotte took it without hesitation.

As the gazebo-like structure loomed before her, Charlotte could no longer contain herself. She ran faster than she had ever in her life, willing herself through the tall grass, until she reached the glass walls. Shadow had inexplicably gotten there before her, although Charlotte never saw the small girl overtake her. She moved next to her and like Shadow, she shielded her eyes from the tremendous glare of the glass walls and peered inside.

Like a scene from a formal debutantes ball, at least half a dozen girls were gathered together wearing gossamer gowns of sheer silk. They sat primly sipping from teacups as incredibly handsome men decked out in black suits stood at attention waiting to refill their cups. They just sat and drank without looking at each other or even speaking.

"I don't see her," Charlotte said aloud, pressing her nose against the glass.

"She's right there," Shadow pointed.

Charlotte took another look at where Shadow was pointing. In the center of a circle sat a girl whose back was to them, her hair was indeed red like Samantha's, but it wasn't Samantha's wild mane of runaway curls. This girl's hair was conservatively piled high on her head, not a stray tendril in sight. She wore an elegant, midnight blue strapless gown that featured a criss-cross lacing in the back from the waist upwards.

"She's beautiful...it couldn't..."

"Are you saying that your friend is not beautiful?"

"No, of course not. It's just that Samantha wouldn't be caught dead sipping tea in a ball gown. That girl is too...it's just not like her."

"Well, it's a bit different here, isn't it? But you'll get used to it."

Charlotte turned to stare at Shadow, fearing the words she spoke. But before she could verbalize any words to the contrary, Shadow backed away from the gazebo, moving to leave. "Well, I've seen enough. Coming?"

"No way," Charlotte answered as she knocked on the glass window. Although the sound rang out clearly to her ear, not a soul from inside even turned toward the noise. Samantha and the girls continued to sit in silence. Charlotte slapped both hands against the windows, pounding harder in a desperate attempt to get Samantha's attention.

"That's a good show," Shadow noted.

"Be quiet," Charlotte snapped. "I thought you were going to take me to her, not tease me with the sight of her."

"That's not the show I'm talking about. It's the one playing in your mind."

A myriad of emotions were indeed bombarding Charlotte's psyche, but there was something about the little girl's words that plagued her. If she knew what Charlotte was thinking, did that also mean she knew the secrets that the Amulet brought her? "Can you see my thoughts?"

"I don't want to see everything, not the boring stuff," Shadow answered, once again sounding more like her age. "But, those..." she said pointing to Charlotte's head, "those are good," she wickedly smiled.

The emotional pull affecting Charlotte was too much. She was having a full blown panic attack over not being able to get to Samantha, and the ramblings of this little girl, or whatever she really was, made her heart pound with intense nerves. As Shadow started to leave, rounding the building to the other side, she called back to Charlotte. "I'm going for a walk; I'll be back after you mind the show."

"What?" Charlotte asked, not understanding her words. Before Shadow answered, everything around Charlotte shifted into darkness. Her eyes saw nothing except the images and thoughts of her own mind, playing in a fast-forward mode, although showing memories of her recent past.

Images flashed of Phineas, his beautiful features, her smile as she looked up at him with longing...the pictures played on, one after the next, in her mind. She tried to shake herself from the thoughts, but as she saw herself obviously in love with Phineas, her heart betrayed her current reason for being in the Romani Realms and returned to feeling love for him.

Just as quickly as this "show" ended, another would start. Again, she saw snapshots of Phineas and she allowed herself to enjoy it until the image shifted to one with Phineas and Raven. A cold chill crept up Charlotte's arms. Feelings of dread, jealousy, and sadness replaced her warm heart, and just as quickly, a new image, worse than the sight of her love with the girl who caused her best friend's death, struck her mind.

She saw the accident. The whole thing played out in achingly slow motion. I had told her how Samantha died, but naturally Charlotte couldn't have witnessed it considering that she was in the past with Phineas. But now, she saw it quite clearly. Samantha, with her red hair and smiling green eyes, was running with a frightened look. Gone was her easy-going attitude, replaced by a look of desperation. Charlotte knew now that her look was associated with her need to find Charlotte and warn her, but it resulted in her careening off the bluffs of Malibu. The horrifying scene continued to play out including showing James and I debating who to go to first -- Samantha or Charlotte.

"Help her!" Charlotte screamed, but Shadow wasn't there and the girls inside the glass gazebo didn't see her. Even worse, she felt the same despair she felt on the day of the accident. She saw James and I choose to help her. That mistake would continue to haunt all of us as now, in the Romani Realms, we may all lose our lives.

Shaking and crying, Charlotte's mind returned to the present and once again she found herself staring into the glass gazebo, wishing that Samantha would look her way. Her mind's show was over, and Shadow had returned to her side.

"Have you made a decision?"

Charlotte looked at the girl cautiously before answering. "I told you what I wanted. I came here for my friend. Are you going to show me a way inside?"

A moment passed as Shadow seemed to weigh up whether or not to help Charlotte. "You know that I got to see your show too."

Charlotte narrowed her eyes, wondering where this was going. "And?"

"I saw the one called Phineas. You weren't in such a hurry to be with your friend when he was around."

"That's not true!" Charlotte shouted, but lowered her voice when she saw Shadow's eyes turn black again. "I'm sorry..." she said and just as quickly, the little girl's appearance returned to normal. "I didn't know Samantha was in danger. None of us did. Well, maybe Phin knew, but he says he didn't. Anyway, that's the past. I'm here now."

"But what about him?"

"I left him and everything in my world to come here and save her. I don't care about him."

Shadow started to skip in circles, irritatingly acting like a small child again and ignoring Charlotte. The girl was playing a game of leap frog, seeming to talk to others although nobody was there.

"Shadow, can we go? Please?"

Shadow turned and waved goodbye to someone whom Charlotte couldn't see, and then sat down and placed her head in her hands looking forlorn.

"What is it now?" Charlotte asked, her patience wearing thin.

"I'm just sad to see my friend go. She was telling me a story about that guy too."

Charlotte hesitated, but in spite of her instincts to protect her feelings, she caved. "What guy? Phineas?"

Shadow nodded her head and smiled. "Come on. It's time," she said indicating the gazebo. The ladies will see us now."

Charlotte pressed her hand to the glass to peer in one more time. Everything was as it was earlier with Samantha sitting among the women, only now a few danced in the center of the room with the men in black tuxedos.

"Beautiful, isn't it?"

"Can we go?" Charlotte asked.

"Sure, but one thing...Phineas isn't allowed. You won't find love here."

Chapter Six

I trailed behind Raven and Phineas. The air in the Realms made my heart pound with even the slightest exertion, much like the way one feels when they're in the mountains although thus far, the surroundings were wide, open meadows mixed with dense forests. But as I followed, I noticed that Phineas started lagging behind Raven, until the three of us appeared to be walking single file. It felt like a weird game of follow the leader with Raven leading us to who knows what.

Occasionally, Phineas would stop and place his hands on his knees, letting his head hang down as if trying to catch his breath.

"You're fighting the Realms," Raven said, turning to speak to him over her shoulder, although not stopping for him. Her voice wasn't the least bit out of breath. "Stop lagging behind."

"I can barely breathe," Phineas complained. "Jeez Raven, what is the hurry?"

I had to agree with Phineas. The pace Raven had set was intense to say the least, but surprisingly, I wasn't as affected as Phineas by the effort to keep up.

"Just try to admire the beauty around you," I said under by breath. Instinctively, I didn't want Raven to know how I was managing so well. James had warned me that she may be able to control my perception -- changing something of beauty into something abominable or vice versa.

"So we're friends again?" Phineas asked, now walking next to me.

"That remains to be seen."

"I'm going to help you find her," Phineas said emphatically, although I didn't answer. I was too absorbed in the sudden shift of my own perception to get into any sort of discussion with him. My senses felt like they were on overload. The sound of birds chirping seemed to be everywhere. The wind in my face felt like tiny fingers brushing against my skin. The colors of the flowers were intense as if someone had come and painted each petal with a magic marker. What was more remarkable was that each one glowed brightly. A beam of sunlight shone down and spotlighted each one.

I stopped and let my eyes follow the beams up to the sky. Moments earlier it was dark and threatening, but now the sun was breaking through a beautiful rainbow, and a delicate, light drizzle of rain dusted my face. It was incredibly refreshing, giving me a second lease on this long walk of ours. I bent my head back and enjoyed the sensation as I closed my eyes.

Suddenly, I heard Raven's laughter and as I opened my eyes, I saw Phineas staring at me with a look of sheer horror. He opened his mouth to speak, but the words didn't flow.

That was when I looked down at my top, which was now splattered in blood. Droplets flowed over my arms. I searched my body for the source of the blood, but I didn't feel any sort of pain. Finally, Phineas moved into action, covering his own head with his arms and throwing his jacket to me.

"Oh, how gallant of you," Raven said.

Blood was raining down from the sky, and now poured off my face and arms.

I looked at Raven, who was calm and unmarked. "Why aren't you touched by it?"

"Because I wasn't stupid enough to welcome it. You turned your head upwards, practically asking for it to drip into your mouth. This isn't a walk in the park. You stupid genie; this is the Romani Realms. I don't know why I even bother with you," she said walking off.

Phineas stayed back with me. "Here," he said handing me a small towel from his pack. "You look like something out of a horror movie."

"I wouldn't be here if it weren't for you...but, thanks."

"I know, and you're welcome."

His voice dropped to a whisper. "You're not going to make it if you allow the illusions here to affect you. Try and focus on...I don't know...something girlie, pretty."

"I was! It shifted."

"Try again."

My eyes suddenly became transfixed on the flora around me. Every plant and flower, even the blades of grass seemed to glow with an intensity as if the sun was sending spotlighted beams directly onto them. I reached my hand out to touch a flower of magnificent blues and greens that had captured my attention.

"Stop it," Phineas said and slapped my hand away.

"Ouch! What in the world?" I stared at him, no longer absorbed in my surroundings. He raised his eyebrow with annoyance and indicated what I had been about to touch. A small hummingbird lay dead atop a pile of rotting leaves.

"Oh, that's so icky."

"Yes, it is," he said taking me by the elbow and leading me away. "Come on. We have to get used to it here."

"How did you adapt so quickly?"

He motioned his chin toward Raven, but didn't say anything.

It was then that I realized just how precarious the situation was for Phineas as well. If Raven was able to protect his thoughts, she was also able to distort them. As if knowing that I had figured out the math, Phineas filled me in more.

"She's helping, but I've also been here before. Knowing what to expect helps. Emotions are heightened; fears are intensified; and, reality can be distorted. Because it's so hard to tell what is real and what isn't, it's going to take a miracle to get Charlotte back."

"And Samantha."

Phineas looked at me for a moment as if he were about to comment, but decided better of it.

"You were going to say something."

"Sometimes, it's better not to."

"Phin, you just got through telling me that the reason you're not affected by this place is you know what to expect. Don't you think a little knowledge would do me good right about now?"

He stared up the path and seeing that Raven was a good quarter mile ahead of us, he told me the hard truth. "I'm not the only one who Charlotte is angry with, and you know it. Raven tormented Samantha's thoughts, and it made her jump that cliff. I unwittingly led Charlotte back in time at that precise moment. But you, Suki...you chose to save Charlotte over Samantha."

"It wasn't like that. I didn't choose one over the other. I saw her running and it looked like she was running from you. Samantha was alone. I didn't know the severity of the situation."

Phineas put his hand on my shoulder. Without realizing it, the blood rain had started to fall on me again. "You've got to stay calm. Raven is in your head and you don't even realize it. Now breathe."

I closed my eyes and did as Phineas suggested. My lungs filled with air, and I visibly relaxed.

"You ready for the rest?" he asked.

"Go for it."

"Charlotte is as angry with you as she is with me. In the Realms, that anger may translate into her not trusting you, or even believing that you have ill intentions toward her."

"How could she think that? She's still my Releasor. I owe her...and Samantha... another two wishes. That doesn't change, even in the Realms."

"In the Realms, everything changes."

"Everything looks okay now, pretty even," I said admiring the flowers once again. "Are these..."

"They're flowers...for now. If Raven decides she's tired of her marathon walk, she may decide to mess with you and then they'll look more like slugs."

I rolled my eyes and we carried on until...

"Suki, listen to him. He knows what he's talking about."

I stopped in my tracks at the sound of James' voice, clear as day, in my head. What was even more surprising than hearing him, was hearing him actually praise Phineas.

"Why are you stopping?"

"It's James. He's..."

"Shh...don't," Phineas tipping his head in Raven's direction. I looked up and indeed she had stopped and was finally waiting on us, but the look on her face made me instantly wary.

"Careful, love..."

My eyes widened at hearing his voice again. It was James. How I wished he was here, but at least in some sense he was with me, protecting me behind-the-scenes as he has always done, even before I realized that he was part of my life.

"Something wrong?" Raven asked.

"No," I answered, perhaps too quickly. "I'm just getting used to the surroundings."

"Let me help you with that," Raven shot back and no sooner did she announce her intention when a high-pitched shriek rang out in my ears, forcing me to hold my head as if it were about to split my brain in half. I fell to the ground and blackness consumed me.

Raven picked up a large tree branch and took a few whacks at my back, ensuring that I stayed put, before she turned to Phineas. "What are you waiting for? Let's go."

"Why did you do that? You're insane."

"By nightfall you'll see me in an entirely different light. Besides, it's obviously better to keep you two apart. Come on."

Phineas took one last glance over his shoulder at me, and saw me struggle to open my eyes. We locked eyes for a brief moment, and then either because he had no choice in the matter or comforted in the knowledge that I wasn't yet dead, he turned and left with Raven. The ringing in my ears started up and once again I slipped into a troubled sleep.

The caw of the birds of prey awoke me, and although my head no longer ached, the sun had grown high in the sky and was beating down with a fierce intensity leaving me feeling weak and feverish. I was both sweating and suffering from chills. With barely any strength, I turned my head and tried to press myself to a seated position. My mouth was dry and I wouldn't have been able to call for help even if I had wanted to. At least I had fallen in the shade of a large willow. It was no use. Even the effort to lift my head exhausted me and I quickly succumbed to closing my eyes again. I concentrated on finding James' voice in the midst of all of this madness.

"Come on," I implored. "I know you said you couldn't be here, but I heard you and now...I need you."

"You're doing fine."

"James! I miss you. Are you here?"

"Come to me..."

And then I saw him. He was here! Looking as handsome as ever in all white, I pulled myself up and stumbled toward him with all the strength I could muster. My sweet reward for persevering was to reach him and feel his strong embrace. His arms wrapped around me and I felt the coolness from his body, healing the burning fever raging inside me from the sun stroke.

"James..."

No answer came, which wasn't like him. My James would at a minimum give me some snappy rapport, but this cold being whose arms were wrapped around my body said nothing, it only started to squeeze me with a force that was taking every last breath from me. I closed my eyes and then opened them again. A pale arm seemed to wrap around my neck, before revealing that it was in fact a light yellow, nearly white snake closing around me. I tried to scream, but no sound escaped me. I was either dreaming and unable to call for help, or this was all too real and I was being suffocated.

Phineas trailed behind Raven, looking back over his shoulder to see whether I had risen and was perhaps trailing them as well.

"Why are you still looking for her? She doesn't matter to us."

"Then why did you bring her?"

Raven stopped to retrieve a blanket from her backpack. Holding it above her head, she let the wind gather and billow underneath it. The clouds moved rapidly across the sky, changing shape from puffy marshmallows to large, black masses until each one broke up into individual pieces that started to take on their own unique shape. Phineas' eyes glanced upward, somehow aware of the threat brewing above him. Raven's own eyes were closed in a trance as she repeated an isolated phrase:

"Presently my soul grew stronger; hesitating then no longer,

That I scarce was sure I heard you – here I opened wide the door;

Darkness there and nothing more."

The dark clouds erupted releasing hundreds of black birds into the daylight sky, blocking any trace of sunlight until they flitted and spread, landing in the nearby trees.

"Come to me," Raven said lustily.

"Is that an order?"

Raven pouted her mouth, but thought better than to start an argument. "I'd like your company," she said reaching her hand out to Phineas.

Phineas hesitated before accepting her hand, knowing what came with her company. The trouble was that in spite of everything, he couldn't deny that he did owe his life to Raven and reason stemmed that if she could bestow it upon him, then she could also have the power to take it away. Although a life with Charlotte was what he most wanted, the possibility of that seemed unlikely if he ended up dead himself. Appeasing Raven may be, he reasoned, his only way to help.

He glanced warily at the black birds watching their interaction, somehow aware that these were no ordinary birds. Rather than sit perched on the tree limbs, they sat with their wings spread wide, touching tip to tip, waiting...but for what, he wasn't sure. He locked eyes with one and watched in horror as the small, beaded black eyes changed shape and lightened slightly to appear more brown than black, more almond shaped than round, and definitely more human than bird like.

It was then that he realized the truth that these were some of the lost souls trapped in the Romani Realms. His unanswered question posed to Raven about why she brought me became clear.

"You never needed Suki here," he said with new understanding.

Raven merely shook her head, a small smile forming on her lips.

Phineas had realized the truth. I was only brought here by Raven to complete a Triad offering. Samantha, Charlotte, and I would be trapped here forever. An offering of this sort would make it possible for Raven to release the secrets from the Amulet of Pollox worn around Charlotte's neck. It would also allow Raven to form a new Triad with Phineas, but who she intended for the third member escaped him. All he knew was that he had to pretend and go along with Raven or he would never get Charlotte back.

Phineas accepted Raven's hand and he felt an instant heat between them. Electric attraction was what Raven used to call it. It was her explanation for how their supernatural powers aligned them to each other, but also for why they were so good together. The most worrying thought plaguing Phineas was how to protect his own heart from this supernatural law of attraction and remain focused on the task at hand.

"That's better," Raven smiled up at him, and ever so slightly moved her body closer.

Phineas took in her smile, the shining dark hair that looked so soft against her smooth complexion. Her black eyes that danced and beguiled him. He had his work cut out for him for whether it was their connection, the realms, or the influence she forced onto him earlier, there was no doubt that he did want her. He took her in his arms, welcoming her into his embrace and when their mouths met, the black birds rustled their wings as if clapping their approval at the union.

Raven's body formed perfectly against Phineas' chest. Instinctively, he reached his hand up her back and then cradled her neck as his kiss grew deeper, more passionate. He struggled to stay focused on Charlotte, and although he knew it wasn't right, pretending that he was kissing Charlotte was in actuality the only way to not become completely aligned with Raven again.

With Raven in his arms and Charlotte in his mind, he made a secret plan to rescue me along with the girls. But it would be risky because he knew that in order to not erupt suspicion within Raven, I would also have to be unaware of his changing allegiances.

My throat burned from dryness and my head was dizzy from the heat. I was back on the ground in the midst of a wide expanse of utter nothingness. No snake, no trees, no black birds. It was as if nothing terrifying had happened, and yet, it had all seemed so real.

"Damn this place," I croaked. I lay on my side, my head still planted on the ground and my eyes searching the horizon for any indication of something that would let me in on the cruel joke that insisted on messing with my mind.

I thought I could hear James' voice, a mere whisper in my head, but I was afraid to let myself believe again that it was truly my love. I had fallen for that trick earlier and I wouldn't allow myself another moment of happiness at the sound of his voice only to become victim to the changing scenery. The Romani Realms were both a thing of beauty and a horrific scene of destruction. Strangling snakes and tarry pits gave way to grassy fields with dancing butterflies only to disappear again and in their place, trees as bare as the dead of winter held threatening black birds on their limbs. What if the words I heard were a figment as well?

I welcomed the cool wind that started to blow through the trees until I saw that the source of the breeze was the maniacal fluttering of hundreds of black bird wings. Their eyes looked down at me strangely as if willing me to stay lying face down and defeated.

"You can't win," I said looking at them through eyes that still threatened to glaze over. "I only have my resolve in this horrible place."

And with that I pulled myself up, only to have first one and then another dive bomb me, their talons scratching my arms and the back of my neck as I made my way to a lake that oddly, I didn't remember being there just moments earlier.

"Nam myoho renge kyo," I chanted the buddhist phrase to awaken my own connection to nature, the butterflies that flew with me, in order to be one with nature rather than against it.

"That's right, sweetheart."

It sounded so much like James. I so wanted to believe. Maybe just for one minute...just one gift of the memory of him would give me the strength to carry on.

Chapter Seven

"**M**r. James, you's not concentratin'," Maebeline's syrupy voice poured over him.

James took a deep breath and clasped hands with Maebeline again. "I'm trying."

"Then try not to be so distracted."

With his hand in hers, Maebeline once again attempted to channel the powers of the Otherworld, the realm that traps lost souls of which the Romani Realms is but one.

"Child, I've known you for your entire life and while you have proven to be an excellent business man and somewhat reliable Shade partner, you are not living up to my standards at the moment."

James smiled in spite of the gravity of the situation. Maebeline was the only person he had met that like him, had the ability to travel forward and backward in time and therefore, could heal and protect. As formidable a force that this made both of them, it was nothing compared to the scolding she could wield.

"Okay truth. I'm coming up with nothing. Are you seeing her?"

Maebeline's round face and chocolate eyes met his as she sadly shook her head.

"It doesn't make sense," James said running a hand through his wavy brown hair, his blue eyes cast downward. "Suki should be able to hear me. We..."

"Uhh, uhh, I don't need to know what you two did outside the establishment of marriage. It obviously didn't bind you to her in the way that a marriage would in the eyes of God and the other spirits we're dealing with."

"If I get her through this, I'll make sure and do something about that," he said and closed his eyes, trying once again to extend his reach into the Romani Realms. "In the meantime, we need to find why my voice is blocked to her."

Maebeline shifted and lit another candle that sat among many others that were lit in a semi-circle in front of them. She extended her hands to the flames, letting them hover dangerously close to the heat. "Let me try something else...an incantation of nature. It will help to bring her and the elements closer together."

Maebeline remained in a trance for only moments before the reality of the situation presented itself. "Raven's influence is very strong in the Realms. Did you see..."

"She's altered Suki's reality. I saw it."

"It's the curse of the Romani Realms. They all do it and then the changes become all the stronger. Every soul that resides there has a bit of mischief in them."

"Not every soul," James reminded.

But Maebeline was quick to correct him. "Not every soul who has yet to succumb to the powers and influence of that dreaded place. Eventually, they all go mad. I saw her James...I saw Raven and her thoughts."

"It's strange. I saw Suki and the others, but my vision of Raven materialized as only darkness -- like a television screen gone black."

"That was Raven. She's planning on trapping all of them within the Realms -- Suki, Charlotte, Samantha. The only ones who are getting out of there are herself and Phineas, and I can't tell where his allegiance lies."

"We need to get a message to Phineas."

"How do you know you can trust him?"

"I don't," James said before falling silent, not daring to speak the polarized thoughts that ran through his head. On the one hand, he was indebted to Maebeline. Each protected the other during time travel, ensuring that there was always someone securely planted in the present to retrieve the other. Yet, if he simply remained here, rooted in the presence, the entire mission may be sacrificed.

"She can't hear me," he said finally.

"And without your voice, she'll eventually succumb to the forces of that crazy messed up realm."

"But she's so strong, Maebeline. She survived centuries without having actually met me."

"Yes, but what made your appearance in her life necessary?"

"Raven?"

"Precisely."

Maebeline took his hand. Although technically she had worked for James as his maid for years, she was also a comfort to him. "James, go to her. You know you want to."

James nodded his head. "You know what this means?"

"We've had a good run."

"Give me a little credit. I'll get her and be back in time for your jambalaya and peach pie."

"Unless you get yourself killed, then I'm eating the whole pie myself."

"Ah, you can wish that all you want, but that doesn't make it true," he said smiling his mischievous glint.

An uncomfortable silence grew between them. Their bond had grown over the years to be more than employer and employee, more than mammy and the school boy she had raised. They relied on each other as only Shades could; they were each responsible for bringing the other back when the portals of time travel closed unexpectedly. If James were to travel into the Romani Realms, there was a distinct possibility that he wouldn't return. Therefore, to go there and ensure my safety put his own life as well as Maebeline's in permanent jeopardy.

"Chin up," Maebeline said. "You won't have to pretend to listen to me or take my advice any more."

"First of all, I never pretend about something as important as your advice. Got any now?"

"Yes. Don't die."

Maebeline smiled at James as he reached and pulled her into a gigantic bear hug with each one competing for the tightest squeeze.

"Well, shall we go inside and give me a proper send off?"

James' voice was still persistently trying to get through to me, even while he crossed through the realms of the present into the hidden and perilous Romani Realms. Although I wanted to hear him, trying to listen intently meant that I also heard the pleas of every lost soul in this god forsaken place. They would cry out for forgiveness, scream with promises to repent, and as if that weren't bad enough, then one had to also hear the cries of the souls who were truly lost -- the ones who had no idea what they had done to deserve such a fate of living among the bizarre and shifting universe that was the Romani Realms.

There were innocents here that were being tempted into going bad and innocents that were being preyed upon for their purity. Charlotte and Samantha's reality and minds could be fed upon, literally eaten alive. Their goodness and dreams captured like television shows for the lost souls' enjoyment or as penance paid to the demonized creatures who used the Romani Realms as their own training ground to create formidable forces used within the present realms.

The grinding of gears sounded in my ears, reminding me of how easy it was to come here in the first place.

"Sure, easy to get here, but impossible to leave. This place is a one-way street," I said aloud to a few butterflies that finally answered my prayers and materialized, gliding just overhead. They flew in a circular formation around me, moving in formation as a protective element while I rested from Raven's latest attack.

"Suki, I'm here," James' voice sounded.

This time, I dared to answer the voice, annoyed at whoever was trying this cruel trick. "Stop it. You think I'm going to cry over the sound of his voice? Honestly, he's not that hot."

"That's not what you said in your living room."

"Still not James," I answered back defiantly. "Anyone can have sex in their living room. We're not in Victorian times anymore. That was just a lucky guess on your part...whoever you are, you perverted little demon."

James' low chuckle sounded in his throat before he spoke into my mind once again, *"That's a nice pet name. I think I'll keep it."*

There was something different this time. Unlike when I heard his voice before being attacked, this

James was clearer. Of course it could mean that whatever threatened me was simply closer, or could it be true? It was too much to hope for, but I had to try...and hope. "What shape is the birthmark on my thigh?"

"Butterfly."

"What color dress was I wearing when I first met Maebeline?"

"You weren't wearing a dress."

"James!" I spun around in a circle, watching for him, hoping that he really would appear. The butterflies, originally all blue, now doubled in numbers and included varieties of green, pink, and yellow. They fluttered with excitement and created a curtain effect that when they finally parted revealed James looking fit and strong, alert and happy, not in the least bit affected by the long and arduous journey into the Romani Realms.

I threw my arms around his neck and he wrapped his around my waist. "You're here."

"Thinking about you getting dressed from behind the partition in my Atlanta home helped give me the last boost to get here."

"So glad I could help jumpstart you."

James bent his head down to mine for a kiss, which I gladly returned. My hand reached for his face, relishing in the familiar tickle that his bit of scruff felt against my palm. He twirled a lock of my long, brown waves around his fingers and then pressed his hand against the back of my head, taking my mouth for his hungry kiss, and with our tongues now intwined we continued to kiss, until I unexplainably stiffened.

"What's wrong?"

"It's nothing, just that my back is a bit sore. But I feel much better in your arms," I said wiggling closer again, hating that my involuntary movement caused our kiss to cease.

"Let me see. Just lift up the back of your top."

When I did as he requested, James' breath caught and a low whistle escaped him. "That's quite a bruise. How'd you manage that?"

"Raven, a large branch, and me. Not my favorite combination."

"Hmm, so much for my hand-to-hand combat lessons. What happened to all of that Krav Maga training?"

"Basically, I fight like a girl."

"And did you think that using your power over the elements wasn't a good idea?" James pressed.

"They've been on the blink ever since I got here."

"Want me to...you know?" James smiled.

"Here?"

"You're here; I'm here. And your back is a mess."

"Yes, but if you do that magic Shade treatment to me, then I'm going to want something more."

"First of all, that's a good thing, but since we're here to get Charlotte and Samantha back, we better table that. You'll have to resist me...as impossible as that sounds."

"I think I can manage."

James turned me around, lightly placing his hands on my shoulders. "You ready?"

"Hit me," I answered back.

"Cute. Now just relax. Feel the energy from me into you."

James hands felt warm on my back. As he moved them up and down the bruised area, a tingling sensation spread not only across my back, but also down my arms and up each leg, leaving me feeling almost dizzy. But James was quick to place one hand behind my head as I started to reel backwards. He gently placed me on the ground face-down and then knelt behind me, slowly pulling up my top to inspect the bruise.

"It's not black and blue anymore, just a hideous shade of yellow."

"Then it's healing. Let's go."

"I can do more; just lie still."

With just one finger James traced a circle around the bruise, and I inhaled sharply.

"You like that, don't you?"

"It's no big deal. I'm not going to be affected by this."

"Sure you won't," he said continuing. "Then you won't mind if I finish."

"What color am I?" My voice suddenly sounded less confident about my abilities to fight the attraction to James.

James lightly ran one finger down the length of my spine. Even that small action was magical. When he gently pressed his entire palm onto my back, the feeling sent a pulsating jump all the way through me. A low rumble sounded from my stomach, indicating that his touch was starting a reaction of sheer pleasure. He continued to let his palm explore the delicate bruised skin while he bent his head to press his lips to the top of my shoulder blades.

"James?"

"Mmm hmm?" he said, still keeping his mouth on my back, but this time he let it trail light kisses down the center of my spine.

"Is this part of the treatment?"

"No, this is extra. You should go with it."

His mouth went lower and was now at mid-back.

"Okay, I'll just..." I closed my eyes, not even able to utter another thought.

James placed a knee on either side of my body and let his mouth move down each vertebrae. His tongue now went to work, weaving delicate circles along my hip. His hands gently caressed each hip as his tongue continued to work magic over the very base of my spine, moving dangerously close to the area that could no longer be classified as my back.

"And you're finished," he said popping himself up to a seated position.

"This is what you call finished?" I asked, feeling frustrated.

"Well, your back is its normal shade, although I must note," he said furrowing his brows and pretending to examine my face more closely, "that your cheeks have taken on a very flushed tone indeed. I wonder what caused that?"

"Indeed. I wonder."

James offered his hand, which I accepted as he pulled me up to standing. "So, there are a few things you should know," he said sounding business like again. His tone was intoxicating and commanding. It made me wish I could have seen him in action during the Industrial Revolution when his factory manufactured an early version of the steam engine and later constructed nearly 500 engines.

"Just like the scenery changes, so do people."

"Charlotte and Samantha?" I couldn't imagine either girl changing, their pure nature was undeniable. "Have you seen them?"

James shook his head. "Not directly."

"What does that mean?"

"It means that I couldn't see them, but I felt the presence of innocent souls when I crossed through. What about your connection to them?"

I paused, not really believing my own insight unto them. "Right now, I don't feel like either is in distress, but then it shifts, and I do. I can't trust my own instincts."

"You have to. That's what will save you down here. If you're seeing them happy and yet you know in your heart that they're in danger, then the risk is greater than you realize."

"I'm not following."

James continued, "The souls that feed on the innocent can befriend someone here. They can convince them to stay."

"Charlotte and Samantha might not recognize who is good or bad?"

James nodded.

"But Samantha's gift? Surely that will help her?"

"It's true that Samantha can spot whether someone is of pure heart -- back in the present -- but she had barely discovered her gift when she was thrown into this place. She would have to channel her gift, focus on it. Only then would she be able to further develop and use it here."

"Maybe Charlotte has found her, and can get through to her."

"We need to hurry -- in case Charlotte has been compromised."

Chapter Eight

"Would you like to dance?"

Samantha looked up to see who had made the request of her. Like the three before him, he was extremely good-looking, and similar to the others, his soul was completely tarnished. She had gotten better at reading souls and developing her ability to realize a person's true essence. There wasn't much else to do in these realms so it was a pastime that she had decided to perfect.

"No, thank you. My feet hurt."

"Alright, maybe later."

Samantha smiled politely, not wanting to upset the man whom she suspected had killed his former lover. Initially, she could only decipher whether a person was innately good or bad. It was quite simple, almost like a thumbs up or down sign that flashed in her mind. But as she practiced, visions would accompany her instincts and now she could also tell what caused a soul to go bad.

She sat twirling one tendril of her long, red hair that managed to spring free of the bun. She had taken to piling her hair on top of her head as she found it attracted less attention than her unruly and wild curls. There was little to do except listen to the music and hope that nobody too terrible approached. She was quickly realizing that in the realms her gift kept her in solitude.

She watched her would-be suitor walk away, swirls of black clouds trailing him and visions of him stabbing his ex-girlfriend to death materializing out of the dust that rose above him. He greeted another girl who accepted his advances. Although Samantha typically needed to speak to someone to read their soul's essence, this girl was so rogue that her misguided nature and inability to conform to society flowed freely from her. Samantha stared in her direction, amazed at how clearly the vision of the girl's guilt puddled at her feet. In the realm of the present, the girl had seduced one man after another only to blackmail them for money after pretending to be pregnant with their child.

"Looks like you dodged a bullet there." She looked up to see a young man with light brown hair that fell in gentle waves over his forehead, wide-set brown eyes that still twinkled in spite of the depressing nature of their environment, and a broad chest and strong shoulders that filled out his suit nicely.

"Yesiree," Samantha admitted. "I'd say those two are meant for each other."

"So, are you ready?" he asked expectantly.

"Pardon me?" Samantha asked with a guarded expression.

"Are you ready to dance? Everyone else is and if you just sit here, the others are sure to ask. I'm Daniel," he said holding out his hand.

Samantha followed his gaze to where a row of young men were standing by the wall of the rounded room eyeing all of the women inside as they sized them up deciding whom to approach. The young guy was right. She didn't want any of them coming up to her as they were all showing essence of evil. It was true that some were less so than others, but she didn't need any type of malignant male in her life. As one man whose essence showed him to have held a girl underwater started toward her, she hooked her arm within Daniel's.

"I'll take that dance now. I've had enough cray-cray for one night."

"Cray-cray?"

"I'm Samantha," she said holding her hand to him in return. "And that's my own little expression for crazy, which I think I'm quickly becoming."

"This place will do that to you...unless you dance."

Samantha shrugged her shoulders in response.

"Come on," Daniel coaxed. "You're not like most people here. I could use the distraction."

"Are you sure? I'm no debutante," she warned with a slight smile, the first one that had graced her face since she arrived in this horrible place.

"I'll take my chances with you," he said and held her hand high above her head, readying Samantha for her first twirl around the floor.

"That's her! Shadow, how do I get inside?"

The girl held tightly onto Charlotte's hand and her voice wavered. "I don't want you to leave me. Please don't go!"

Charlotte's heart melted. The more time she spent with Shadow, the more of a pull she felt toward the girl, a deep need to take care of her was growing within her. She bent down on one knee to look the little girl in the eye and readily pulled her in for a hug. Whispering soothingly in her ear, she said, "I won't leave you. I don't know how you ended up alone, but you've got me now. I just don't want my friend to be alone either."

Shadow looked into Charlotte's eyes, sizing her up and weighing whether to risk losing her to another. "You promise me?"

Charlotte made the sign of crossing her heart with her finger.

"Follow me," Shadow commanded before running around the building to a side that wasn't covered by windows, but with a mural. The painting depicted a lake with one solitary swan and a bridge that disappeared into the mist.

"There," Shadow pointed. "That's how you get in."

Charlotte shook her head. "Where?"

"Don't you see it?"

And then, as if Shadow willed it to appear, the outline of a small door suddenly became visible within the base of the bridge. Charlotte placed her hand on the small, wooden knob, disguised as part of a tree branch in the mural. She tried to turn it, but it wouldn't budge. Feeling desperate to get inside, Charlotte rapped on the door, but barely a sound echoed from her touch.

"Wait," Shadow stopped her, placing her small hand atop Charlotte's. Charlotte immediately recoiled her hand, the touch of the child feeling oddly cold to her.

"What's wrong?"

Charlotte recovered herself and took a deep breath. "Nothing....nothing's wrong."

"Just don't forget your promise."

Charlotte hugged the girl ignoring the cold chill running through her as she did so. Shadow placed her own hand on the knob and with barely any effort, it turned and the door swung open, releasing the sound of the orchestra's waltz.

Shadow outstretched her arms and turned in circles. She began dancing with abandon, exhibiting the exuberance of youth. Only somehow with Shadow, it came across as more of a manic act. She stopped only when she had twirled herself into a dizzying fit and stumbled into Charlotte.

"That was fun. Now it's your turn," she said and indicated that Charlotte should go into the next room where the music could be heard.

Charlotte took a tentative step in the direction that Shadow indicated only to have her stop her once more. "You're not going in like that, are you?"

Charlotte looked down at her casual and now rather dirty outfit. "I don't have anything more appropriate," she reasoned and started toward the room again.

"Not really the best way to make an impression."

"Listen, I'm not here to make an impression. Samantha is my best friend. It's not like she doesn't know me."

"She won't know you." There was something about the emphatic way in which Shadow spoke the words that made Charlotte take notice. "You'll look like some sort of street urchin and the guards will throw you out."

"So what do I do?"

Shadow pointed to a long hallway with a door at the end that read: *Salon de Beaute.* "Go in there. They'll get you sorted."

Charlotte glanced down the hallway, and then back at Shadow, who had miraculously changed her appearance and was now wearing a light blue party dress with a black sash, white tights and black shoes.

"How did you..." Charlotte looked at Shadow, who was taking a brush to her curls.

"Your necklace is pretty," Shadow said admiring the Amulet of Pollox that hung on a delicate chain around Charlotte's neck. "It would look so pretty with my dress. Can I..." she started to ask while reaching her hand toward the pendant.

Instinctively, Charlotte batted her hand away. "No!"

Shadow looked up in surprise, her eyes growing large and filling with tears.

"Oh, I'm sorry, Shadow. I'm just so jumpy. I can't even remember you changing clothes, and this necklace is very special to me."

Shadow's eyes cleared of tears and changed to a hateful red before she blinked them back to their regular ice blue. "I'm going to go inside now," she said sullenly.

"Okay, I'll get fixed up and see you soon. You'll be okay?" Charlotte asked, but the little girl had already left.

Samantha watched the murals of the room go by as Daniel led her around the rounded room in what seemed to be a never ending waltz. They passed the same couples repeatedly, each displaying varying degrees of evil wafting up behind them. Samantha wished she could close her eyes and lose herself in Daniel's arms as he was the first person she had encountered in the Romani Realms who didn't send off warning messages in her mind. Whether that was safe for her remained to be seen, but for the moment she decided to go with it and enjoy the mental salvation.

"You okay?"

"Yeah, why wouldn't I be?" Samantha asked.

"Well, you're here for one thing, and from what I can tell of your soul it isn't tainted. Want to talk to someone who is good at listening?"

Samantha's need to confide in someone was great, and yet, she hesitated. "How do you know I'm not...tainted? And besides, why would I trust you?"

"Your soul is pure. I can read it...just like you can with me."

Samantha stopped dancing and focused. Since being in the Romani Realms all of her instincts were heightened and she was learning to trust them. She took Daniel's hand once more, a silent acceptance that he was telling the truth.

"So how did you end up here?"

"You mean if I'm not...evil?" he asked, maintaining a low whisper because of their proximity to other couples who did not share their purity.

Samantha nodded, also not daring to speak aloud.

"Some mistakes are irreversible. I made a big one," he said and shrugged.

"Me too," Samantha added sadly.

"Do you miss your friends and family?" Daniel asked.

Samantha wrinkled her brow. "It's strange, but I don't remember any of them. I see snippets of myself somewhere else, but I don't know what I'm looking at. I see myself running and I'm terribly scared. No, I'm worried about someone, but I don't know who. And then, I think I'm falling, but maybe it's just like one of those dreams where you feel like you're falling. You know?"

Daniel nodded, and pulled her closer against his chest. Samantha looked up in surprise. It felt good to talk to someone openly.

"I'm sorry," he said and released his hold slightly. "Hearing your story makes me want to keep you safe. I've seen so many people here succumb to the curse of this place."

"How long do I have?" Samantha asked, knowing that he spoke the truth. Even she had felt her hold on reality slipping away, before he mentioned it. She suspected that the fact that she couldn't remember anything about her former life to be indicative that the Romani Realms were already affecting her sanity.

"If you can learn to channel your thoughts by keeping a foothold in your former life, you can be okay indefinitely. It's just not easy," he said, indicating a couple that breezed past them, each one spewing vision clouds that displayed heinous acts of malicious intent. "Those two arrived here together three years ago. He had been in a car accident and was on life support. She took his life in the hospital and then her own believing they would end up together. They did."

Samantha furrowed her brow in question as she watched the couple. She saw them committing a myriad of other acts against innocent people.

"So the crimes they committed..."

"All of them occurred here," Daniel explained. "Their souls were so lost that it was easy for the evils to prey and feed upon them until no goodness was left. Now those two do the same...eating away at the humanity of the newcomers so they can feel just a bit more human and good, to feel some semblance of what they once were. It's why they spend so much time at these dances."

"Why are you here?"

Daniel shrugged uneasily. "I guess I want to find someone too. But not for the same reasons."

Samantha looked at him warily.

"Tell me that you believe me."

"I want to...but you have to be honest with me...and trust me." Samantha stopped dancing for a moment to look into Daniel's kind eyes. She wanted so much to believe that there could be one other person here who was good. "What caused you to be here? What did you do?"

"Voodoo," he answered simply.

Chapter Nine

As Charlotte entered the Salon she was immediately greeted by two beautiful, young women in their mid-twenties. Identical twins with blonde hair and blue eyes, both wore their hair in a chic and tidy chignon and were immaculately dressed in crisp, clean linen robes.

Charlotte was handed a similar robe, hers in a rather ugly shade of blue that resembled a hospital gown, and led to change into it behind a partition. When Charlotte came out carrying her clothes, the girls looked at each other as if weighing who had gotten the short end of the stick and would be forced to touch something as disgusting as the dirty clothes. One of the girls finally rang a bell and within seconds another girl appeared. Unlike the girls attending to Charlotte, this one was brunette and wore a robe of burlap. Charlotte's eyes immediately went to the girl's throat, where a hideous scar weaved across where her voice box would normally be.

One of the girls shouted in a foreign tongue at the new one, when she accidentally dropped one of

Charlotte's shoes. The brunette bowed low immediately in front of the twins, who merely let her remain in the subservient pose for a good minute before dismissing her.

Once she was gone and Charlotte's clothes taken along with her, the twins whispered to each other as they circled Charlotte. After a few turns around her, one stopped in front of her and reached for her hands to inspect her nails, while the other gingerly touched her hair and examined the pores of her skin. Although Charlotte was a natural beauty by anyone's standards with skin as smooth and pale as alabaster, blonde hair so light it was nearly white and her delicately small facial features, but in spite of her good looks, the girls shook their heads and made clucking noises with their tongues as if making Charlotte over would be the challenge of a lifetime.

Finally, the twins, known in the Romani Realms as Nephilim, the product of fallen angels and human women who had been trapped in the realm, came to an agreement. Deciding on the course of action they would take, they led Charlotte down another hallway to a stark, white room filled with sinks and salon chairs, a large table covered with colorful bottles of every shape and size, and various instruments to either curl or straighten one's hair.

The Nephilim continued their unusual language at times sounding guttural and then turning into a bird-like chirp. At one point, Charlotte recognized a few words of Spanish, but no sooner did she show a look of recognition did the girls catch her eye and changed their dialogue to French. Once again, a look of understanding crossed Charlotte's face and the twins again switched to something that sounded like Dutch. Charlotte casually moved her hand up to her necklace to activate the powers of the Amulet of Pollox. Visions of the men who had the pendant in their possession came to mind, but alas, none were Dutch and so she was at a loss to figure out what plans the girls were cooking up for her. They watched closely as she fingered her necklace and when satisfied that Charlotte had no idea what they were saying, they continued, only now obviously more relaxed about their conversation as they seemed to be arguing about their course of action.

One of the girls touched a lock of Charlotte's hair and shook her head in disgust. The other objected and pointed to her face and then waved a finger up and down, pointing out the flaws she found with Charlotte's entire body. Finally, the first one threw up her hands and nodded. It was decided. They handed Charlotte a towel and three bottles: one pink with a silhouette of a woman's body, one turquoise that had an image of a woman running her hands down her long hair, and the last one, a pale green bottle that had a similar picture of a woman massaging her head with bubbles floating up into the sky. They pointed to a shower and then left the room.

"So I guess they think I stink. Okaaay," she said to herself and turned on the water. "I'm guessing body wash, shampoo and conditioner. If I had a razor, I'd be all set."

As if able to either read her mind or hear her voice within the confides of the shower room, one of the girls suddenly appeared, rapped on the door, and handed Charlotte a razor that was hygienically sealed in a plastic wrapper.

"Thank you," Charlotte said, trying to cover up her body at the same time.

The girl glared at Charlotte and made a face as if she were trying hard not to vomit, and simply pointed at Charlotte's legs.

"Yes, I'll take care of it," Charlotte answered.

The ball was still in full force with the floor full of couples dressed in elegant clothing, the tuxedo clad waiters standing in the shadows waiting to bring drinks or replenish the multitude of dishes at the buffet.

Samantha indicated to Daniel that she needed a rest from their turn on the dance floor, pointing to the table of canapes.

"Deux champagnes, s'il vous plait," Daniel requested.

"They're French?"

"Only tonight," Daniel replied with a shake of his head and shrug of his broad shoulders. "The elders of the realm thought it gave the ball an air of elegance so they brought in an entirely French staff for this event. Trouble is, they don't speak a word of English so unless you've studied, you go hungry."

"Where did you learn?"

"I grew up in New Orleans," he explained. "Yeah, it was an interesting upbringing. My grandmere fed me tales of voodoo and bowls of dirty rice."

Samantha laughed. It was easy to be with Daniel. He put her at ease in spite of the fact that something he did landed him in the Romani Realms, but who was she to pass judgement? She was here as well, although the reason that sent her here still escaped her memory.

"Why is everyone whispering? I feel like I walked out of the ladies room with a piece of toilet paper attached to my shoe or somewhere worse."

Daniel looked over Samantha, taking in her long, midnight blue gown that made her red hair look even more fiery. He reached out and gently placed the runaway tendril that she had earlier fiddled with behind her ear. "Trust me, you look beautiful."

"Thank you. I don't normally dress up so I'm out of my element, but I have to admit this is pretty amazing," she said taking in the surroundings.

"They're all wondering who will be offered for the Reckoning. That's why everyone is whispering and staring. Over there...in the corner," he said pointing to where a beautiful, young woman in a black catsuit stood behind a high fronted desk, "that's where you can place bets."

"What's the Reckoning?"

Daniel looked at Samantha in surprise. "How long have you been here?"

Samantha shook her head slightly. "I don't think very long. I can't remember anything."

"Then you're probably in your first six months. If you had been through a Reckoning...well, you'd remember," he said grimly.

A bell sounded at that moment causing Daniel to check his watch.

James held tightly onto my arm. "We need to hurry," he said. "But, I don't think we'll get there in time with your leg the way it is. May I?"

I raised my eyebrows and James no sooner lifted my skirt above my knee, exposing part of my thigh along the way.

He winced at the sight of my thigh, which was covered in bruises with a long gash down the center that was swelled and showing signs of infection. He closed his eyes, placed his hands delicately on my thigh and almost instantly, a cold sensation flooded through the cut and the throbbing of my pained flesh ceased. Miraculously, the river of blood started to dry, the skin that was deeply wounded began to close and the bruising changed from a dark blue-green to yellow and then back to its normal shade of pale.

James paused momentarily to ensure that the cut didn't re-open and then, comforted that my leg was healed, he bent his head and gently kissed the affected area. "Good as new. And now, we need to get going."

"To where?"

James picked up a branch from the ground and broke it into two. With the sharp end, he carved the symbol of infinity onto the nearest tree branch. "To mark our spot," he explained. "Now, first to get us some proper clothing and then...The Reckoning."

Before I could reply, the sound of gears turning and clocks chiming sounded. The wind rushed past my face as I felt myself pulled through time with James' strong arm securely wrapped around my waist.

"We're here," Raven said pointing to a small house in the midst of a forest clearing.

"Who lives here?"

"Consider it our little home away from home," Raven answered and plucked a dandelion from the ground. Phineas watched as she brought it to her lips and blew the fuzzy petals into the wind. It immediately turned black, sending ashes into the air as well. She smiled and pulled an intricately carved key from her pocket and opened the cottage door.

Phineas stepped over the threshold behind her, following as she led him through the main room and into a small bedroom with a large four-poster, oak bed. She flopped onto the middle of it and stared up at him expectantly. "We still have at least two hours before the Reckoning."

"That's happening now? It's too soon. I thought..."

"Tsk tsk," Raven smiled. "You thought we were coming here to give Samantha a gift for her new home? Or, maybe we were here to make sure that Charlotte had a safe flight back into the present realms? Come on, Phin, I love your innocence, but full out naivete is just not that appealing in a man. We're here for the Reckoning so you can put these silly fantasies about Charlotte behind us once and for all. I can see now that this is totally necessary, which actually makes me happy. I'd hate to think that I orchestrated this major event without a need for it. The lifeless souls are still digesting that sweet girl of two months ago. The elders thought there wasn't really a need for another Reckoning so soon, but as you can see...there is, at least in my book."

"Are you finished?"

"Quite, but not with you." Raven crooked her finger at him.

"Not in the mood, Raven."

"I don't believe you," she answered in a sing-song tone. "I love you."

"You don't. You love manipulating me."

"Come here. I want to share something with you," she said, patting the bed beside her, her tone changing from demanding to actually sincere.

Phineas rolled his eyes, knowing that the chances of Raven telling him anything that could actually change his impression of this place or what she had proven capable of in the last month were an impossibility. He thought of Charlotte, his need to see her and the plan to go along with Raven in order to make the first goal a reality.

"What's wrong?" he asked, his attempt at sincerity making him feel ill.

"I know you think I'm horrible for the way I've treated Suki, and perhaps letting my anger affect her Releasors was immature..."

"That's putting it a bit mildly, don't you think?"

"Phin, I have my reasons. I'm trying to tell you..."

In spite of wanting to appease her and her volatile temper, Phineas couldn't help but roll his eyes. The only surprise was when Raven ignored his insolence and continued in a voice that was both sweet and almost wounded.

"She did take everything from me."

"You told me about the witch trials. I know that she turned in your lover, but she was doing that to save you. Why can't you get over it?"

"If it were just about what happened in the 1400s then by now, I probably could forget. But she took something else from me. She took *someone* else. And the loss of that relationship I can never forgive because we were going to have a child."

"I'm not following you. Who are you talking about, Raven?"

Phineas knew Raven to be a shrewd demon gypsy who had perfected her ability to control the elements, to cross-over into other realms, and defeat death. He had ceased to be surprised at her ability to turn off her human emotions as that was what she had worked so hard to perfect. She was a complex woman who had lived many lives, but what he never expected was the simplicity of her next comment.

"James."

The woman at the podium rang a bell and indicated for everyone to take seats that surrounded the perimeter of the room.

"Before we commence the Reckoning, we will be showing a brief film about the rich history of the Romani Realms. I do hope you will enjoy it."

Samantha and Daniel sat next to each other as a grainy film with shoddy sound began. It was reminiscent of the propaganda films dating back to McCarthyism.

Time travel through the Romani Realms is a skill that many have tried, but few have perfected. Like everything in the realms, senses are heightened and therefore, as one moves through different times the realization of the hardships of those times is associated with it.

Those who first settled in the Romani Realms were unaccustomed to its treacherous landscape of lost souls. Our founders worked hard to create an open door policy where lost souls would be welcome and able to make the forgotten marshes and forests into their new home. Our earliest inhabitants were people of the land, who knew how to forage for food. However, as more people came, the animals that many survived off of were long picked over. In order to survive, food came in the form of new souls.

At that moment, Raven's face appeared on the screen in what looked like a model's headshot pose, followed by images of her in various athletic and casual poses. She was shown on horseback playing polo, in a gourmet kitchen preparing a souffle, and then on a yacht, tacking during a regatta. The narrative continued...

One of our great founders, Raven Underwood, saw an opportunity for growth in our realms. By feeding upon innocents, the Romani Realms' inhabitants could once again become self-reliant and a destination of choice for demons of all races and breeds.

Under Raven's tutelage, our community built the magnificent glass gazebo in which you are all seated as well as recruited the finest landscape architects to create the illusions that newcomers see. We thank Raven for her vision -- to create a break in the pattern of bleakness and turn the Romani Realms into a vacation retreat.

As you enjoy the upcoming Reckoning, take note of our peaceful bodies of glass-like water surrounded by willow trees... Our grassy meadows with flowers and fauna... Like an oasis, these areas are meant to be enjoyed until the time comes that soul can no longer appreciate beauty. You will find these areas located in strategically placed spots to give founders and innocents a welcome break in an otherwise gloomy and horrific scenery. We hope you enjoyed this bit of history.

The woman who introduced the film returned to the podium. A round of applause followed her. "Wasn't that a gem of a film? I've got one more surprise...I'm told that none other than Raven will be here later."

The crowd erupted again, this time with even more enthusiasm.

Daniel leaned over to Samantha. "Are you okay?"

"Yes...it's just...I don't know it's probably impossible, but there was something so familiar about that film. I felt as if I knew that woman they spoke of -- the one called Raven."

"Give me your hand," James instructed, but I still felt as if I were flailing through time, being pulled through the good and the horrors of our recent history.

"Suki, try not to focus on the negative." He was doing his best to shield me from any atrocities, but still my sensitivity and perceptive abilities made it difficult to not see and feel the emotions of the people who have entered the Romani Realms.

"Come on, Suki," he urged. "You can hear me."

Although trembling, I extended my hand forward in space and reached for James. He not only grabbed my hand, but immediately pulled my entire body into his strong chest, holding me closely against his beating heart. "I've got you," he whispered into my ear.

I felt the warmth of his hand stroke my hair, felt his arms around me, and immediately the fear dissipated and I opened my eyes to see his clear, blue ones smiling back at me.

"Welcome back," he said against my lips as he brushed them with his own. "I was so worried about you. What happened?" he asked, and I realized that we were now safely planted by the banks of a quiet lake, somewhere on the outskirts of one of the Realms' tar traps.

For a moment, I just shook my head in sorrow. Then, wiping a tear from my cheek, I took a deep breath and spoke. "I passed by so much sorrow and pain. I expected it from what you said, and I thought I could handle it, but then there was something else..."

James pulled me onto his lap and let me rest there with my back firmly planted against his chest, his arms holding me closely until I calmed.

"James, I saw one of my past Releasors...a man named Brian Mickelberg. He was a good man, but falsely accused of robbery in which multiple bars of gold bullion was stolen from the Perth Mint in Australia. There was a trial and he was sent to prison for it."

"Did you grant him all of his wishes?"

Sadly, I nodded. "The last of his wishes was granted upon his release. He wanted to fly a twin-engine plane. It seemed like such a simple request and because of what he had been through, I granted it. And then, he died in a crash."

James' eyes met mine, and I was thankful for his attentiveness.

"His wish wasn't a selfless plea, and still, I granted it. I shouldn't have been swayed by circumstance. His death was my fault. And just now, I saw that he suffered and ended up here."

"It's out of your hands, Suki, and you have to move on. Charlotte and Samantha need you to be strong."

I nodded, knowing he was right, but the after effects of seeing what could happen to a trapped soul stayed with me. "What if I can't help them?"

"Don't think like that. This place will throw everything at you, and you have to fight it back with everything you have."

"Nothing can be worse than what I just saw," I said. "He was innocent -- in both lives."

I stared across the lake at a lone swan that glided gracefully in circles, its mate no where in sight, and involuntarily shuddered at the cool wind that was suddenly picking up. James' words shook me out of my quiet reverie.

"We better get to the other side of the lake now. It's quiet there and I'll be able to channel us with Maebeline. We'll get some proper clothes and join the others. Are you ready for this?"

I nodded, and took his hand, unaware that my own trials were only beginning.

Chapter Ten

When the Nephilim finished with Charlotte she was perfection personified. This had been like no makeover Charlotte had ever experienced. The twins took computer images of Charlotte's face, ran it through a program, and were instantly rewarded with a program designed to bring out Charlotte's features in the most effective way possible via makeup techniques and colors, clothing and hair styles.

Charlotte stood poised at a side door leading to the grand ballroom. The girls instructed her, thankfully this time in English, not to draw too much attention to herself until the bell sounded that the Reckoning would begin. Although Charlotte had no idea what the Reckoning was, she was thankful to enter the ballroom and search for Samantha in a circumspect way. But anyone looking at Charlotte would know that for her to enter a room undetected was an impossibility. In a word, she looked breathtaking.

A hush fell over the room and a crowd gathered in the center, blocking Samantha and Daniel's view of whatever was the attraction. As the crowd parted, they could see why everyone had grown silent. Charlotte walked hesitantly into the room, taking in the staring faces and ornate decor. She moved slowly, which only made her entrance seem more majestic. Dressed in a long white off-the-shoulder gown with a form-fitting bodice and a train that draped behind her, she was a vision of beauty. The body of the dress and its train flowed gracefully over Charlotte's petite frame and onto the floor. The white fabric had an ethereal quality to it, appearing as if it were made of delicate silk adorned by soft, downy feathers. Her hair hung straight, gently caressing her shoulders and its color practically mirroring that of her dress.

Across the room, Samantha was carrying a plate laden with tapas and petit fours, her first appealing meal since coming to this Realm, to her spot with Daniel. She struggled to move through the multitudes of people who had now gathered at the ball. As she made her way back, the hushed whispers she passed were more than a distraction, they felt like a warning.

Samantha paused by a wall to listen to the conversation of two women from the Elite Founders Circle, those who are given first access to the mind of a new Reckoning.

"Have you placed bets on who is to be the Reckoning?"

The woman standing adjacent to the first shook her head. "The younger minds are all so full of technology, it's difficult to get a true reading."

"One of the Nephilim girls knows it to be a young woman. Apparently, she's here looking for someone. They say she's quite pretty."

"How peculiar. So she wasn't actually sent here?"

"No, but apparently she has no idea of how to return. There's others who are expected to meet her."

"Others?" the second woman asked with disbelief, only to have her question returned with a nod.

Samantha jumped when a hand touched her arm. "There you are," Daniel's smooth voice reached her.

"Here," Samantha offered him her plate, "they looked wonderful so I stocked up."

Daniel raised his eyebrows in amusement at the mounds of food she had selected.

"Can we go somewhere more quiet to eat?" Samantha asked indicating the women around her.

She and Daniel found a corner of the massive ballroom that wasn't near the food or bar. Samantha visibly exhaled as she slid into a plush wingback chair away from the noise and crowds. It was then that Charlotte made her way deeper into the ballroom and locked eyes with Samantha.

"That must be her," Daniel whispered.

"Who?" Samantha asked with no trace of recognition in her voice.

"The Reckoned."

With James by my side once again, I began to feel my

energy levels improve. The traveling through the Romani Realms had greatly depleted my powers, leaving me without the strength to control the elements and mentally, feeling too defeated to not give into the sounds and urgings of the darkness.

"You can do it now," James said encouragingly. "I'm watching you."

I closed my eyes and felt the cold wind of the realms rip through my body. The shivering was intense, but I embraced the feeling knowing that to give into it now, especially with James, my Shade, by my side, would mean that Raven had won. Instead, I focused on heat, the sun, the air warming, the ground absorbing that beautiful heat and releasing waves of warmth back to the animals and plant life that struggled against the cold wintery feeling that was suddenly ripping over these Realms.

Nothing.

"Come on, Suki," he encouraged.

I looked up at James, feeling a tear weave down my cheek. "It's as if hundreds of years have been taken from me. I see the sorrow of my Releasors, but none of their strength and I feel all of their struggles."

"You're focusing on the bad. Listen to me," he said taking me in his arms. "We trained for this. Here, it's not a matter of just using your power over the elements, but physical strength too. The Krav Maga, the aerial training...I told you that you would need it. Practice your moves and this time, don't do it as an exercise. Do it to feed your very soul." He indicated that I should move into a clearing, and he stepped back to watch me step forward, moving with grace in spite of the circumstances.

It was cold outside, but still, I removed my sweater to have more freedom of movement. The thin camisole I wore today clung to my body and my skirt billowed with the wind. Raising my arms above my head, I started a slow and precise sun salutation, lifting my head skyward and closing my eyes. Then, I placed my hands in prayer and lifted my arms once again. Determined to regain strength and power, I bowed forward with a flourish placing my hands on the ground to stretch my calves and then quickly and without a sound, jumping back into plank, moving almost seductively into cobra pose and then pulling my body back into downward facing dog.

I performed the sequence twice more keeping my eyes closed throughout. Gaining fluidity and grace, my practiced movements improved my circulation, heating myself from the inside out, and allowing me to channel my thoughts and affect the elements. Although the air was still cold and the field was still cast in ice and shadows, above there was sun, shining a spotlight on this beautiful, moving meditation.

James stepped behind me, placing his hands on my hips while I still remained in downward facing dog. "Wow, that was hot."

"That was just the warm-up," I said with a laugh, looking up at him from under my shoulder. "Shall I continue?"

"I suppose you should," he said pressing his hips forward, closing the distance between them -- his front with my backside.

"Then you better stop that," I replied, feeling my heart rate accelerate and not from the mild movements of the sequence.

James released his hold on my hips and I stood, turning to place my arms around his neck. I allowed myself to plant just one small kiss on his lips before pulling away. "That was a prelude."

"The kiss or the sun salutation?"

"Both," I said, a twinkle returning to my eyes. "I felt you as my Shade, watching me, believing in me. I've felt that over the years, but never knew it was you."

"It wasn't just me, Suki. You can do this. You can fight Raven. I've just been there when you need me. So, show me what else you've got."

Once again, I moved into the clearing and crouched into a low warrior pose. With eyes closed, I summoned the elements and when the crack of lightening that I had commanded commenced, I started a new routine. It was a show of force as I practiced kicks and punches and even parkour stunts, literally turning a kick into a back flip and landing with cat-like grace.

James watched with amusement, as much a proud teacher as he was my lover. "Hey, I've got an idea. Can you hold on a minute without getting cold again?"

"I'm fine. What are you up to?"

"We're running short on time, and it looks like you'll be okay without needing a trip back to New Orleans."

"I can always use one of Maebeline's meals, but you're right. I'm okay now. What about my clothes?"

"I was looking forward to accidentally walking in on you dressing again, but that'll have to wait too. But the dress that I picked out for you is still part of the plan. Do that thing again."

"This thing?" I kicked my leg high, nearly touching my forehead.

"And the rest," James instructed.

As I repeated the kick into backflip, James moved in circles around me, silent and with the wind until I heard the grinding gears of time ring in my ears. I stopped my movements and stood still as James commanded the wind to rush around faster and faster, particles and ions moving with increasing speed until finally, all became still again. James looked at me appraisingly and said simply, "You are beautiful."

I looked down at myself and took in the pale pink ball gown that now inexplicably adorned my body. A plunging neckline accentuated my decolletage and moved into a tightly fitted waist that then gave way to a full skirt. When I twirled in front of James, he was greeted with the sight of the back of the dress -- another plunging "V" that went down the back.

He moved toward me and took my hand, holding it high above my head and encouraging me to spin once more for him. "My turn; now close your eyes."

I did as I was told and when I opened my eyes once more, I found James standing before me in a charcoal grey suit and crisp, white shirt. Usually found with a slight beard, he was clean-shaven. James didn't need another boost to his ego, but I couldn't help myself. My breath hitched when I stared at him. Maybe it was the clothes, or perhaps his square jaw and high cheek bones. But if that wasn't enough reason to go weak in the knees, his blue eyes were enough to set any girl's heart pounding. Add to that a strong body that looked more than capable of a few dirty deeds, and I was reduced to biting my lower lip and trying to remember how to speak. He may have complimented me by saying I was beautiful, but truer than true, James was downright dashing in his dress clothes. Without thinking, I stared and bit the end of my index finger, holding it in my mouth while staring at him, willing myself not to say something embarrassing.

"Don't do that," he said taking my finger from my mouth and gently placing it into his own, weaving his tongue slowly around the tip, "...it gives me ideas."

"Oh my."

"Let's go before we get distracted."

"Too late," I replied while taking his hand and heading in the direction of the grand gazebo.

Phineas stared at Raven and then looked away. "I don't believe you."

"You have to believe me. It's the truth."

"You and James? How? When?"

"If ever he had a fatal flaw, it would be that he's such a softie for the damsel in distress," Raven said pacing the room and shaking her head.

"I met James long before I actually met Suki, which is why it's so killing to me. What sort of loyalty must I show her when I saw him first?"

Phineas raked his hand through his hair, taking in this news. "So we hadn't met?"

"No!" she said reaching for him. "You weren't even a thought on God's mind at that time. You hadn't even been born and so you hadn't yet died...or been saved by me."

"Okay, so go on with it."

Raven sat down on the bed and took a deep breath. For the first time, Phineas actually saw her humanity come out. Always so controlled, so careful with her emotions and her choice to push them aside in favor of developing magic that controls people, Raven had always rebuffed any behavior that would interfere with her ultimate goal of power -- until now.

"I told you once that I wasn't always like this...determined, powerful. I was just learning to develop my magic. I was a gypsy, but without any trace of demonism. I lived like my ancestors before, learning to read people, entertaining the crowds with simple acts of magic, but I hadn't crossed over. But death is such a powerful aphrodisiac. When face to face with it, people start making deals -- senseless covenants."

Raven did something that utterly surprised Phineas. She cried. Her body shook and although practically silent and still trying her hardest to maintain her cool demeanor, the tears flowed down her cheeks until she lowered her head into her hands.

"Tell me more," Phineas said softly.

She took a deep breath and continued. "My parents were already dead and gone. The only remaining family member was my grandmother and she meant everything to me. But tragedy would strike her as well. She was suffering from scarlet fever and I was told by the doctor not to go near her. She had maintained a full house staff for years. Now, they became her nurses. They wore masks whenever near her; I was never allowed to go into her room. They insisted that I only speak to her through the door. But I knew that she was too weak to eat. So, one day, I snuck into her room, just to be with her. I brought her chocolates, but of course, by then even those didn't interest her."

Raven paused and Phineas watched her face, etched in the pain of her memories.

"It was horrible seeing her body, so frail and unable to even lift her own head. I brushed her hair, wiped down her face and body to ease the heat of the fever, and laid my head down on her chest just to feel its rise and fall -- to know that she was still with me. She was suffering and worst of all, the doctors expected it could go on like that for two more weeks. For me, watching her for two hours was torture. I didn't want her to be like that any longer. She looked at me and her voice barely a whisper, begged me to make it all go away. I knew what she meant."

Suddenly, she took a hold of Phineas' hand and bent her mouth to kiss it, a rare show of subservience and love.

"I snuck out and went to the marketplace to find some herbs that the gypsy community said were poisonous, but aided in a smooth transition to the next world. I just wanted to take away her pain so I sought out James."

"What did he have to do with it?"

"I had heard many stories that spoke of his powers to heal and protect. I knew there was no helping her at this point, but I thought...if he could heal, then perhaps he could end her suffering as well."

"Go on..."

"He was already a powerful Shade, but nobody knew whether he was actually aligned with anyone. He had made appearances at Shalaman ceremonies, and was revered for the way he helped burgeoning gypsies learn their lessons. One touch from him," she paused clearly remembering, "it was like receiving a jolt of energy."

Phineas rolled his eyes, in spite of the circumstances, only to receive a glare from Raven. "Sorry...go on, tell me more about James the Amazing."

"Thank you...as I was saying, I had seen him help others before me. Like when someone was just on the edge of being able to move an object with their mind, the object shaking and trembling, but not actually flying. James would touch that person and center them, and then when they tried again, it would work. Once they knew they were capable, they were well on their way. Nobody ever knew how he got his powers, but he was generous with them, so..."

"You asked him for help?"

Raven nodded. "I knew that my grandmother needed to pass on easily, and I had no malice in mind, so he agreed. He told me the incantation that would ensure she ended up in a beautiful, peaceful place, and he even showed me it. If ever there was a heaven, that was it."

Raven bowed her head and slowly shook it at the memory.

"You loved her," Phineas said simply.

"Is that so hard to imagine," she chuckled. "That I am or was capable of love?"

"What changed?"

"We were living in England and in the midst of the Thirty Year War between the Catholics and Protestants. It was a brutal time with fighting, disease and famine. I was raised Catholic and my father had been a high ranking diplomat. Knowing that I was in need of a caretaker once my grandmother passed, one of his top advisers suggested a marriage between myself and the Protestant son of my father's biggest rival."

"If you can't beat them join them?"

Raven nodded. "Exactly. They wanted to take over my family business now that nobody was left to stand in the way -- except for me. It didn't matter that

I never even met the boy. My picture had been passed to the family and apparently, he became quite taken with me."

Phineas smiled in spite of his present feelings toward Raven. "That doesn't come as a surprise."

"Well, it just goes to show that if you fall for someone based on their looks, that isn't a sound platform for a relationship. Just one week after my grandmother passed, I came down with the fever, and my dad's rivals called off the wedding. I can understand that the son didn't visit me as mere inhalation could cause the spread of the infection, but he never even sent his footman with a note of condolence.

"My advisors were so angry at the idea that their political future was ruined that they blamed me, especially when they found out that I had visited my grandmother on her deathbed. They said that I brought this upon myself, and I would deal with it by myself."

"How can anyone deal with it during Victorian times? There were no vaccinations."

"Ahh, don't forget, we had arsenic," she said bitterly.

"So, that's when you crossed over? I mean, obviously you survived."

"I almost didn't. I was cast out of the home. You can see why when I met and saved you centuries later, I never showed any love loss for my family -- it's why I was so desperate to create a family with you."

Phineas looked at Raven, their eyes meeting. He tried desperately to weigh out the truth from the propaganda that she fed him. He had loved her once, but had grown tired of her treachery. He nearly wanted to tell her of the plan to save Charlotte and how he was part of it, but he still didn't dare. One story couldn't make him a sell out, but then he worried that he had done just that to Raven.

"What happened to you...if you weren't yet a demon gypsy?"

"I had no where to go and the fever was ravaging my body. Nobody would go near me, so I found myself crumpled in an alley, huddled with other infected women and children. I passed in and out of consciousness, until one day I woke up in a beautiful bedroom, clean and feeling weak, but on the mend.

"I can still remember being given a vile of medicine that momentarily cleared my head, and then placed me in a deep sleep once again. I regained consciousness at times, and when I did, always there was a pitcher of clean water next to my bedside along with chicken broth and homemade bread. I ate and drank until I became stronger, never knowing how I ended up there until one day when I felt...well, human again, and James was sitting by my side with what I thought was a cool cloth against my forehead. Only it wasn't a cloth, but his hand, gently removing the last bit of fever from my body."

"And Suki wasn't in the picture?"

"Not entirely," Raven admitted. "James was already Suki's Shade, although she had never met him. She didn't need to," Raven added wistfully. "Suki was strong. She inspired men. She didn't need one to guide her. But James took his role seriously and watched over her from afar. I think he even fell in love just by watching her, but like me, he was alone."

"So you hooked up?" Phineas asked incredulously.

"It wasn't a hook up," Raven insisted. "I moved in because I could easily relapse. James insisted on it. He spent his days teaching me about my gypsy heritage, teaching me magic. Our evenings were spent like a married couple. We prepared meals together, talked, and…"

"Unbelievable," Phineas shook his head.

"But Suki was always in the background. It quickly became obvious that I could never compete with his idea of what she was…this amazing muse, the only woman truly worthy of his heart.

"He admitted to me that there would come a day when they would meet in person and he would go to her."

"So you…" a hush fell over Phineas, unsure he wanted to hear how Raven ended up dying. In spite of everything, he didn't want to imagine her in death.

"I had been studying about crossing over. My magic was already so strong because of James' help…and his touch. That gave me an edge over other gypsies who wanted more power. But what really inspired me was a broken heart. He was so angry one night and I asked him why. It turns out that Suki slept with one of her Releasors."

"But she hadn't even met James so what's the problem?"

"Exactly! But he hated it and being with me wasn't enough to get his mind off Miss Bottle Stopper. So I decided that night to end it all. If I could cross over, great. If I couldn't, then at least I was finished feeling like second fiddle. Well, I was filled with so much pain, sorrow, jealousy, rage...should I go on?"

Phineas shook his head. "Powerful emotions lead to powerful results."

"It worked," Raven said nodding her head, "and I haven't looked back once."

"You never spoke with him after that?"

"Right afterwards. But he was so '*disappointed*' in me that it only fueled my anger. He told me that I was strong and I could just as easily have channeled goodness, but I did the opposite. I told him that he could have been happy with the girl he had in his bed, but he did the opposite. I realized that our love was one-sided and that's no basis for a long-term relationship, even though it seemed well on its way toward that. I truly thought we would end up together -- with a family.

"Eventually, I met another man, John Proctor, but Suki managed to screw that one up for me as well. Turned him into the council who was seeking out witches during the Salem Witch Trials in order to save me. She thought we were friends, but I had only started the guise of a friendship to meet the amazing creature that James had dumped me for."

"Weren't you ever friends? I thought...," Phineas stopped himself, aware that he might reveal something he learned in confidence.

"Well, she was okay to hang out with and she hadn't met James yet because all of her Releasors were fine with just her help, although she did manage to kill off a very large number of them. Rather amusing, if you ask me. Anyway, I suppose I could have been friends if I wasn't always aware that somewhere out there, James was watching. I had gotten over him, sort of...not really. Suki was always so full of life and happiness, taking what life dished out and then making it even better. It's hard not to like her, and with that thought, it became hard not to hate her because I could see why I never really had a chance with James."

Phineas remained quiet, obviously brooding at the edge of the bed. Raven moved up behind him, wrapping her arms around his waist and resting her head against his shoulder.

"Are you mad at me?"

"I don't understand why you chose this moment to tell me all of this. Are you trying to justify what you're about to do?"

"I'm just trying to explain myself to you. I do love you Phineas, and the idea that I've come close to losing you to Charlotte is reliving losing James to Suki all over again. She brought those girls into our lives and then to see you actually fall for Charlotte..."

"Maybe if you were different, more..."

"More what Phineas?" her voice took on an edge. "Perhaps more human? Is that what you were about to say?"

"Raven, I don't know what I was about to say because you jumped down my throat before I could get it out, but I do know this....I only wish that I got to see the girl that James knew back then."

Phineas got up from the bed to leave, but Raven held on tightly to him, pulling him back down. "Please."

"Why don't you just influence me again?"

"Because I want to know..." her voice broke and to Phineas' surprise the tears flowed down her face again. "I want to know that you still want me. For real."

Phineas looked at Raven, clearly distraught over the history between them, her vulnerability, and his determination to bring Charlotte back. But he couldn't deny that the centuries spent with Raven couldn't be forgotten easily.

"Phineas?"

"What is it?" he said still turning away from her.

Raven bore her eyes into him, willing him to turn around. "Please, Phineas. Look at me."

Phineas did as she requested and allowed her gaze to connect with his.

Never taking her eyes off him, Raven spoke in not more than a whisper, "Let me show you something. Give me your hand."

He held out his hand to her without hesitation and she took it, placing it over her own heart, which beat strongly. As he held his hand there, he felt something that didn't often occur when he touched Raven. He felt warmth radiate from her.

With their hands still intertwined, Raven moved slowly toward Phineas, her eyes on his mouth. Her kiss wasn't filled with its typical urgency. Replacing the heat and passion was a vulnerability that was new...and intoxicating. Phineas allowed her mouth to remain on his, felt her hands cradle his face, and in return, he slowly, rather instinctively, wrapped his arms around her waist and pulled her entire body into his.

Raven turned her head to the side and sighed, a long happy sound of comfort mixed with growing desire that Phineas immediately picked up on. He bent his head to her neck and layered the kisses there, unaccustomed to being able to do as he wanted with Raven rather than being instructed. It was having an effect on him, which Raven took full advantage of by moving onto his lap, her legs wrapped around him, her neck fully exposed to his hungering mouth.

She threw her head back and arched her back, pressing her breasts against his chest. His kisses left her neck and trailed along her collarbone, her decolletage, and between her breasts as his hands caressed each full mound, releasing them from the already plunging neckline of her dress and gently leading each one in turn to his mouth.

"Please don't stop," Raven breathed heavily.

Never had Phineas heard Raven utter the word 'please' especially during moments like this. Although her request was demure, the result was the same as in the past. Phineas was unable to resist her.

His hands traveled down farther to her waist and held her firmly while their kisses continued to build. She felt him harden against her and Raven squeezed her legs around his waist stronger in response until Phineas pressed against her and lay her down on the bed, prone between her legs and ready to move down her body. Raven let her hands feel the strong muscles of Phineas' arms; she felt the hardness of him elsewhere as well. Straddling her, Phineas expected Raven not to remain silent and to tell him what she wanted. He knew what she wanted. But she only returned his gaze, and with that one look, he felt the surge of desire course through him. The tables had turned suddenly and Phineas grabbed each one of Raven's wrists, pressing them into the bed. He held tightly onto her and looked down at her exposed breasts, rising with each breath she took.

"Don't. You. Move," he said carefully, a warning of sorts.

Raven looked up at him wide-eyed and simply shook her head. He released her wrists and waited to see what would happen and when she remained still, her arms splayed outward, he moved down her body, lifted the long trail of her dress and let his finger toy with the light fabric of her panties, carefully moving it aside to expose her.

A quiet whimper momentarily escaped Raven's mouth and she wriggled ever the slightest bit. He immediately stopped the movement of his finger that was just seconds earlier sliding against her in a slow, agonized movement. He gave her a look of warning and she stiffled any further movement until he rewarded her by pressing his mouth against her there. Phineas reached underneath her hips and lifted her towards him.

Raven murmured something that sounded like 'oh god,' but Phineas let the comment go and continued to let his tongue explore her with luxurious, long strokes and quick flicks that made her body shake. He performed like a man with something to prove and he didn't stop until he felt every inch of her tighten and release.

He reached for Raven's dress and straightened it back into place before holding out his hand to her, knowing that she would need it. "Let's get to the ball."

Raven didn't say a word, but looked at Phineas with wonder and nodded.

Chapter Eleven

The guests of the ball waited for the Reckoning. One could feel the excitement build as couples began to dance a bit closer, speak more suggestively, and anticipate the freedom from suffering that would befall them when Charlotte was sacrificed. It was an intoxicating aphrodisiac.

As Charlotte continued to peruse the room searching for Samantha, whispers followed her. Samantha and Daniel both felt the mood of the room take on a new charge.

"I think this is it," he said, taking hold of her hand unexpectedly.

Samantha looked up at Daniel in surprise, although she didn't remove her hand. It felt good to feel someone warm as she hadn't felt anything but a cold, bleak sense in weeks.

"That girl...she's..."

"That must be her," Daniel confirmed.

"She looks somehow familiar."

"Don't say that," Daniel said and squeezed her hand a bit harder. "Someone might hear you."

"But what's wrong with what I said?"

"Nothing, it's just that they could get the wrong idea."

Samantha wore a confused look that only increased when someone clicked a spoon on the side of a glass. Others followed suit, and no sooner, the lights lowered and the movie screen was once again displayed.

The same woman returned to the podium. "We proudly present the second part of our evening." With her announcement, the projector started up and another documentary of sorts began.

"The Reckoned and its corresponding Reckoning Ceremony of the Romani Realms enjoys a complex and rich history dating back to the early Druids. These priests of Celtic paganism would save the souls of their flock through human sacrifice, but as society began to frown upon the loss of life, a wicker man emerged as a substitute. Burning a man in effigy dates back to the days of Julius Caesar."

Samantha gasped when a figure suddenly sat beside her...the girl who the crowd had spoken about as the Reckoned.

"Samantha? My god, I never thought I'd find you," Charlotte spoke, leaning closer to Samantha as if to embrace her.

Samantha automatically stiffened. "Do I know you? I don't think we should be talking."

"Of course you know me. It's Charlotte. Let's go."

The film's voice droned on and Samantha turned her attention back to it.

"But in the spirit of restoring us to a simpler time, the Romani Realms' High Commission endorsed the idea of sacrifices for the greater good. Initially, these sacrifices were deemed only to be of the male species as a symbolic nod to the historic Wicker Man."

The older men in the room grumbled amongst themselves. One even interrupted the film by calling, "What about the movement on equality?"

As if hearing the man's complaint, the voice droned on.

"Although the figure of the Wicker Man is still used in modern ceremonies on the other side, in the Romani Realms such comical imitations of history have been banned and replaced with more authentic means. True sacrifices that reflect our liberated society are performed annually. Women were added alongside men as offerings to the Realms in 2013."

The film stopped and a woman dressed in a forest green long dress and an elaborate hat that looked like the branches of a pine tree approached a podium near where the screen was now retracting.

"Good evening," she said in greeting. "I am Evangeline, Chairwoman of this year's Reckoning ball. I would like to welcome you all and just ask that

you remember to treat our Reckoned with respect.
The Reckoned is to be revered because this one soul
will satisfy the gods of the Romani Realms and keep
them satiated for months to come. Our chosen one is
in no way to be considered a food source. We have
evolved from that pitiful blot on our history."

Applause exploded among the crowd, and
Charlotte leaned in closer to Samantha again.
"Samantha, I've got a bad feeling about this. You need
to come with me, now. I think they're talking about
you. Please listen to me."

Samantha turned to Charlotte. "I don't know you
and I can assure you that they aren't speaking of me."
She indicated the screen, which had descended once
more and now showed an image of Charlotte.

"Oh my god." Charlotte brought a small fan up to
her face and hid behind it. "What is this place?
Samantha, don't you see? It can't be safe for you
either."

Daniel looked between the two girls. "She speaks
the truth, Samantha. I can feel that you two have a
history...you felt it too. And if they find out...," his
voice trailed off.

Samantha looked into Charlotte's eyes, but spoke
to Daniel. "How do you know?"

"Samantha, I'm like you...I recognize purity and I
see it in you. And, like you, I innately know someone's
true nature. Take her hand and tap into your skills.
They led you to me in this god forsaken place, so let
them continue to lead you."

Samantha extended her hand to Charlotte. As their fingers intertwined, Samantha closed her eyes and concentrated. "We need to make a run for it," she said urgently.

"You know me?" Charlotte asked with obvious relief.

"I'm not sure, but I know of you -- of what you are. And, you don't belong here." Samantha looked from Charlotte to Daniel. "None of us do."

As the girls rose from their seats, Daniel scanned the exits. "The Selkie are blocking the exits."

"Those girls?" Samantha asked looking at each door, but only seeing beautiful, young women.

"They're powerful shapeshifters and they work for the High Commission. We'll have to go the way you came in, through the salon and kitchen. "Let's go," he said, wrapping an arm around Samantha's waist.

"Wait..." Samantha and Daniel followed Charlotte's gaze to where a couple was dancing slowly on the floor. They were a devastatingly handsome couple, a girl with raven black hair and the young man, blond with a chiseled face and strong arms that held the girl close.

"Isn't that the girl from the film?" Samantha asked.

"She's the one who sent you here, and the boy who broke my heart."

"Ladies, we have to get out of here," Daniel said as he noted the Selkie speaking into walkie-talkies. "This way..."

"James, over there!" We had no sooner arrived at the ball when I spied Charlotte and Samantha from across the room.

"It looks like they're leaving....with..." James craned his neck to catch a better glimpse of the girls.

"I don't know who that is, but they're following him. And, look who else is getting chummy," I said pointing out Raven and Phineas on the dance floor. Although every couple in the room had now donned elaborate masks to cover their eyes, Phineas lowered his for a split second, his eyes boring across the room and connecting with mine.

"He's following the plan, making Raven feel that he's still with her. I don't think they've seen the girls yet, so let's not draw attention to them."

"But if the girls leave..."

"We'll find them. It's best they get out of here."

As they spoke in hushed whispers, Phineas twirled Raven across the floor, speaking into her ear while he scanned the crowd.

"He sees us," I noted.

Phineas' eyes came to rest on James and myself, as he gave us a surreptitious nod and continued to lead Raven through the dancing couples.

"Can you hear what she's saying?" James asked.

I shook my head. "There's too much noise. I can only pick up words here and there. Can we get closer?"

James leaned down to find two masks discarded on the floor. "Here," he said handing one to me and placing the other over his own eyes. As we glided closer to Raven and Phineas, my connection to Raven and our history over the years allowed her voice to resonate.

"It's almost time," Raven said noting a clock mounted high on one wall.

Phineas scanned the room, no doubt checking to see if Charlotte had made her way to leave. "Time? For what?"

"The Reckoning."

"Everyone's in masks. How do you know Charlotte is even here?"

"It doesn't matter if she's here or not. She'll be found. Back in 1990, the Reckoning lasted two weeks, but eventually they're always found."

I shivered involuntarily at hearing Raven's words. There was no doubt that we were in new territory. The Realms. The Reckoning. My powers slightly disabled. If it weren't for James and the support he provided, I would feel totally lost.

"Did you hear..."

James nodded gravely before I even finished my thought. "We need a distraction, something to give them more time to get to where they're headed. You can do it."

I nodded, more to myself than to James. "Back home controlling the elements is as easy as swallowing a warm slice of lemon merengue pie, but here...more like trying to shell crawfish with one hand behind my back."

James leaned in and kissed my cheek. "Here, take my hand. Pretend you're taking me on the most amazing journey. We're going to fly on the wind. Now, make it happen."

I closed my eyes, but rather than immediately try to control the elements, instead I focused on the changing weather conditions of the Realms. Like trying to catch the perfect wave, I let my mind ride the tides of the wind until I felt its rhythm and was able to summon it.

First it came as a light breeze, gently stirring just a tendril of the brown waves of my hair, then it grew and a blast of frigid air struck me directly in the face. Keeping my eyes closed and raising my chin, I welcomed the assault and then finally, focused it onto the rest of the party-goers.

James held tightly to my arm, leading me to the side entrance, so that I could continue stirring the wind. What felt almost like a small tornado started in the center of the room and rotated in a circle, pulling in dancers to its center eye, and thrusting those who were on the outskirts of the dance floor against the wall of the rounded ballroom.

"What does she think she's doing?" Raven hissed, her attention immediately drawn to me. If not for Phineas' arm around her waist, she would have stumbled.

But rather than answer, Phineas noted Raven's surprise and let go of her suddenly, allowing her to spin with the wind to the center of the dance floor.

Phineas found himself standing at an equal distance between Raven and myself. Fully aware that his next move would either solidify or destroy what remained between he and Raven, he met her questioning gaze and remained in place for a moment.

Raven's words were more than angry. "I will have those girls' heads on a platter."

"You'll have to find them first," I countered. "And it looks as if you don't have quite the army you expected."

Phineas had made his decision and could be seen leaving out the same door that Samantha, Daniel, and Charlotte had used.

"What makes you so sure, you naive genie? Just look." Raven had controlled the wind rushing around her and was now standing quite serenely, arms outstretched as if waiting to take flight. She pointed in the direction that Phineas had left before shifting into an enormous black bird.

"You don't know that he's with you," I cried out.

"And neither do you!" Raven shot back. "But I do know whose side they're on."

The Selkies, a half dozen in total, had organized and were now walking in formation, flanked by two grey wolves who walked alongside them with chain link leashes around their necks.

A loud gong sounded and confetti rained down from the ceiling, both breaking my concentration. My ability over the wind stopped and the gathered crowd moved back into the center of the ballroom where the film screen was once again being lowered. Images of Charlotte flashed on the screen, along with those of Samantha and Daniel. *"The Reckoning has begun,"* a robotic voice announced. *"This year's Reckoned is being accompanied to her sacrificial conclusion by two of our own Romani Realms residents. Although they are not included in the Reckoning ceremony, their lives are expendable. We invite you all to reconvene outside where the hunt will begin."*

The crowd no sooner made their way out the doors of the ballroom, whispering about the dance and the food as if they had all just gone out for a Saturday evening.

"This is insane!"

"Be careful," James warned. "This way," he said taking me by the hand and leading me through the employees' entrance where he had seen the Selkie arrive. We hurried through the corridor leading to the kitchen and then turned to the entry to the spa area where Charlotte had been made up for the night.

"James, I have to ditch these shoes."

"Find something in there," he said pointing to the salon.

I ran down the hall while James kept watch, although it wasn't necessary as everyone was occupied with the morbid festivities.

"Bingo," I said returning having found a pair of ballet flats. "Let's hurry."

Charlotte struggled to keep up with Daniel, who after having years in the Romani Realms was experienced at dodging the human soul obstacles that lashed out at unexpected moments. Even Samantha had learned to ignore the disturbing pleas that could be heard in the surrounding forests and marshes.

"Just focus on something pretty," Daniel yelled over his shoulder. "It's all about your perception."

Charlotte screamed as a hand reached out from the marshy mud and skimmed her ankle.

"And keep it quiet," Samantha urged.

"I need to stop."

"No!" Daniel and Samantha both spat out simultaneously.

But it was too late and the air was too thin for Charlotte to catch her breath. She sat down in an open trail.

"At least come over here," Daniel called to her from behind a large, beaver lodge made of logs and sticks, just off from the lake.

Charlotte felt a blast of cold air, urging her forward. *Go, don't stop. You're stronger than you realize.* She looked up as if questioning whether she really heard me. My voice sounded close, but it was just so cold. Charlotte willed herself to stand and met Samantha and Daniel behind their hiding place.

They could hear the cry of the wolves in the distance. "We've only got a mile at best on them," Daniel said. "We have to keep going," he said lightly touching Samantha's arm.

She shivered at his touch. It was warm and yet, it sent chills down her spine reminding her of the pleasure of jumping into a pool on a hot summer day, cold glasses of lemonade after running, and her first high school crush. In short, better times.

"Where?" Samantha asked.

"To my place. It's safe...and hidden. Do you trust me?"

Samantha looked at Daniel and using her special gift, she innately knew that he wouldn't lead her astray. "Yes. I'll go with you."

He smiled in spite of their circumstances. "Well then, let's keep on."

"Come on, Charlotte. You've had enough time to rest. Charlotte?"

She was no where to be found. "Where is she?" Samantha's voice rose in a panic.

"There!" Daniel pointed to a fallen tree just three hundred feet in the distance. Charlotte leaned up against it, deep in conversation with a small, blonde girl. "I don't like this."

You can help her.

"Did you hear that?" Samantha looked all around her. "I recognized a voice. It was so familiar."

"It doesn't matter. We have bigger issues," he said pointing toward Charlotte, who was now walking closer to the shores of the lake with the little girl.

"Charlotte!"

Charlotte turned toward Samantha, but didn't meet her stare head on. Her eyes seemed unfocused, unseeing. "I need to go now."

Daniel stepped forward, but the girl who appeared quiet and meek, held up her hand in warning. "Stay away from her."

Samantha and Daniel looked at each other, unsure how to react. Finally, Daniel whispered to Samantha, "The little girl -- she's not what she appears. She's an Encantado and this newcomer...your friend, if that's what you believe, is in serious danger."

"She's mine. You can't have her."

"Shadow, don't be rude," Charlotte answered the Encantado, whose hair turned from blonde ringlets into writhing snakes before their eyes.

An involuntary gasp escaped Samantha, who took a step backwards, but Charlotte, unaware of the change, lovingly ran her hand over the small girls' head. Within seconds of receiving her touch, the Encantado's appearance returned to normal.

"She's really quite sweet. This is Shadow. She found me when I arrived. Just give me a minute," Charlotte indicated that she wanted some time alone with the creature that was sending warning daggers with her eyes at Samantha.

The Encantado smiled at Samantha and Daniel, her grin changing from pearly white teeth to a gaping hole of black.

Charlotte moved out of earshot and Daniel gripped Samantha's arm firmly. "Your friend is falling for the traps of the Romani Realms. The others will be here soon. We need to leave."

"What will become of her?"

Daniel shook his head and looked to where the Encantado was laughing and whispering with Charlotte. "I don't know. Maybe that...that thing will give her a hiding place."

"She *is* my friend," Samantha said firmly as if only now believing the statement. "Just as I know that you are of pure heart, I know this to be true about her as well. You believe me?"

Daniel gathered Samantha up in his arms. Although she had never spent time in a man's arms before, she didn't feel nervous. Instead, she exhaled and felt her body relax against his strength, feeling stronger herself because of him. "I've lived in this hell for over a decade, waiting for something. I know now that it's you. I don't want to lose you."

Samantha didn't move from his arms, nor did she raise her head from its resting spot against his broad chest. There had been days when she was hungry, cold and so terribly alone that she didn't relish experiencing that again, but when she thought about turning her back on Charlotte, she just couldn't. Something innately told her that they had a history.

"I can't ask you to sacrifice yourself, but for me there is no choice. I can't explain why I know this, but I think the fact that I can see what people really are deep inside is how I've survived here before I met you. It won't be easy, but I could continue on my own."

"What are you saying?" he asked, placing a hand under her chin so that their eyes met.

"I can't leave her to...to them," she said glancing toward the muddy ground that bubbled and brewed, threatening to take over one's emotions and sense of reality. "Samantha, what they do during the Reckoning ceremony...you don't want to witness that. Ever."

I'll be there soon. She heard a voice speaking directly to her. My voice. It gave her strength.

"I'm going to get her away from them. I'm sorry, Daniel. I'll do it with or without your help."

He wrapped his arms around her again. Holding onto her tightly as if his very soul depended on her. He twirled a lock of her red hair around his finger and smiled. "You are a spit fire. I need you."

Samantha shimmied her body from her shoulders to her hips, smiling as if she had just been told that she was being given a new puppy. "I knew it!"

"Confident, aren't we?"

She gave a defiant nod and stretched her arms out widely, inviting him toward her once again. As he held onto her waist, Daniel whispered in her ear. "I admit that I need you. I might even admit something more...one day...if you're lucky."

"Oh really?"

"Mmm Hmm. But, you're sure going to need me to pull this off."

Matching his now serious tone, Samantha whispered back. "Thank you."

Feeling decisive about her need to help Charlotte fueled a need within herself as well. She turned her chin upward and met Daniel's gaze without wavering. Up until now, their longing looks had always ended with Samantha changing the subject or pointing out something about the ever changing scenery, but this time...she waited.

Daniel's warm brown eyes smiled as they met hers. He didn't let another moment lapse to confirm their shared intention. Placing one hand under Charlotte's chin, he moved her face slowly toward his own. His eyes stared at her lips, which she bit with anticipation.

"Daniel...," nerves were beginning to take over, but he wouldn't allow her to break the spell between them.

"Shhh...just be," he said, his words barely above a whisper.

And then, taking his message to heart, Samantha closed her eyes, forgetting all fears, all memories of what she had been through over the past months or weeks or however long each god forsaken day would play out in her mind, and she just allowed herself to be...resting in his arms. She closed her eyes and felt his lips ever so gently touch her own.

A warmth spread throughout her body. For the first time that her memory served, she wasn't cold. Daniel's hand stayed under her chin, guiding her mouth more firmly onto his, before he dared remove his hand for fear of this moment ending. Instinct took over inexperience and Samantha wrapped her arms around Daniel's neck and held on as if her very life depended on it.

When their mouths separated, their arms still held each other tightly. Daniel let his head lean forward to rest on Samantha's forehead. For a moment, they stood like that in silence, until a woman's voice interrupted them.

"Samantha, looking at you is like taking a long sip of sweet tea. I never want it to end."

Samantha looked up and unlike the experience she had with Charlotte, when she laid eyes on me the recognition was instantaneous. "Suki?"

"It's me, honey plum," I held out my arms and Samantha ran into them. "I can't believe we found you."

"We?" Samantha turned to see James standing to the side.

"You remember James?" I asked.

Samantha stared at James, who smiled easily.

"Come on everyone, let's get Charlotte and get outta here," I indicated the docks where Charlotte still sat next to Shadow.

James and Daniel introduced themselves while also refilling canteens from the stream that ran through the woods. Everyone was suddenly bustling about, but Samantha remained quiet. The fact that she hadn't answered my seemingly rhetorical question went unnoticed by everyone, except James,

who turned his head over his shoulder and met
Samantha's gaze head on.

Chapter Twelve

The sun was strong as it beat down on our little group that was already weary from the rough terrain. "If we can get to the woods it will help camouflage us," Daniel spoke more to Samantha than the others. "We can head to my cottage. We'll travel by night and if we're lucky, we'll get there by morning."

James picked up his pace, taking me by the hand, and moving easily in front of Samantha and Daniel. "We stick with the plan. Follow us."

"Umm, Sugar? We've already veered from the plan," I reminded him, and indicated the end of our line where Charlotte was trailing, still holding Shadow's hand.

James stopped and ran his hand through his hair. "It's not going to work. Not with all this extra...," he held his hands out in front of him, searching for the right word, "baggage."

Daniel faced him and standing as tall as James at six feet, he looked him straight in the eye, placed his hands on his hips, his legs planted apart. But he said not a word. Samantha and I eyed each other, knowing that few packs had more than one alpha dog. One would have to back down.

Finally, Daniel spoke. "Did I mishear you?"

James shook his head, more at himself than Daniel. It wasn't like a Shade to lose his temper and it gave credence to the fact that the Romani Realms affected every inhabitant. He whipped off his t-shirt, revealing his tight and toned abs, and mopped his brow with the fabric. Then, he held his hand out to Daniel.

"New plan," James finally said.

"What's this plan?" Daniel asked.

"It's not totally unlike the first, which was to find the wormhole back to the present. As long as we are all in our right minds, we can get back safely. But if any of us are dealing with a false reality, and we were to be pulled away, the fears and paranoia would always remain -- regardless of where we end up here or back home."

Daniel nodded, now understanding what set off James. "It would be impossible for a group this large to be sane at the same time. Not here."

As if proving the point, Charlotte's voice could be heard although she was still quite a few meters aways. "You are so good to me, Shadow. I'll never leave you." They turned to watch in disgust as Shadow dug in the ground for beetles and mealworms, and then offered them to Charlotte, who happily popped them into her mouth.

"Eww Charlotte, no," I called out.

Daniel placed a hand on my shoulder and I immediately calmed. "It's okay, Suki. I mean, it's gross, but it's the red beetles that cause dangerous hallucinations. The black ones? At least she'll get her protein."

I turned my mouth downwards and shuddered, but willed my mind to leave Charlotte for the time being. "Daniel, what are you? Samantha sees the good and I can feel your calming nature. Are you...a wizard?"

"No, that's not the source of my powers," he said looking downward, ashamed. "I was a practicing voodoo priest and I was good at it. But I never used my abilities to erupt evil onto others, only goodness. Primarily, I saw paths where evil could crawl and I would block it. Sometimes they were love spells..." he said, his eyes going to Samantha.

I nodded, satisfied that some good might be on the horizon. "You are good, Daniel. Remember that, always."

James held out his hand, which Daniel accepted. "We haven't seen Raven or Phineas, the demon gypsies who placed Samantha here, but they're near," James explained. "Phineas is supposed to be working to help us, but who knows..."

"You don't know that he's betrayed us," I answered.

"No, but it's no coincidence that they're hanging around," he said lifting his eyes to the treetops.

Samantha gasped and grabbed a hold of Daniel's arm, while I instinctively summoned the element of

wind to envelope our party in a private whirlwind.
Hundreds of blackbirds lined the branches of the
trees. They sat still and quiet as if listening in on the
conversation, which of course they were.

"What has she done?" I asked.

Samantha instinctively bowed her head into her
shoulder. Although she had no recollection of the
tragedy that took her life from the present,
somewhere in the recesses of her mind, she knew to
fear the birds. "Who? Why are there so many?"

"They're disciples," James answered.

I nodded, knowing that he was right. "Raven's
followers. She attempted this once before, many years
ago. It was during the second world war and she saw
the power of fascism and wanted it for herself. She
went all the way to Greece where she could work her
evil without prying eyes of the world leaders and
concocted the National Youth Organization, there
known as Ethnikí Orgánosis Neoléas, or EON.
Fortunately, it was a failed attempt."

Samantha took a deep breath and raised her eyes
to the birds in a show of defiance. And then, to show
she couldn't be intimidated, she bravely turned her
back to them and walked toward the edge of the
forest.

"Sam, where are you going?" I called to her, still
controlling the wind that whisked Samantha's red
mane around her face.

"I'm going down there to get Charlotte and then
we're getting out of here."

"What about Shadow? The Encantado?" Daniel asked.

"What is she?" Samantha asked, suddenly turning around.

"It doesn't matter," James said forcefully. "She's coming too. We're going to need her."

Appearing in bird form, Raven glided easily over the tree tops, reveling in the sheer number of followers gathered. She soared higher feeling the exhilaration that comes from weightlessness and the freedom from emotions that plague humanity. Noticing that Phineas had already returned to his body and was lying on the ground staring up at her, she returned and shifted before his eyes.

"Do you feel better?" she asked, stroking his cheek.

"Much," he said turning on his side to face her. "It's been awhile since I've flown; the air is so pure here."

Raven smiled to herself. "Purity isn't easy to come by -- especially here."

"What's with them?" Phineas asked, indicating the throngs of black birds that still perched above them, hovering closely together.

"You know how animals can sense changes in energy? Whether it's a hurricane or earthquake...domesticated animals can even sense heartache or happiness on the part of their owner.

They're excited. Waiting to see what I'll do with the Amulet of Pollox, once it's mine."

Phineas stared up at the birds his anger causing the branches to bend and sway. Raven reached for him. "Easy tiger. Looks like you need another dose of happy."

He knew she was right...somehow she had made him happy, and it wasn't welcome, not from her. He turned his head, struggling not to give into whatever influence Raven was dishing out.

"Phin! I never expected Charlotte to do something so crazy as to enter the Romani Realms on her own. Believe me. I knew you had your little infatuation growing."

He turned back to her, and shot out, "An infatuation that you encouraged and built in order to get to Samantha."

"I know," she said, her eyes trained on him, concentrating on calming him. "But it is exciting. It's proof that the Amulet of Pollox has given her the power and insight to do so much more than an ordinary human could. She even harnessed the mind of Charles Babbage, Suki's greatest Releasor ever."

"I'm not so sure he was her greatest Releasor," Phineas said.

"Well, he may not have Charlotte's legs, but he did invent the first computer and used it to develop the principles of time travel."

At the mention of Charlotte's name, the Celtic Knot that Phineas wore around his neck grew warm against his skin, giving him hope that there was still a connection between them. He put his hand to it, hoping. Knowing that Raven was watching him, he did his best to empty his mind of thoughts for her.

"Phin, would you do anything for me?"

"Yes."

"I want things to be back the way they were."

Phineas rolled onto his side once again and pulled Raven in closely. He nuzzled her neck and she turned and relished in the feel of his kisses along her collarbone. "Isn't this better?"

"Hmm? Better than what?"

"Just better together. You and I."

Phineas looked upward toward the birds again as if trying to gauge whether they would strike if his answer wasn't to Raven's liking. "I don't feel drugged any more, if that's what you mean."

"It doesn't seem necessary to influence you any more. You're...pleasantly pliable."

Within a second, he easily rolled her onto her stomach and then straddled her, perched just over her hips with his weight on his knees, placed on either side of Raven's thin waist. He leaned forward to kiss the back of her neck and ran his hands over her shoulders, gently massaging any tension away. She could feel his hardness pressed strategically between her legs as he allowed himself to rest it against her.

"So, if that's the case, then why are you still maintaining such a close watch on me?" he asked, enjoying the fact that he had her pressed faced down under his control.

"Am I?"

"Well, who are they and why are they here?" he asked forcefully rolling her onto her back. He kissed her mouth with a fervor, until she parted her lips, welcoming his tongue to intertwine with hers. His hand found its way over her chest and roughly cupped one breast. "Tell me."

Raven wrapped her legs around Phineas' waist and allowed the weight of him to press against her. It was difficult to know who had the upper hand. When she believed that Phineas was right where she wanted him, she answered. "Disciples. Followers. Friends. There's so many names for hopeless souls who are easily manipulated."

Phineas pushed up the hem of her dress and let his hand work magic against her. "You see how nice it can be -- if I have full control of my own mind?" he said as he gently pulled her lace panties aside and ever so lightly allowed his fingers to caress her.

Raven sighed with the delicious torture of his slow movements. "Just hold that thought," she said pushing herself up on her elbows. She looked to the hundreds of birds above them, raised her hands skyward and closed her eyes as she began an incantation.

"Gathered friends born to serve. Let my words touch a nerve. You may leave, but your thoughts will remain. Once a follower, but never sane."

A sharp crack sounded, much like a lightening bolt sounding, and the birds scattered in every direction, darkening the sky. Raven smiled at Phineas and lay back down, pulling him atop her once again.

She didn't speak, but loosened his belt buckle and tugged on his pants.

His eyes stared at her, slightly glazed over, either from desire or influence.

Her hand reached down and found him, strong and hard, and she wrapped her fingers around him.

"The others...they could turn up any time," he said protesting.

She didn't answer, but continued to run her hand up the length of him, milking him with an intention of making him forget. She guided him toward her and allowed just the tip of him to touch her, although she would have welcomed all of him.

"Phin?"

"Mmm?"

"Are you of sound mind? Do you want me?" she asked teasing him, mercilessly.

"I wouldn't know the truth now, would I?" he answered.

Phineas used every ounce of willpower to pull himself above Raven. He removed her hand, pressing both of her wrists to the ground and holding her prone. Then, he regarded her, taking in her shiny, black hair that fell in waves below her shoulders, eyes that were dark as coal, but bright as obsidian. She matched his stare and begged him to release his hold on her. "Please, Phin..."

He loosened his grip and she sat up long enough to shimmy out of the light dress she wore. When she lie back down, she was completely exposed to him. She wriggled a finger toward herself, inviting him atop her once more, and when he took his place, she raised her hand to his face and pulled him toward her. She kissed him with the desire of a woman who knows one too many secrets about her man.

"Phin, you know about James...you must agree when I tell you that truth is overrated."

With his body pressed against hers no words came from his mouth. Only a hunger that was out of his control, his mind and body not his own, worked against him.

"The Reckoning will take place by morning," Raven declared. "So without any obligations to truth or what your mind tells you is right...tell me what you want."

Phineas stared at Raven, his eyes showing a myriad of emotions from lust to hate, and as the last of the black birds scattered from the darkening sky, he entered her with one strong thrust.

"Gosh I hate that sound," I complained as yet another black bird cawed from above. "This place is just plain creepy." My comment elicited an angry glare from Shadow, who was holding onto Charlotte's hand.

Knowing what she was thinking and equally unable to dissuade their newcomer from sharing her intentions, James fell into step next to me. He gently placed an arm around me, his touch instantly calming my nerves and making me feel safe.

"When is she going to leave?" I whispered, referring to Shadow.

"She's cursed."

"Aren't we all?"

"No, I mean really cursed. Maebeline would know what to do."

"You mean, voodoo?"

James nodded. "Either that, or she's born from an abomination."

"How can you tell?"

"Her changing features -- both horrific and innocent. This Realm claims people before their pre-destined time. If that were to happen in the present, our world, it's called an accident, but here it's only due to black magic. Voodoo."

"You're saying she still had life to live."

"Yes, and here, the bad souls feed on her lifeblood and remaining innocence. It gives them happiness that they aren't likely to give up. What's worse, they can befriend her and convince her to stay."

"Just as she's doing to Charlotte?" I asked, worriedly.

Daniel, who was just behind us, joined the conversation. "Samantha is immune to it, which is how I found her. It's unusual here."

"At least she's okay," I added, "but Charlotte...we can't get her home if she's not willing to leave."

"She's got her necklace. Samantha lost her memory, but maintained her gift. The same is true for Charlotte," James reassured. "She just needs to access the memories of the others before her...your past Releasors, Suki. Don't worry, she'll come around."

I nodded, deep in thought. "It takes deep concentration, and a guide. With my help, she can do it again. She could access the mind of Charles Babbage and get herself out of here. But it's not going to happen with Shadow hovering over her. James, you need to get to Maebeline."

"I'm not leaving you. You can't travel backwards and there is no going forward in this place."

"But my other powers have been restored. I'll be okay until you get back with more information."

James looked at our party of misfits: Charlotte who brushed Shadow's hair, which changed from beautiful golden ringlets into writhing snakes, Samantha and Daniel, who held hands as they trudged through swampy mud, careful to step over the hands that emerged and reached for them, and me...the woman he had protected throughout time.

"I don't want to leave you," he said finally. "It's just not what I do."

I thought for a moment. "You've always been there. Even if you're not next to me, I know you can feel me. That won't change. You do your job. Find out how we get Charlotte away from Shadow's grip. Besides, Phineas is with us. Isn't he?"

James shrugged, and like me, was unsure of the answer.

Perched in bird form with her minions around her, Raven emitted a show of strength, although she felt ill at ease. Surrounded by her followers, she wanted to lead them into action against Charlotte, although the conversation she had just overheard made her wonder if there wasn't a more pressing issue to attend to...Phineas. As usual, he was proving to be difficult and far more trouble than she was expecting from someone who she had lived with for centuries.

Hearing his name on my lips did more than ruffle her feathers. She let out a loud caw, feeling furious that she could succumb to human emotions of jealousy. It was this Realm that forced souls into eternal damnation and wreaked havoc with their mind. Even those without emotions, which to her was a blessing. She sat quiet once again, allowing her mind to relax as one of the other birds groomed her. It soothed her nerves and then just as quickly, with one sloppy peck, caused her great irritation. She snapped her beak at the other bird, easily drawing blood, and then swooped down to ground level to return to her magnificent human body.

She turned her face skyward, searching the trees for the other blackbird that was larger than the rest, the one that would turn back into Phineas. And upon seeing him and watching him be nuzzled by a smaller bird, she angrily threw a stone at the offending fowl. Within seconds Phineas dropped down next to her.

"You know what they say about throwing stones at glass houses," he mocked, but quickly lessened

Raven's testy emotions by planting a kiss on her cheek.

"That glass house, as you refer, was another female. And even if she is feathered, you still have the ability to procreate with her while you share that characteristic."

"During my London days all the guys talked about going out to bang a bird."

"Cute. But that's not going to happen on my watch. But speaking of birds, stones..."

"Yes?" he asked, and then dropped silent. He had seen this look on Raven's face before. Determination. Ambition. Drive. She had a plan and he knew that somehow, it involved something from him.

"Suki wants James to pay Maebeline a visit."

"Maebeline? Whatever for?"

"Well, she's a Shade, just like him, only older. She knows every religious spell,   voodoo curse, and shaman incantation under the sun. For all of them to get out of here safely, they need unity and that's not going to happen with Charlotte acting whacked out over that creepy...god, what is she?"

"Shadow? Some say she's an Encantado because of her beauty on land and yet, she shifts into a demon with snakes for hair. Others have seen her take to the waters and immediately shift into an animal of the sea."

"You're kidding."

Phineas shook his head. "Dead serious."

"That's even messed up for this place," Raven admitted, and then started laughing. "God, I have to love it. I couldn't even have planned for her to fall for a half-girl, half-dolphin creature. What would an Encantado want from Charlotte?"

"The birds think that she's just lonely and wants a companion."

"So, she picks the first lost human who stumbles into the Realms? Why Charlotte?" Raven asked, now suspicious. "And why did they tell you about it?"

"You know, Raven, if you ever took the time to get to know people, you might just find your own humanity again. They just wanted to talk and I was there. As for Shadow, she just wants someone to love her, and Charlotte can't help but give that."

"Ahh, you're breaking my heart. Well, get over it. You're going on a trip."

"What? You wanted me here. I'm watching Charlotte and trying to get the Amulet of Pollox off her. Remember?"

"Of course I do. But you also remember that the prophecy mentions a Triad. Once that amulet is given to an owner, only the rightful Triad can ever use it next. And I'll be damned if I'm going to go through the rest of eternity with her."

"So, it's you, me, and..."

"Our baby, of course." Raven smiled at Phineas, whose complexion had grown decidedly paler. "But first, I need you to take out Maebeline."

"Whatever for?"

"Because if Suki and James figure out a way to save Charlotte, they'll take her and Samantha back to the present. James can travel alone, but those two girls and Miss Bottle Stopper will form a Triad. I need to make sure that James is sufficiently delayed with any information he plans to bring back."

Phineas turned away from Raven, trying to figure out how to play his cards. Staying in the Romani Realms and acting to save Charlotte would put her in danger if Raven realized what he was up to, and the likelihood of that was pretty high. Similarly, if he left, he was helpless to do anything to support my efforts. The idea of both he and James being gone was beyond dangerous for me. He wondered if ultimately, that was Raven's plan.

Hoping to persuade Raven otherwise, he took her hands in his own.

"Are you sure, you don't want me to stay? We could watch The Reckoning and then go for a fly? Come back and spend a quiet night in the cabin."

Raven's eyes narrowed. It wasn't like Phineas to be so transparent in his motives. "How sweet."

Phineas visibly exhaled, believing that he would keep Charlotte alive for another day. He knew she wanted him gone so he pretended to want to see The Reckoning. Yet he knew that if there was one thing he could count on, it was Raven being so stubborn that she would never do as someone else suggested. This time, he was fatally wrong.

"You know what, sweet Phin? We can watch The Reckoning and then, then you'll leave."

"Raven, that's just not a good idea. I mean, you're going to want me here to complete the Triad."

"I can wait. I mean, it's true that Demon Gypsies ovulate twice a month, but it's not my time. You'll be back in time to do the deed."

Phineas shuddered with the idea of creating a child with Raven, someone who only wanted an offspring to fulfill her own ambitious dreams. But before he could come up with a compelling argument to further his own motives, Raven reached for him and placed a hand under his chin. She turned his face toward her own and held his gaze while speaking the Latin phrase that would compel him to travel back to seek out James' housekeeper, Maebeline.

Da mihi in animo.

Vos ex pura mente.

Faciam scelus.

Et peregrinari cum celeritate.

Give your mind to me.

You of pure thought.

Do my deed.

And travel with speed.

Raven looked at Phineas' pupils, which grew large and dark, and then, when they had returned to normal, she released his head. Momentarily it dropped and hung forward, the incantation brewing in his own mind.

"You're alright now," she said and placed her arms around him in an embrace. "I'll miss you, but you better hurry."

"I'll be back as soon as I'm finished," Phineas replied without any trace of resistance. He placed his arms in the air and a soft rustling of the leaves initiated, the breeze gently blowing his tousled blond hair across his forehead.

Raven watched as the clouds began to roll in slowly across the sky.

"Here, let me help you," she said with a tone that was mildly impatient. She no sooner took his place in the circle that she had previously drawn on the ground when everything began to speed up. The branches on the trees bent with urgency toward them, the wind pushing their limbs to the limit before a few even snapped and broke, then spun out of control into the twirling vortex of the gale force. The clouds that had previously moved slowly across a mainly blue sky now seemed to be changing from white to black like stop gap photography, the transition immediate and strong.

As Raven closed her eyes to the sky, the ticking of clocks indicating the passage of time began and Phineas was caught up in the dust and movement around him. She stepped away and observed as his image became less visible -- the whirring around him growing stronger, until it stopped thus completing his travel and leaving the circle completely empty.

Raven exhaled from the effort and muttered with annoyance to herself. "If you want something done..."

A branch snapped behind her, and Raven turned to see one of the Nephilim, the girl who had prepared

Charlotte, indicating they should walk toward the lake.

"Is it time?" Raven snapped.

The girl merely nodded and then placed her forehead against Raven's so that her thoughts could be easily read.

"Yes, it's happening right now. I've just sent him on his way," Raven confirmed. "He'll kill Maebeline and James will run after to save her. James will still be out of my hair, leaving Suki alone. And if Phin is successful, and he kills Maebeline, James will also eventually perish because nobody will be around to bring him back to this life. It's like killing two birds with one stone."

Finally, the girl spoke, albeit not much above a whisper. "Why are you displeased?"

Raven thought for a moment, still reeling with the reality that she, too, was feeling emotions. "Phineas may have responded to an image of Charlotte when I sent him away, but I'll be damned if I'll let him remember anything about her when he returns."

"That's what makes you so kind," the girl said meekly.

Raven turned to the girl and nodded. "You know, you're right. I haven't been appreciated fully." She looked at her watch before adding, "It's time people started seeing that I'm only working for the greater good."

The girl smiled and clapped excitedly, then reached out tentatively for Raven's hand. Raven rolled

her eyes, but finally accepted and the two headed
toward the lake to wait for The Reckoning.

Phineas' mind may have been compelled by Raven,
but there was no doubt that his heart still belonged to
Charlottte. Raven's irritation was due to the fact that
it actually took many silent attempts to get Phineas on
his way to the present Realm. Her annoyance spread
on so many levels. First, the idea that Phineas was
capable of calling the winds and stirring the energy
fields on his own. She watched his feeble attempts
thinking to herself that his powers were no match for
hers when in reality they had been working overtime.
But eventually, he succumbed.

He found himself just outside of James' house,
resting from the journey before continuing with the
mission that Raven had implanted in his mind. The
time travel left him weary, particularly since he had
worked so hard to make it appear as if he were
summoning the winds. Building them up, only to
remain in place was a tricky endeavor and he had
nearly won until Raven planted image after image in
his mind, accosting his thoughts until she found the
one that sent him over the edge and into the present
Realm.

Pushing his thoughts toward ideas of riches and
power did nothing to motivate him. Nor did the
images that Raven left of myself and James living our
life in happiness. He didn't wish revenge on us and

frankly, he had no desire for more powers beyond what he already was capable of, but what he did want was Charlotte. To Raven's chagrin, it was the one image that sent him over the edge. An image of Maebeline supporting the work of the Nephilim with voodoo and shaman prayers caused Phineas to give up the fight he had launched against the elements and instead, give into them. Raven was naturally fuming that the one image that gave his mind fully to her was that of Charlotte, but if it served her well and she could keep Phineas pliable, then so be it.

Phineas stood and approached Maebeline's door, ready to fight the woman who he believed was fully responsible for Charlotte's pending death. He stopped for a moment and walked back to the street to the mailbox where he gathered up the day's letters and bills.

An older man from next door saw him and being a neighborhood watch type of street, took it upon himself to find out what Phineas was doing. "Hey, you there. Something wrong with Maebeline?"

"She's just out of town. I'm watching her place for her," Phineas lied easily.

"Hmm, she usually asks me to do that," the man said scratching his head. "I can save you the trouble."

Phineas turned and in a split second raised his hand in the 'stop' motion, sending the man careening into the picket fence that bordered his property. The man stumbled to rise, but Phineas refocused his sights on him again. Within seconds the man clutched his chest and slid back down to the ground. Phineas slowly walked toward the man. "Sorry sir, but the only trouble I'm experiencing here is with you."

"Please, call an ambulance. I think I'm having a heart..."

"Shhh, I'll do better than that. I'll bestow some neighborly kindness unto you. This will be quick. Phineas left him and turned toward Maebeline's walkway. After knocking on her door, he turned and saw that the man had now closed his eyes in death.

Chapter Thirteen

The air was still and the woods were quiet. Too quiet. Daniel pulled Samantha closer to him and looked into the sky where the blackbirds had suddenly scattered.

"Something isn't right," I noted. "It feels..."

"Wrong," agreed Daniel.

Charlotte finally joined the group, moving the furthest from Shadow since they had left the ballroom. "What could be wrong?" she said in a dream-like haze. She bent down to run her hands through the mud and sludge.

James gently pulled her up by the elbow and led her back to me. He leaned in and whispered. "I need to leave you with Daniel. You'll be alright. He knows this place and you've trained for this moment."

"I know that I'll be okay on my own, but why do you have to leave?"

"I think what you're feeling is my energy. Something is happening to Maebeline."

I saw that his brow was tinged with beads of sweat and his voice sounded raspy, not at all like its usual, silky smoothness.

"You're not well." Alarm tinged my voice.

"That means she's not well. I...I need to get there."

"Go! James...go now." The fear in my voice didn't go unnoticed. We held each other tightly. James running his hand down my spine, soothing me and calming his own nerves. We held each other like that for a moment, mutually accepting the other one's support.

"Don't panic. Not about me, not about anything. You keep your wits about you here. Understand?"

I nodded.

"And Suki...remember that I love you."

There was something sad about his tone, something off, but I just clung to him a bit tighter. "Of course."

"Let's try something," he said, and then focused his energy on projecting his voice into my head. *"Do you hear me?"*

"Yes silly. I always do."

"You didn't when you first arrived. Now don't be a smart-ass."

"You love bringing up the subject of my ass."

James gave me a loving little smack across my backside. "You. Me. We're One. I've always been there for you and that's not changing now."

"I know."

He leaned in slowly, hesitantly as if he needed to memorize every changing expression on my face. When I tilted my head up to his, he met my mouth with his own, gently letting his lips graze mine.

Again, I felt his hand move up my back and rest behind my neck, pulling me in closer. Even traveling on foot through the mud, he still gave off his clean scent like warm sunshine after a light rain. I sighed against his mouth and let his tongue interweave with mine. My leg wrapped around his, pulling him in closer so that every inch of our bodies pressed against each other. God, I didn't want to left him go.

The wind picked up and he pulled away from me. "It's time. If I can catch the wind just right, the continuum of time will pull me back exactly where I need to be."

"And that's not with me," I said sadly.

He gave me a sideways, sad smile and pressed two fingers to his lips and then to mine. I felt the jolt of electricity run from his body directly into mine when he touched me. He gasped suddenly and placed his hand on his heart.

"James!"

"It has to be now," he said suddenly weaker.

"Can you make it?"

Without a sound, he was gone, riding the wind and the gears of time in search of his childhood home in New Orleans where Maebeline still resided.

I sat on a tree stump, taking a moment to assess the situation. On the positive side, I was reunited with both Charlotte and Samantha. But there was still much to be done if I were to get the three of us home safely. The Triad needed to be fulfilled and there was no telling how to do that. Charlotte was the only one who could access information from the Amulet of Pollox and her mind was not her own. Even if I were to draw upon the information that I had learned from each of my past Releasors, Samantha seemed reticent to leave Daniel. As for myself, I too worried about leaving for fear of James suddenly returning and being alone. If we were to form a proper Triad, each of us had to be aligned simultaneously with the same goals and thoughts.

I turned to watch Samantha quietly holding hands with Daniel, while Charlotte was once again enamored with Shadow, gently combing her fingers through the little girl's blonde locks and then pulling them away before the strands turned to snakes and nipped at her wrists.

"Charlotte dear, maybe you should let Shadow comb her own hair? Her snakes seem hungry." I tried to keep my voice even, but my look of disgust gave the game away.

"I won't hurt her. I love her," Shadow argued.

"But do your snakes know not to bite?"

"They won't hurt Charlotte. They know how I feel about her."

"That's all very fine and dandy, but..." my voice was rising.

"Shh," Charlotte placed a finger to her lips. "Be polite. You should know better than to raise your voice to an innocent child."

I rolled my eyes. That was ripe. I had been to finishing school, ladies teas, debutante balls and more, and now I was being given etiquette lessons from a teenager with identity issues and an unhealthy relationship with an Encantado.

Before any more discussions could ensue, a low rumbling could be heard, interrupting the strange stillness of the air. Daniel instinctively pulled Samantha closer and I carefully scanned the horizon for signs of danger.

"Run!" I hurriedly grabbed Charlotte by the arm while Daniel moved toward Samantha, his eyes showing as much concern as my own.

"Samantha, Sam...come on, come on!" he urged. "What? I don't see anything? What is it?"

"There's no time. Come on."

"We can't out run them," I screamed. There isn't time. Go up," I urged pointing to the trees that surrounded us with their strong branches, wide enough to hold even a grown man.

"Charlotte, come on," I urged, but the girl planted her feet solidly underneath her, unwilling to be led away.

"Not without Shadow," she said quietly, with little concern for anything happening around her. Neither the shaking of the earth or the sounds of rumbling seemed to sway her. What started as just a warning now gave way to the sound of scampering claws as raccoons and squirrels climbed trees, deer bounded by, and wild horses pounded the ground toward us at full gallop.

I desperately tried to pull Charlotte out of harm's way, but she merely turned toward the oncoming stampede, looking for Shadow, who was nowhere to be seen.

"We have to go!" I pleaded.

Daniel helped Samantha grab a hold of a tree, interlacing his fingers as a step and then pushing her upwards. She had always been athletic and her old skills came back to her easily as she climbed higher and he followed, ready to grab her if she lost her footing.

"Suki!" he called down to me, extending his hand to mine.

"Not without Charlotte!" I shouted above the rumble.

"Alright then. You go for Charlotte. I'm going back to the Gazebo," he said looking upwards to ensure Samantha was safe.

"Daniel, no," Samantha begged. "I can't lose you."

"I need to stop the time. Don't you hear it?"

The sound of gears, grinding and moving and a ticking clock could be heard. It was barely audible, but if one focused it was most decidedly there.

"Daniel, if you stop the master clock it will buy us time before the Reckoning," I confirmed.

"Be careful," he said as he ran into the clearing.

Samantha watched him go and then shook off her sorrow. The fiery redhead was back and she turned her attention back to me. "The people who live here are motivated by innocence and happiness. They feed off of it," she explained. "That's what the Reckoning is all about."

I looked up at her. "Samantha, how have you managed to maintain your mind? Why haven't they taken control of you?"

"Because Daniel keeps me sane and when they are near, I remember all of the loss I've experienced. I didn't know the specifics, but I felt it. Now that you're here...I remember. My parents. Charlotte. You. It's enough to make them think that I no longer have any hope. But I do."

I smiled up at her. "You certainly do. You were always..." but I didn't get to finish my thought. A large buck bounded within inches of me, but I swiftly rolled away, using one of my practiced Krav Maga moves that fortunately came back with necessity and instinct. As I hit the ground, the hands from underneath the muddy surface protruded through, reaching and grabbing for my legs.

"Samantha, you always knew of a person's true essence. You need to focus on Charlotte. Help her remember. Focus on the Amulet of Pollox. If we both focus our thoughts, she has a shot."

I called upon the elements to help me and with each angry glance I shot in the direction of those offending hands, bolts of lightening thrust them away. "Come on, Charlotte. I can't keep this up forever."

But Charlotte was lost in her own misery, chasing after a girl who wasn't one. "I have to find her...Suki, I just have to."

I turned at the sound of my name. It was the first time since having arrived in these Realms that Charlotte had spoken it. I looked at Charlotte's eyes to see if I would be met with real recognition or if she were only repeating what she had heard from the others.

"You remember me!" I asked with hope, and then called up to Samantha. "It's working!"

"I do." Charlotte looked down at her ball gown, once a beautiful creation of white, now stained and muddied. "What has happened to us? Where's...where's...," but she only buried her face in her hands and shook her head, unable to complete the thought.

"Phineas?" I said, reading her thoughts, although it pained me to do so.

Charlotte wiped the tears and nodded.

"He's here. At least he was, but he was with Raven."

"He couldn't be, Suki. I have to believe in him."

There had been a break in the stampede, but the rumbling had started up again and this time it was ten times louder, if that were even possible. There wasn't time to answer her unspoken question. "Charlotte run!"

I stepped over the dead, white limbs of the souls who resided underneath us and grabbed Charlotte's hand. The two of us ran until a voice, sweet and that of a child, rang out... "Charlotte!"

Charlotte stopped in her tracks at the sound of Shadow's voice.

"No Charlotte, we have to go. You can't stop for her...for *it*," I said with emphasis.

One of the hands, regenerated yet still mangled, reached for Charlotte, only to be zapped powerless by me once more. "Charlotte, we don't have time. You have to help me. Concentrate on the Amulet. Think of all of the powerful messages and information it contains."

"But I can't leave her," she said looking out toward the lake. "I think she's that way."

I spoke in my most soothing tone. "Just try."

We moved further into the forest, away from the main path that the animals seemed to run through, and Charlotte focused her mind on those who had come before her.

"I know how we can get out of here. All of us!"

The loud caw of a blackbird overhead called as it forced a branch to crash down upon us. The distraction broke my hold over Charlotte, and in turn, her ability to see into the greatest minds of the past. Charlotte became captive by one of the ghostly white hands from underneath. It grabbed onto her ankle and no sooner, another hand reached even higher, climbing upwards onto her leg and scratching a terrible gash down her calf. She fell, giving more hands the opportunity to hold onto her, working as best they could to drag her deep within the mud.

I sent one electrical bolt after the next, and while they temporarily halted one hand from its hold over her, there were so many and my assault had to be continual if she were not to succumb. I sent one more charge at a nearby hand, working carefully to avoid Charlotte's leg with my own attack, when the same blackbird, a particularly large one, cawed and caught my attention.

Yet, truth be told, it wasn't just the bird that captured my attention, but a vision that was suddenly planted in my mind as well. Suddenly, I saw Phineas and Raven together -- very together, lying in their room before joining the ball. Phineas' intimate exploration of Raven's body was right before my eyes, giving me the answer once and for all of whether or not he was still aligned with Raven.

I did my best to shake off the image, telling myself that maybe it happened years earlier. I wouldn't put it past Raven to fool my mind with an old image, in spite of the fact that my mind's eye most distinctly saw her in the same dress that she had been wearing earlier that night at the ball.

Still, I fought the offending display and focused on Charlotte's needs. But Raven was relentless, planting one image after the next, just as she had done to Samantha when she plummeted over a cliff to her death. Each visual became more graphic than the prior, taking all of my attention.

Phineas' mouth kissed the side of Raven's neck, then met her mouth with his own as his hands wandered as well. I summoned the elements, allowing a cool rain to fall down on us, hoping it would jar me out of this horrific home movie, and it nearly did...until Raven twisted the knife.

"No!" I called out and suddenly lost my grip on Charlotte's hand.

"Suki! Suki!"

But what I saw was too shockingly painful. Phineas' face hovering close to Raven's suddenly wavered and shook, his image changed and contorted. Trying hard to see what was happening, rather than try to move away from the scene, I became riveted by Raven's antics.

Unable to turn off the images, I instead tuned into them and watched each one flow from one to the next. First, Raven lying in bed with Phineas, breaking my heart for Charlotte.

"It doesn't mean anything," I kept telling myself. *"So what...I know they were together once. It could be a scene from years earlier."*

But there was one niggling thought that I couldn't ignore. The dress. The one that Phineas lifted above her knees was the very same she wore in the ballroom.

"She could still distort the timing. She isn't the Queen of Sheba. Lots of people wear a dress more than once."

But even if I could convince myself that Phineas was still aligned with James and I, and intended to remain faithful to Charlotte, I couldn't ignore what I saw next. The image of Raven lying on top of the bed, her face sighing in ecstasy as a man's form was prone above her, his head between her legs. It was so...intimate.

As he rose up, his strong arms holding himself above her, there was something familiar about him. The movie screen in my mind shifted and I no longer saw things from above, but rather from Raven's point of view, looking upwards into the face of her lover...looking upwards into James' face.

Chapter Fourteen

"No!" I gasped again, further losing my focus on Charlotte. The image of James making love with Raven was too much to bear. The bird above cawed again, this time sounding almost gleeful as Charlotte, lost without the guidance of the Amulet or my support, became captive by two even stronger hands that held her legs in place.

"Suki!" Charlotte shouted as the sounds from the stampede were nearly upon us.

With the damage done, Raven released my mind back to me. I immediately retched and vomited, but forced myself to focus on the situation at hand -- Charlotte faced an even worse predicament. "Release her, you abomination of hell," I shouted, knowing that Raven was behind the images, this painful distraction.

"Where's Shadow? Where is she?" Charlotte screamed in panic.

I shook my head. "It's you we need to worry about..." and then I plunged my hands into the mud, trying to free Charlotte, but the hands wouldn't take me as bait -- their hold on Charlotte remained.

He was amazing. Raven's voice rang out from the treetops, but when I looked skyward all that I could see were the blackbirds gathering. That momentary glance proved to be a terrible mistake.

Cattle ran through the clearing, one knocking me over with a fierce kick to my ribcage. I doubled over in pain and rolled to the side of the clearing where the muddy patch, now resembling a small but steady continual movement of sludge, had moved Charlotte downstream. I reached for her, trying at least to hold onto her by the shoulders as she was now nearly completely submerged.

The blackbirds cried out from above and following their shrieks came the rest of the forest animals, running at top speed. Some of the smaller animals were trampled, left to die by their own kind. But the horror didn't stop.

For a moment the steady stream of animals running let up only to give way for wild, black stallions. The horses were different from the other animals. These ran in formation, their stealth-like grace and rhythmic galloping drawing the attention of the souls trapped below the surface of the earth. Gaunt and white faces popped up like disturbed flowers to eye the beasts that ran by.

And once a large enough audience had gathered, the horses' appearances seemed to fade and ripple. For a moment I felt relief, believing the end of the procession was upon us. But the end was a more apt description. Each horse shifted from black to the same deathly white as the trapped souls and then the amalgamation of the animal became even more gruesome as its horse head remained, but in place of its body and legs, those of a man appeared.

The head of a horse attached to the strong body of a man, a beast known as a Buraq, running on all fours, veered off the course of the midway, and came straight for Charlotte.

"Stop!" I screamed, holding up my hands and releasing bolts of electricity. My control of the elements didn't falter, with each strike growing stronger against the offending horse-men, and yet, their grossly disfigured forms kept coming closer.

"That's quite impressive, Suki," Raven's voice sounded behind me. "Just not impressive enough."

I knew better than to turn my attention away from Charlotte. *Good girl. Don't let her get to you.* James voice sounded in my mind.

But the sound of James' voice only served to upset, rather than comfort me. *Had he betrayed me? Could he have once been involved with Raven?*

I would have to do this on my own.

A cloud of blue butterflies released into the air, my energy guiding them toward the beasts. They fluttered around the horse-men's faces, hovering closely and tickling their nostrils causing them to stumble, but only slightly.

"Suki, watch out!" Samantha shouted down from her perch high in the trees. She pointed to one of the horse-men, causing her weight to shift and the branch to break. She would have fallen had she not grabbed another just in time. Although for me, time had run out.

The first Buraq turned suddenly and returned, running straight for Charlotte, who by this time had sunk even deeper into the mud. The Buraq ran up to her and stopped, staring at me defiantly. He stood on its manly legs and reached its arms around Charlotte, paying no attention to the electrical waves I sent in his direction. Charlotte screamed as its hold on her tightened.

Although it was saving her from sinking completely into the muddy abyss, she was by no means out of danger. The Buraq lifted her onto its back and ran into the clearing with her. I was helpless to stop it.

I sent the butterflies in their direction, but the visions of peace and beauty that the delicate creatures delivered did nothing to stop the fast running Buraq. Within seconds it had disappeared with Charlotte.

I looked upward to ensure that Samantha was still safe. "You stay there. I'll find her."

Samantha nodded, tears flowing freely down her face. She suddenly waved her hands frantically, trying to warn me of another Buraq's return, but her voice was muted as she became gripped in total fear for there wasn't just one returning for me, but five.

The front runner bucked me from behind, forcing me to fall into a tree stump. I went down hard, a trickle of blood running from where my temple struck the stump and the brambles on the ground. I struggled to my feet only to find that the five Buraqs had positioned themselves around me in a circle. Their bluish white skin glowed slightly; their horse heads raised upward and one after the next let our a loud whinny of excitement.

You know what to do.

I took a deep breath, wanting to take comfort in James' support, but also not trusting his words. *Were they his words or was it another trick of Raven's?*

The confusion of my thoughts caused me to lose ground with the Buraqs. The first delivered a strong punch directly into my abdomen and I bent at the waist, winded from the experience.

Suki, you can do this. Be strong.

I wasn't comforted by his presence, but angered. Raven could distort time; she could plant an unrealistic fear in one's mind; but, surely she couldn't distort an image. At some time, she and my James had been lovers. The reality hurt me far more than the continual pounding of the Buraq's fists against my back and kidneys.

Anger would have to be my friend. If James' words didn't comfort me, then at least they could help me fight.

I rose and immediately spun and extended a roundhouse kick to the first beast. It went down easily, but only drew the attention of the others. One immediately stood up on its human back legs, its naked male form moving at me in a menacing fashion. Muscles upon muscles, legs spread showing no shame, and all the while, its horse's eyes wide on the side of its head taking in any movement from its team mates.

Raven flew in bird form and then swooped in low, her talons grazing the side of my cheek, before she landed and shifted into herself. "Isn't he remarkable?" she commented of her favorite Buraq. "Gives new meaning to the phrase, 'hung like a horse.'" She sidled up to the Buraq, and allowed her hand to slide over his chest. "Take her."

The Buraq immediately grabbed me, holding my shoulders roughly, his head staring at me with keen interest.

"What do you want with us?" I hissed.

"You know what I want," Raven chided.

"The Amulet....well, you have it. You've taken *her*. Just bring Charlotte back to me and we'll go."

Raven smiled. "But this is fun for me. And by the looks of things...for him," she noted the Buraq's excitement. "He reminds me of someone...oh I remember..."

I twisted against the Buraq's hold, but he only tightened his hands around my waist and then lasciviously pressed himself against me.

"Yes...yes I remember," Raven taunted. "You probably can guess, now that you're getting to know each other better. I'll give you a hint...he has a thing for a girl in distress. At least that's how James and I ended up, you know. But maybe that's not what turns him on any more because I don't see him coming to your rescue. Maybe he loves me more?"

"Stop it, Raven."

"Sorry, I just felt the need to share."

Raven moved behind the Buraq and took out a riding crop, which she used against his back side. The Buraq exhaled loudly and snorted, jumping forward and pinning itself against me.

"You're delusional. What's in the past stays in the past," I said trying to prove how little she could affect me -- even if it were a lie. I kicked the Buraq where it counted, but it only served to excite him. He rallied his other horse-men, who moved in each one taking a stand and surrounding me.

Although I had surprised the first, the others were ready for combat. Two sent simultaneous kicks into me, one from behind sending me reeling into the other, who struck back at my chest just as hard. The wind may have been knocked out of me, but I wasn't about to give up.

"Nice try," Raven said with a smirk.

"Suki!" Samantha shrieked from above. "They're coming!"

Take them. Now.

I hear you. My thoughts went to James, wishing the sentiment I threw at Raven could indeed be the truth. I wanted an explanation, but couldn't deny the fact that he wasn't here, just as Raven said.

"Suki, you can do this," Samantha's voice rang down to me.

I may have been down, but I would use it to my advantage, doing as James taught me -- lying in wait, composing myself, all the while estimating each

Buraq's position and how I would fight off the remaining four. I recalled our training sessions.

Move from a position of defense into one of offense.

The next Buraq also abandoned its stance on four legs and instead rose up on two. I jumped up and immediately reached for its torso, grabbing around its neck and pulling my knee into his side. Winding him, I didn't hesitate to finish him off. With a swift lift of my knee, I plunged it upward into his gut and when he doubled over, I forced my elbows into the back of his neck and back. One down. I exhaled deeply as it dropped to the ground.

Three left. As the next approached, I didn't wait to be the victim. I sent a kick upwards, landing my boot against the side of its head and then continuing my assault.

Strike hard and fast as many times as is needed to take down your attacker.

I put James' words into action, kicking repeatedly until the third also succumbed to my battle attack.

"There's no such thing as a one-punch knockout," I said more to myself than the beast that lay by my feet. I looked up at the remaining two, who had both stood like men, their horse heads watching me, weighing my next move. One walked slowly to my left, while the other went to the right. They weren't going to chance the one-on-one battle. This time, I'd have to fight them both.

Knowing that in this fight there were no rules, I leapt into action and attacked my opponent's most vulnerable spots. Kicking one in the groin, he neighed loudly and doubled over. I lifted my knee into its face hard and when he reached his human hands toward his face in pain, I finished him with a kick to the abdomen that threw him backwards. I looked to the tree tops and concentrated on a particularly large branch. With a narrowing of my eyes and the fire that burned anger within me, I sent the branch falling onto the Buraq, ensuring that he wouldn't rise again.

But the reprieve was short lived as the last and final Buraq approached. He was also the strongest standing at six feet tall, with muscular arms, a wide chest, and legs like tree trunks. He circled me, moving with the grace of a stallion. His trot soon turned to a gallop as he moved around and around at a dizzying speed.

He grabbed me from behind suddenly and thrust me into a nearby tree, like a shot put. The back of my head hit the trunk hard enough to cause a black out, but as I started to succumb and slide down toward the ground into the muddy sludge where the hands reached hungrily upwards, the Buraq walked threateningly toward me.

"Enough! Finish her!" Raven's voice sounded from every which way as if on loud speaker.

Raven's whereabouts being unknown were tremendously disconcerting and caused another momentary lack of focus, but it was enough. The Buraq changed course suddenly and came straight for me, butting me with its head more like a bull than that of a horse. I was tossed onto my back and he immediately galloped toward me. Without hesitation, he straddled my body. I thrust my fists against his chest, but his strong torso accepted the assault as if it were nothing.

"Get up, Suki. Fight!" Samantha looked down in fear.

I tried to pry my legs up from underneath the Buraq, but he only began to crush down upon me with his strong body.

"I can wish for your safety," Samantha called down.

"No!" I answered. "No Samantha. It's not a privilege to be used on me."

The Buraq whinnied as its nose nuzzled the side of my neck, drool dripping down my throat. His naked form forcing downward onto me as well. The sight caused jealousy to rise in the other that had just come to, and it approached as well.

"Suki! Let me help you!" Samantha screamed, her anguish growing as the situation became more perilous.

I closed my eyes, willing the elements to take control, and as I relaxed, the Buraq took my expression as acceptance and grew more excited. This only served to anger the watching Buraq, which kicked its back legs into the head of the first, forcing him off me.

The fighting among them ensued. Each kicking and punching until the fatal blow was delivered and they fell to the ground in exhaustion. The hands of the dead, grabbed for them and used their heavy forms as leverage, allowing themselves to rise out of the mud. Raven quickly changed into bird form and left the scene, flying toward the lake.

From the safety of the tree where I joined Samantha, we watched in horror as the lost souls formed a procession and walked in a solitary line in the direction that Raven flew.

"Where are they going?"

"I don't know, but I don't like it," I responded, still exhausted from the battle. "We need to get down and find Charlotte."

"Can you handle it?"

"I have to."

At that moment, Daniel materialized from the forest, which had grown eerily quiet. "It's too late."

Before we could ask for clarification, the bell from the ballroom sounded loudly, piercing the quiet wilderness. Raven's voice rang out from a loudspeaker:

"The Reckoned has been found! You are cordially invited to witness the festivities lakeside."

"It can't be true," Samantha cried. Daniel held her tightly, covering her ears and trying his best to shield her from the sounds of the party-goers, cheering with elation.

I closed my eyes and focused. I may be hurt, both mentally and physically, but this was no time for pride or stubbornness. I needed to get a message to James. We needed to find Phineas and end Raven's control over him.

"What are you planning?" Samantha asked, aware of my concentrated look.

"If you can find love in this horrible place then I have to believe that Phineas will help Charlotte...and James...well..."

"Well what? You two are like destined...he waited centuries for you to arrive."

"I guess even a Shade can get tired of waiting."

"Not James," Samantha said emphatically.

I gave a slight smile. Now wasn't the time to think about myself. I took Samantha's free hand in my own. "This isn't over. Come. I know what to do."

Chapter Fifteen

When Maebeline opened the door to her Georgian-styled home, the residence that she had maintained since James was just a child, she was half-way expecting him to be standing outside.

The duality she brought to James' life and he to hers, meant that their very lifeblood was connected. James may have been tasked with protecting me throughout time, but Maebeline was the only one who could do the same for James and without her, his life hung in the balance. She had known that the journey back into the Romani Realms would be difficult, but even she had underestimated Raven's trickery.

She had spent the morning baking bread when she felt the presence of a supernatural at her door. "James? You know you could've given me some warning if you were going to bring Miss Suki back for a visit," she called out.

But the man waiting for her was not who she suspected. When James told her that he would be trusting Phineas with this rescue mission she had her doubts. Now that the demon gypsy was staring her in the face, she knew she had good reason to feel that way.

"What are you doing here? Aren't you supposed to be..."

Phineas shoved past Maebeline sending her flying into the alcove, before closing the door behind him. He strode toward her, unseeing eyes staring straight into hers. Maebeline had dealt with enough people possessed to know that he wasn't of his right mind, which put her in a precarious position.

She was a rotund woman better suited for baking than fighting, but she did have the powers of the spirits to guide her. Her visions had foreshadowed an unexpected and unwanted visitor. When Phineas shoved his way past her, she caught a glimpse of her neighbor, Mr. Talcott, lying on the ground outside and knew immediately that he was gone.

"Mr. Talcott didn't mean no harm to you. Why'd you go and do that?" she scolded.

Phineas laughed. "That's something. I'm here to kill you and you have the chops to tell me off."

Phineas approached Maebeline head on, his eyes glazed, but determined. He reached his hands for her neck and gripped her tightly. His somewhat dreamlike state didn't go unnoticed, and Maebeline realized that she had mere moments to react. Although instinct made her want to pull his hands from her throat, her strength was no match against Phineas' muscular form. Keeping her head together was her best hope and so, she quickly gripped the talisman she had placed in the pocket of her housecoat earlier when the spirits indicated that trouble was brewing.

She held the symbol up to him and with barely a whisper, she uttered an incantation that caused the wind to force the shutters against the house and the sun to disappear behind the clouds. Phineas turned in shock, his release faltering. It gave Maebeline enough of her voice back to be able to complete the first part of the incantation:

"Darkness and cold from nature's earth...mirror the demeanor of a centuries old birth. Once human, now demon...an amalgamation."

Maebeline spoke calmly and Phineas' hold on her neck receded, his arms fell by his sides as he stared into her round face with unblinking, green eyes. A nasty cough escaped him and with it, a snake weaved its way from his mouth. All the while, Maebeline continued to speak in soft, calm tones.

"Impure intentions are driven away. Your energy now a clear path to what I say."

Phineas stared at Maebeline. With his eyes fixed and words escaping him, he waited until Maebeline broke her hold over him and waved the talisman in front of his eyes.

"Now that we've put the nastiness behind us, you mind tellin' me what this is all 'bout?"

"What is this?" he said, indicating the talisman.

"You gonna be good or do I have to send that snake back into you? Cuz if I do, it ain't gonna go in the same place it came out."

The snake laced its way up Phineas' leg and he jumped backward, flicking it across the wooden floors. Maebeline reached down and the serpent wrapped itself around her arm. She stroked its back gently.

"I'm cool," he said, more than a little shook up.

"Is that all?"

Phineas stared at her, like a child being scolded. "What do you want?"

"What do I want? You come in here like a bat outta hell, kill my sweet neighbor, the very one who always enjoyed my sweet rolls and then some, and you tried some no good nonsense with me too? I want an apology."

"That's all? I'm sorry."

"I'm sorry...what?" Maebeline asked, her tone angry.

"I'm sorry, Ma'am."

"That's better. Now, follow me into the kitchen; I need a glass of sweet tea. You want some?"

Phineas shifted uncomfortably. "I think I should be getting back...to..."

"Yeah, you need to get back, but you're going to need James for that and he's gonna be spitting mad when he finds you here, so I suggest you sit and have a glass of sweet tea with me because I damn as sure want one and you've given me enough grief for one afternoon."

"Yes Ma'am," he answered and shuffled behind Maebeline into the next room. Maebeline crossed to the refrigerator and retrieved the pitcher. After pouring two glasses, she grabbed a hefty knife from the butcher block and waved it in Phineas' direction.

"You know, I've got a mind to..."

Phineas gave her a wary glance, but didn't dare speak a word.

"You and that harlot Raven have enough crazy in y'all to fill the world's asylums. What were you thinking?" she asked and finally took the knife to its intended -- a brown sugar pound cake.

Ignoring her question, Phineas indicated the cake, "Can I get a slice?"

"Boy, you have got some nerve about ya." Regardless of her annoyance, Maebeline cut a healthy slice for each of them and then sat down across from Phineas at the table.

She accepted a hefty mouthful and after swallowing and wiping her lips with the embroidered serviette she preferred to use at tea time, Maebeline handed Phineas her talisman.

He turned it over, inspecting the intersecting triangles that made up its form. "The Seal of Solomon?" he asked.

"That's right. You know of it?"

Phineas nodded. "Raven showed it to me years ago...told me that it was used by the king who ruled the Genii -- the Jinn."

"And she told you this because..." Maebeline prodded.

"Because she has researched everything there is to know about genies, from their whims and weaknesses to their history and hopes."

"Then you know that this protects the wearer from all evil. The interlaced triangle consists of one apex tilted upwards, thus representing good; and other one...," Maebeline paused and like a school teacher, waited for Phineas to finish her thought.

"The other is inverted, indicating evil," his voice dropping, not wanting to recognize his part in the equality of the symbol.

With the last sentiment spoken, a harsh wind rushed throughout the kitchen and with it, in swept James. He stared at the scene in front of him, not believing his own eyes. Never could he have envisioned the time when his partner and fellow Shade would be entertaining a rival like Phineas.

"Afternoon Maebeline," he said smoothly. "Everything alright here?"

Phineas stood and extended his hand.

"I don't want to shake your hand," James said evenly. "I just want to know what you're doing in my home."

"Phineas came to pay me a visit," Maebeline said, pouring James a tall glass of his favorite minted lemonade.

"James...let me explain..."

"We had a deal. I can only imagine that if you're here, you came looking for trouble."

"I might have been, but...I was compelled and that was before..."

James shot him a look that could have scared a shooting bullet back into the barrel of a gun. Phineas ran his hand through his hair, suddenly feeling much more ill at ease than when Maebeline released a snake from his system.

"James, why don't you sit down and we can finish this conversation in a manner suited for civility," Maebeline purred.

Still glaring at Phineas, James grabbed the nearest chair, turned it backwards and straddled it, leaning his muscular torso against the wood frame. "You've risked the entire operation. You come here to do who knows what to Maebeline, forcing me here as well?

"You can see that I was perfectly capable on my own," Maebeline chimed in.

"Yes, but had something happened to you," James replied, eyes on Phineas, "then I'm a goner as well. Did you ever think of all that before you decided to jump in the sack with Raven again?"

"She's quite convincing in that regard, isn't she?" Phineas goaded.

James grabbed his shirt collar and pulled him up to standing, not liking the implication.

"Hey, I'm not going to fight you. I'm just pointing out the obvious."

James sat back down and rested his head in his hands. After a moment, he let out a big sigh. "It's not a coincidence. Nothing ever is."

Phineas took a long sip from his glass and asked, "What part?"

"When did you find out about..." James shook his head, not wanting to finish his own question.

"About you and crazy doing it?"

Maebeline looked up to the heavens as if her ears could be saved from the pending conversation.

James stood up and paced to the other side of the kitchen. "Yes, when did Raven tell you that we had been together?"

"I'd say it was about five minutes before she jumped me."

Maebeline made the sign of the cross over her chest and poured herself another glass of tea.

"She planned for us to both be here, separated from the others at this exact moment," James met Phineas' gaze. "She wanted something to drive each of us away from the Romani Realms."

"It's happening, isn't it?" Phineas asked, the worry palatable in his voice.

Maebeline took both of their hands in hers and nodded. She held up the talisman symbol again. "There's one more piece of information associated with this triangle. With its apex pointed upward, it's also a symbol of the Trinity."

James and Phineas both stared at each other, trying to make sense of the situation.

Suddenly, James pounded his fist into the table. "She's going to launch the Reckoning."

"Raven's been hedging her bets this whole time, trying to figure out who will form the Triad," Phineas said. "She said she wanted it to be with me and get this...our future child."

"But that would never happen if the girls triggered it with Suki," James added.

Phineas shook his head. "It doesn't make sense. Why would she force both of us out of the picture now?"

"She couldn't possibly think that our little truce meant that...you, me, and Suki? God, it's too disgusting to even contemplate."

"Right back at you, James."

Maebeline listened quietly to their bickering while letting her hands rest lightly on the triangle of her ouija board. Finally, she spoke up. "You two wanted to know who would make up the Triad, so it seemed sensible to let the triangle guide us."

"Did you get a reading?" James asked.

"Yes, but you're not going to like it," she answered, eyebrows raised.

Maebeline looked from James to Phineas, who also sat anxiously for her answer. "Please tell us; what is it?"

"Does Shadow mean anything to either of you?"

The Buraqs had no intention of letting Charlotte escape the Reckoning. If they made that mistake, Raven would ensure that they remained in their hideous form indefinitely. As it was, they had hopes of carrying out the sentence inflicted by the magistrates of the Romani Realms and being granted the freedom to return to fully human form and then perhaps they would one day find love and escape this place completely. Until that time, they were determined to test Charlotte's ability to survive the Reckoning.

Two walked ahead of her, two behind, and the last carried her on his back. The long path they took extended through the forest to the frigid lake and for the nearly two miles of its expanse, the citizens of the Romani Realms lined either side of the dusty thoroughfare.

When they finally reached the dock, a makeshift dressing room had been erected where the Nephilim were waiting to prepare Charlotte once again. They tsked to themselves when they saw her muddy dress, annoyed at the effort they had made earlier and the fact that they would have to repeat their efforts. If there was one thing that was expected in the Realms, it was an attractive Reckoning complete with pomp and circumstance. Nobody took any enjoyment from watching someone ugly get their comeuppance. So as a small band of musicians tuned their instruments and readied to entertain the crowd, the girls immediately got to work on changing Charlotte into more appropriate attire.

Re-doing her makeup wasn't necessary as she would soon be plunged into the frigid lake, but there were sure to be photographers at the onset of the show so every effort was made for Charlotte's dress to be perfect.

It didn't disappoint. When she was led out, a hush fell over the crowd and the band immediately stopped playing.

"If we weren't in the Romani Realms, I'd swear there was a bit of civility among these people," Raven said to a girl as she landed beside her and transformed out of black bird form.

It was no wonder that the crowd was rendered speechless. Charlotte was a vision of beauty like none that had ever been seen in these Realms. Her dress was off the shoulders with a form fitted bodice that gave way to a flowing skirt. The soft, white silk was layered resembling the feathers of a swan. Charlotte's own creamy pale skin and long, straight blonde locks completed the look, giving her an ethereal quality apropos of the circumstances.

"She looks like an angel," another murmured.

An old woman stopped to admire the scene and replied, "She's as beautiful as the swans that will take her to her death."

"It's lovely, isn't it?" a third agreed.

"What's wrong with them?" Samantha asked in horror. "Don't they know that their thoughts will condemn all of them?"

"There's no hope for them. But there is for you so keep your eyes down," Daniel warned.

"And make sure your hair doesn't escape from that cloak," I warned. "We need to get close enough to help Charlotte channel her thoughts."

As they inched along the perimeter of the crowd, blending in by wearing cloaks Daniel had stolen from the Nephilim salon, they positioned themselves within a stone's throw of Charlotte. So close to her that they could see the fear in her eyes, and yet unable to help or they would risk all of them being captured.

The crowd broke out into polite applause, greeting the sight of Charlotte and showing their appreciation to Raven for finding such a worthy specimen to sacrifice for their own souls.

Raven took that moment to climb to the top of a small podium and greet the crowd. "Thank you all for coming to our annual Reckoning. You know how important this event is to our future here. So without further ado, please join me in repeating our motto."

The crowd spoke as one: "One life sacrificed saves many souls."

"And let the Reckoning begin!" Raven's voice carried out loud and clear, and as her hands rose in the air, punctuating her statement, the Buraqs and Nephilim bowed to the crowd and then forced behind Charlotte, huddling close to her, shoving her closer and closer to the edge of the pier until she was forced to step off and plunge into the dark water.

Chapter Sixteen

Neither James nor Phineas were thrilled at the prospect of traveling back to the Romani Realms together, but it had to be done. Passing through time would bind them until eternity.

"Unbelievable. Now I've got you in my system as well as your psycho lover," James muttered as he begrudgingly readied himself to leave with Phineas.

"Ah, sweet nothings. Is that the type of stuff you whispered to Raven when the two of you..."

James stood inches away, his stance threatening. "Don't say it."

"You did it."

"She was dying. What choice did I have? I didn't know what she would become."

"Does Suki know?" Phineas asked, while fastening Maebeline's talisman to the inside of his coat.

James looked to Maebeline, the regret clear in his eyes.

"I haven't been able to get a message to her. She's closed off all of her channels to me. Maebeline can't get through to her either, so I'd say that Raven took pleasure in letting her know."

Phineas patted James on the back, a bit harder than necessary. "You'll get her back. Just look at you...all muscles and manliness. I'd jump you...that is, if I didn't already have plans to save Charlotte and kiss her from here to Sunday."

"You know, after that declaration we're doing this my way. Turn around," James instructed. "Hands behind your back."

"James, you don't want to lose him," Maebeline chided.

"I'll take my chances."

After giving Phineas an 'after you' wave, James bound his hands behind his back.

"Is this really necessary?"

"You came here with the intention to harm Maebeline, and in effect, to do the same to me. So, yeah...until we get there, consider yourself bound to me...literally. Besides, the trip tends to bring out people's emotions, so it's for your safety too. I wouldn't want to forget our deal and decide to kill you."

Turning so that they were back to back, James gave the signal to Maebeline. She tied James hands with the same cord he had used on Phineas and then fastened both men to each other so their hands were behind their backs, each tied to the other's wrists.

"You're all set, gentlemen. Have a pleasant trip."

"See you when I get back," James answered with a nod. "Have a slice of coconut cake waiting for me."

"The one with the cream or the custard?"

"Surprise me."

"See ya, Maebeline," Phineas added. "Thank you for your hospitality."

Maebeline raised one eyebrow, but nodded nonetheless. "Be safe and God speed."

James closed his eyes and instructed Phineas to do the same. Each concentrated on the loved ones they had left behind and hoped to return to soon. James also summoned the wind energy that would transport them past horizons, in and out of space, over oceans and to the Romani Realms.

A darkness fell over the sky and the leaves started to rustle. Birds scattered and the street became quiet. The air grew cold and as the wind started to pick up, the leaves lifted from the sidewalk and spun around them, forming a dust cloud that attracted even more energy until they could hear the clocks of time ticking.

Wails of passed souls followed them through the darkness, along with the sorrowful cries of the innocent lost. The sounds were excruciatingly painful, more so than the last trip as each time brings greater clarity. When they landed, both were silent for a moment as the memories of the trip still plagued them.

Phineas dropped his head and rubbed his temples. A drop of blood dripped from his left ear.

"You're bleeding," James noted.

"Like you care."

"I don't. I just don't want your weakened condition to mess up this mission," James smirked and then took a deep breath of air, his chest billowing out with his inhalation.

Phineas wiped his ear with the back of his hand, rolled his crystalline green eyes, and made a show of coughing while uttering, "Poser."

"Cute. Let's do this."

The bitter cold of the water made Charlotte gasp for breath. After less than five minutes, she sank under the surface. Most of the crowd moved to leave, but a few had been given the honor of fishing her body out of the lake. Samantha stood between Daniel and I watching as three men in wetsuits jumped from their small row boats to pull Charlotte up.

"Why did they bother throwing her in if they are only going to pull her out again?" Samantha asked, her eyes remaining on the lake for signs that Charlotte had survived.

I looked to Daniel for an explanation. "Some people's lungs won't survive the extreme cold for even a moment. If Charlotte is still alive, they'll pull her out and leave her alone here in the woods overnight without shelter or a change of clothing. If she doesn't die during the night of hypothermia, they'll burn her at sunrise."

"Samantha, take my hand," I instructed. "Give her strength."

I focused my thoughts on Charlotte, causing a flurry of butterflies to release into the air with thoughts of love and hope. Their wings beat frantically, creating a vacuum to ward off some of the cold air.

"I don't know what to do," Samantha cried.

"Just focus on the goodness that you see in people. It will materialize and help her," Daniel said, reaching to take Samantha's hands in his own.

Samantha closed her eyes and focused her attention on anyone who might help Charlotte from the present, while I concentrated on the Amulet of Pollox that Charlotte wore, urging her to use its power and retrieve pertinent information from the past.

"Shadow!" Samantha exclaimed excitedly, releasing my hand.

Charlotte lay in the center of a solitary stone that jutted up from the center of the lake. The crowd had dispersed leaving her alone to die under the watchful eyes of the Buraqs that stood as sentries around the lake.

As hypothermia began to set in so did the hallucinations that plagued Charlotte's mind. Memories of her time in London flooded her senses as if it were occurring at that very moment. She closed her eyes and allowed herself a moment of happiness, remembering the day Phineas brought her back in time. She remembered the day she fell in love with him. But that was before Samantha died.

She shuddered in the cold as her thoughts turned from something wonderful into a memory of utter sadness and with her change of spirit, the hallucinations grew. From walking happily hand-in-hand along the streets of London, her mind shifted to a time when she was younger and lost in Oxford. Initially, she saw them turn down an alley and enter Oxford's Covent Garden. His smile warmed her and she felt her insides glow, but as is typical of hypothermia, the extreme cold can make one believe they are burning with heat. With this thought, the pleasant day of shopping shifted to an experience of horror as the maze of shops within the Covent Garden shifted and rather than being shops selling pottery and keepsakes, the shopkeepers changed form into creatures selling horrific wares: humans for trafficking, bodies to inhabit. Throughout the ordeal, the worst feeling imaginable hit her psyche. She felt utterly alone.

James and Phineas trudged through the sleet and snow.

"When did it become Winter?" James complained.

"Raven's favorite season," Phineas noted.

"The cold...figures. You know her better than anyone. What's she planning?"

Phineas stopped in his path for a moment to concentrate. "I honestly don't know. It's as if the connection has been severed. Ever since Maebeline...well, whatever she did. I wonder..." he said, his thoughts drifting off.

James picked up a stick and threw it, annoyed with the situation. "What?"

"If I can't feel her thoughts, then perhaps she can't read mine either."

"That's an improvement over your previous...*connection*."

"You're one to talk," Phineas replied snidely. "Any word from Suki?"

At the mention of my name and the reason for our own cold front, James stiffened. He stopped momentarily and concentrated on the bond we shared. For centuries he had been watching over me, always waiting for the time when I would be his. With intimacy, our bond grew more complete, and yet, our time together had been limited because of Raven. James realized now that she had made sure to cause diversions at the most inconvenient of times.

He walked in silence remembering the way it used to be -- to feel my skin under his touch, cradle my small frame and hold me tightly against his chest until my thoughts permeated his entire being. But that was before. *Suki, let me help you.*

James shook his head when no response came. "Nothing."

"Silent treatment? That sucks."

"Thanks for the astute observation. What about you?"

Phineas closed his eyes and focused on Charlotte. He saw her clear blue eyes, he felt her soft, straight hair, the smoothness of her skin. He could even smell her perfume. But then, as he went deeper into the connection, he felt her heart beat -- at first strong, pounding with fear, and then what he felt was even more worrying for it started to dissipate as if...fading away.

Samantha and I trailed behind the crowd as they made their way back to the ballroom. Fitting in had never been so easy or so difficult. By being one with the crowd, we managed to avoid casting suspicion onto ourselves, but having to endure listening to the conversations left both of us despondent.

When we finally made it out of the forest, Daniel was there to greet us. His eyes met mine and he nodded; our plan was already in place. Turning to Samantha, I spoke the words I never imagined would come from my mouth.

"You are so special to me, you know that, right?"

"Of course, Suki."

"Samantha, that makes it even harder for me to tell you what I need to say...especially since you are my Releasor."

I took Samantha in my arms and burying my face in her shoulder, I whispered, "Please know that I have no choice. I must keep you safe."

Samantha pushed away and forced me to look her in the eyes. "What are you asking?"

"Daniel is going to take you deeper into the Realms -- to where you'll be safe. Someplace where Raven won't be able to find you."

"How is that possible?"

"Because you will appear dead -- even to her."

Samantha's face went pale, and Daniel quickly placed a protective arm around her waist. She swallowed hard before bravely raising her chin, and then looking upwards at the gathering black birds in the trees, she answered. "I want nothing more than to show that bitch that she can't manipulate us any more."

I threw my arms around Samantha. "We will get out of here. I promise you."

Quiet up until that moment, Daniel finally spoke. "It's getting late. When the sun sets completely, Charlotte is going to get even colder and you'll need to put this plan into action."

"You're ready?" I confirmed.

Daniel nodded.

At the mention of Charlotte's name, the Celtic Knot that Phineas wore around his neck grew warm against his skin, giving him hope that there was still a connection between him and Charlotte in spite of Raven's treachery and his unwilling indiscretion.

"I never intended nor wanted to be involved with Raven during this trip," Phineas spoke aloud.

"Why are you telling me this?" James asked.

"I assume you came back to Maebeline's home because you thought that I was aligned with her again -- fully."

"I came because you were influenced by her, in more ways than one. Phineas, she had you completely under her spell. You might have brought harm to Maebeline, to myself, and then indirectly to Charlotte."

Phineas bowed his head and ran his hand through his hair. "The Knot...it's warm, which means that she's still alive. I have to believe that we're still meant for each other."

"We need to get there before it's too late."

"You aren't totally without blame, you know."

James clenched his fists and pressed his lips into a thin line. It wasn't a subject he was proud of. "That was a very long time ago."

"It doesn't mean it didn't happen. I just don't get it. You and Raven?"

"She was dying. I couldn't let that happen. Not on my watch."

"If that's how you feel, then we better hurry or you're going to have Charlotte, Samantha...and even Suki on your head."

The thought of losing me was more than James could bear. He looked skyward, taking in the movement of the clouds and birds. "The energy is too calm. It's eerie."

Phineas reached for the Celtic Knot and held it tightly while closing his eyes. Almost immediately the wind picked up, rain began to fall, and suddenly, as if looking into her very eyes, he saw Charlotte clearly in his mind.

"It's so damn cold!" he said urgently. "And this rain, it's just going to make it worse."

"Don't be such a pansy. Your perfectly coifed hair will survive."

"Do you have to be an ass all the time, James? I'm talking about Charlotte. I can *hear* her."

In and out of consciousness, Charlotte vacillated between calm and frenzy. The Buraqs had fallen asleep and huddled together for warmth on the far side of the lake, but something was moving under the surface of the water, swimming in circles around the stone that was her perch. She tried to pick up her head to look over the edge, but her weakened state nearly made her fall into the frigid water. Bracing herself against the stone's hard surface, she put her head down and wept.

Charlotte, be strong.

She quickly picked her head up again and looked around, confused by the clarity of the voice. It awakened her thoughts, giving her hope. *Phineas?*

How she longed to go back to the way it was, but wasn't it her own selfishness that landed her in this precarious situation? She went back in time with

Phineas, leaving Samantha alone and now they were all paying the price.

Find your strength.

The same words, a similar message. She so wanted to believe. There had to be a way out of this, if not for herself then for Samantha. "This isn't going to be for nothing!" She declared, shouting to the heavens. At that moment, she felt a small burst of heat from the Amulet of Pollox, the pendant I had left for her, which she found while traveling in the past.

"Of course. I may have been wrong for going back with Phineas, but it brought me this," she told herself, grasping the pendant and rubbing it between her thumb and index finger. She prayed that she could still access the wisdom of those who had possessed it before her.

Try Charlotte. Your pendant burns with mine. Try!

Phineas!

There was no doubt; she heard his voice. And with the sound of his voice, the one she still loved in spite of everything, she would do as he said and try with all of her will. Details and facts fluttered through her mind like the pages of a book until her brain, practically in computer mode, paused on one piece of information: "Suki and James...Phineas' bond with Raven..." she spoke her thoughts aloud. "As their intimacy grows, so does their bond." Her mind was a whir with thoughts. *But where does that place me and Phineas? We've never fully been together, at least not in that way. Can I trust you?*

She hadn't intended the question to be heard by Phineas. It was merely a cry for help and a plea that escaped her mind as she looked to the shore where the Buraq still slept and all the while, she was tormented by some other creature swimming around and around her stone.

Let me help you.

The answer both surprised her and gave her hope. When she and Phineas had time traveled back to London and been caught in his former employers' office, he had gallantly referred to her as his wife. She smiled in spite of the cold and her circumstances, remembering the way he winked at her, the way the men who had paid a visit to the office had tipped their hats at both of them upon leaving. And when they were alone once more, Phineas had wrapped his arms around her, held her close and given her a kiss that could only be described as supernatural for the way it left her legs weak.

But in spite of the thrill that she felt with him that afternoon, she had never heard him speak to her telepathically. Their bond hadn't allowed for that...but Raven's did. At that moment, she knew he had betrayed her. Her mood shifted once again from feeling elated to the hopeless reality of her situation. The water splashed her, cold and icy, as if that creature swimming around her wanted to remind her of her current predicament.

You don't love me. She thought to herself hopelessly. *You'll always be with Raven.*

Trust me, please. Charlotte, what do you have to lose by just trying?

She wanted to trust him, to fall in love with him again, but she didn't want to be a fool. And yet, if she threw away her life, then Raven would win. It was exactly what she wanted. Determination rang through her again. She came here to help Samantha and now she had landed herself in trouble. Picking her head up, forcing herself onto her elbows and then feeling even stronger and pulling herself into a seated position, Charlotte looked out to the shores. The Buraq were sleeping; the water was calm. She had no choice or she would die from the waiting.

Tell me what to do.

I'm coming for you.

Charlotte was both calmed and inspired with the thought that she could still hear Phineas. With one hand on her Amulet, she focused on the mind of Charles Babbage, the genius who created the difference engine and made it possible for her and Phineas to travel back in time together. "That was a time when I was happy and as God is my witness, I will not die here in sorrow."

Although still unsure of Phineas' intentions, she focused on the positive believing that there was little chance for her life or Samantha's if she did nothing. And with that positive imagery, she imagined herself and Phineas in love.

I do love you, Charlotte.

She gasped. The words were so clear, but the sentiment was not one he had ever expressed prior.

With her hope, her mind soared to new thoughts and images including seeing Phineas kissing her tenderly and a flash forward that was most curious -- an image of herself holding a child.

The water around her splashed again, bringing her out of the surprising image, and before she could regain her positive thoughts, a dolphin jumped the rock, its sudden appearance causing her to slide off it and into the frigid water.

The shock of the water caused Charlotte to inhale sharply, the cold water hurting her lungs. She felt herself growing heavy and realized that the dolphin was pulling her under. Losing her battle, she allowed herself to be dragged deeper under the water. But before losing consciousness, the dolphin shifted and Charlotte caught a glimpse of a mythical creature -- the Encantado. Although she tried to hit it, her punches were futile under the water and when its hands reached for her own and she stared at it, all fight within her stopped. She looked at the Encantado face-to-face, their eyes meeting and she found herself looking not into the eyes of a dolphin, but into those of Shadow, before blackness took over.

Chapter Seventeen

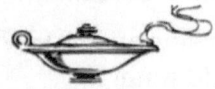

I held onto Samantha's hand while Daniel led us through the woods, along the back trail past the lake and even farther past the glass ballroom. Our trek took five hours, during which time we saw the changing landscape of the Romani Realms from the brutally cold and dead woods to the lush pastures.

When Daniel finally stopped, it was only a momentary reprieve. Within seconds he pushed away a large boulder that hid a safety line he used for the difficult climbing of the mountainous terrain. One could cross the forests and pastures, but his hidden line gave him access to an otherwise impossible route, one that kept the demons and dead away from the quiet retreat that he called home.

"What now?" I asked taking in the fact that we stood at the edge of a canyon with a massive drop downward. A narrow, but fast-moving river ran below us, between the two rock formations.

"How do you feel about rock climbing?"

Samantha and I looked at each other before staring at Daniel in shock. "You're kidding," I finally answered.

"I told you that it was secluded."

"Yes, but you didn't tell us you lived in the boonies," Samantha spoke at last, squinting her eyes to see if she could spot his elusive cabin on the other side.

"If you're trying to see my little abode from here, you won't be able to. But I assure you it's quite a place," he said taking her in his arms. "You'll just have to wait -- and come with me."

I nodded, more to myself than the others. "We can do this, Samantha. We've certainly been through worse."

Suki...

James' voice. How I longed to have him here right now. I bowed my head, nearly letting him in, wanting to use our connected powers to speak with him. Only I couldn't bring myself to do it.

"Then let's hurry. You probably only have until daylight to get back to Charlotte. The Buraqs will come for her then."

We made our way down the steep mountain formation, holding onto the rocks and relying on the ropes that Daniel had in his pack. He had carefully tied them in loops and then harnessed each of them together for added leverage. Down the rocks we went before crossing the river bank and making our way through a meadow.

"This is beautiful," Samantha noted.

I nodded in agreement. "It's not unlike the meadow where I landed."

"But this one is very different. It's hidden in plain site. There is no portal to access it. When I said we would be safe, I meant it."

For a moment, I stopped to listen to the sound of our surroundings. "There's no sound of birds, insects, anything. How can we be so alone?"

Daniel took a deep breath before answering. "It's part of the reality that I am cursed with -- I was sent here to dwell forever in total solitude."

Samantha took his hand and brought it to her cheek. "That was before," she reminded him.

"It's not all bad," he said, seeming to reflect on something in the distance. "You get what you deserve, I guess. Black magic and voodoo, even if performed with the intention of doing good...it's still going against nature."

A grave look crossed Daniel's face, and although he tried to hide his feelings, it didn't get past my prying eyes. "You alright? You look all catawampus."

But before he could answer, Samantha exclaimed. "Just look at that!" She pointed to a darling cottage with a thatched roof, flower boxes on the window sills, and a well cared for garden that ran around the side. A giant oak tree stood proud in the center of the lawn that made up the front garden.

Daniel led the way to a bench that graced his front porch and sat down. Samantha skipped up the front walk behind him and happily took her place beside him. "I could get used to this place," she beamed happily.

"You're going to have to get that out of your pretty head," he chided her.

"You don't know that."

"I do, Samantha."

I looked at both of them -- now understanding the distress I saw in Daniel's eyes and realizing that I had stumbled onto their first squabble. "What's going on between you two?"

"Don't..." Samantha said instinctively.

"Samantha, do I have to remind you that I am your genie? I should be privy to matters that involve you."

"You won't like it."

"Like it can be worse than landing in this place?" I asked rhetorically.

"Much worse," Daniel added.

It wasn't often that I found myself surprised, but this was one of those moments. "What could possibly be worse?"

Daniel took a deep breath before answering. "Worse would be staying here, even when you have the chance to leave."

"I don't know if I want to go," Samantha added quietly.

I gave her a 'you've got to be kidding look' before involuntarily pressing my fingers to my temples. "You don't look so well, Suki."

"I've got a bit of a headache coming on, but crazy ideas and silly notions tend to do that to me.

Samantha, I know you'll be safe here with Daniel...until I come back. And then, mark my words...we're all leaving."

I turned to Daniel. "Take good care of her."

"Be careful yourself. When you get Charlotte, you come back here. I'll get you out."

I nodded.

"Oh and Suki...one-way portals...they only open once."

Finding my way back to Charlotte was much easier alone without worrying about Samantha's safety as well. I merely envisioned the butterflies that brought peace to the troubled and within seconds, I was one with nature, floating in and out of time on the wind like a winged beauty until I was back in the dark forests where I had last left Charlotte.

I made my way to the lake and crept around to the side closest to the rock. It was still at least an hour before dawn and the sun had yet to materialize, but the rock where Charlotte had been placed jutted up empty causing an immediate panic to stir in my soul.

If only you were here... I thought to myself, wishing for James.

I am here.

I shook my head, not wanting to hear his velvety voice, not wanting to feel the longing in my heart.

Suki, let me in.

"How can I?" I shouted aloud.

It was only a momentary lapse in judgement, but it was enough. Raven's disciples, hundreds of birds, flew at me, attacking from every angle. I tried to cover my face with my arms, but they continued to dive bomb me, their sharp beaks breaking the skin and with every drop of my blood that escaped, another would join in to lap it up.

The cuts emerged now on my face and shoulders, my neck and upper back. The birds were relentless, forcing me backwards to the same pier that brought Charlotte to a frigid suffering.

"What a predicament." Raven's voice sounded from above.

I turned suddenly, but saw nobody. Still the birds forced me farther and farther along the pier until I found myself mere inches from the edge when Raven chose to materialize before me.

"You should have never come here, Suki. You were under no obligation. Leave now and I'll let you live."

"Listen to you...you think the sun comes up just to hear you crow. Charlotte and Samantha are my obligation -- my Releasors."

Raven took a step closer. Her dark eyes burned with hatred. "There's been no wish cast, no desire for your interference."

"The very fact that you think my presence is only warranted if they present a wish..." I shook my head in exasperation. "That's indicative of why you are so void of humanity."

Raven laughed. "Save your preaching. You know Charlotte is gone."

"You're lying. I would have felt it. I'm their guide, their muse. I provide more than wishes and I'm happy to serve them. The fact that my part in their life ends when their wishes are used up is the one thing that weighs heavily on my heart -- for I love them."

Raven clapped her hands in a slow rhythmic beat. "Believe what you want, but take a look."

She pointed to the rock, completely void of life. "She's gone. Gone to the bottom of this lake where she'll stay until the end of time."

"It's not true," I insisted.

"You are such a martyr, and as such, you will be martyred." She threw her hands up in front of her and a bolt of electricity hit me square in the chest, bringing me to my knees.

"I came here willingly, Raven, and nobody is going to send me home without them!" I narrowed my eyes and fought back, just as James had taught me. I summoned the elements and rain poured down upon Raven, every droplet punctuated by a bolt of lightening. The electrical storm was far more impressive than Raven's attack and it took her attention off me long enough for me to regain my footing and move a safer distance from the edge of the pier.

"No you don't," Raven said, her patience obviously wearing thin. "That was a warning. This is your end."

The blast took me completely by surprise. It was so strong that I wasn't even sure what hit me, but I felt the wind knocked out of me and the bright light that followed left me momentarily blinded. It was enough time for the Buraqs to charge the pier, with one after the other, pounding against my body. They kicked me down to my knees and then took turns stepping on my small frame until I could no longer move. Just before I was rendered unconscious, the last gave me one final, swift kick, and then rolled me into the water.

Raven smiled at them, and allowed them to nuzzle her neck. "Well done, boys."

She looked at them appraisingly. Their muscular bodies showing their excitement and glimmering with sweat from the endeavor. "One more assignment and I'll release you from this existence."

They snorted and butted their heads against each other, showing their disappointment. Raven moved toward one of them, opening her arms wide in an offering. He immediately wrapped his leg around hers, his hardness pressing against her. "Yes, I'll make it worth your while."

They stood at attention, once again pledging their allegiance to Raven. The message was clear. They were at her mercy. Their disfigured bodies -- half men, half horse -- belonged to her along with their instincts. They mellowed and waited for her instructions.

"That's much better," she praised. "Now, we just have the little matter of Phineas to deal with. It would certainly be a shame if he betrayed me."

I plunged into the lake, hovering between consciousness and sleep. My body grew heavy and I began to sink lower and lower. Hands reached around my waist and began to drag me through the murky water at a speed faster than was humanly possible. The force of the water caused me to regain consciousness and I instinctively fought against the pull of whoever or whatever had its hold on me. Although I tried to train my eyes on the object that had me within its control, focusing at such a high speed was impossible.

I tried to reach for the hands that I had felt before, but now all that I saw was a shiny, smooth body of grey with a round girth, much like a dolphin, but stronger and faster. It continued to draw me through the water, pushing me above the surface at regular intervals at which time I would draw a quick breath of air.

The air helped me to regain my bearings. But, as much as I tried to catch a glimpse of the watery world rushing around me, I just couldn't make out whether Charlotte was nearby. The creature shifted its body against me suddenly, pulling me under once more and ending the small reprieve that I felt against all hopelessness. Again, I fought against the creature, trying desperately to kick and bring myself back up, but it was futile.

Forced under the surface for what felt like an incredible distance, I felt myself thrust both down and forward until to my surprise, the creature released its hold on me. I found myself in an underwater cavern, where the water was notably warmer and there, sitting on a rock as poised as she could be was Charlotte.

"Oh my god, Charlotte!" I swam to her and threw my arms around her. "You're okay. How did you get here?"

Before I heard the answer, a splash sounded behind me. The slate grey animal bounded near, and I instinctively placed myself between it and Charlotte. The previous moment of warm water and the chance to rest had restored my energy and I put up my hands, ready for another fight.

"No Suki. It's okay. We're safe."

"What is it?"

"A dolphin, so to speak."

I watched it with wary eyes and indeed it moved like a dolphin, but there was something different about it. It was somehow a bit faster, stronger, and then the real change occurred and it jumped onto the rock next to Charlotte and nuzzled her face.

Charlotte smiled serenely and patted its back. "Show yourself. It's okay."

The dolphin shifted and wavered, its massive body flitting in and out of reality until it seemed to reduce in length and girth, and once noticeably smaller, it shifted completely into the form of Shadow.

"An Encantado?"

Charlotte nodded. "But that's not all."

"There's more?" I took a closer look at Shadow and noticed for the first time, the little girl looked much more human like, in spite of the fact that she had just transformed from a dolphin. "It's kind of ironic, but she actually looks...normal."

"She's wonderful," Charlotte said with more emotion than I felt comfortable with.

I leaned closer to Charlotte and whispered, "What happened to the creepy snakes that used to make up her hair?"

"That's only in the Romani Realms. It was Raven's tricks to make me stay away from her."

As if the very idea of Charlotte's leaving upset her, Shadow moved closer, sitting on Charlotte's lap as they perched on a rock.

"Come with us; we want to show you something," Charlotte said and then with Shadow they dove back into the water and swam to the opposite end of the cavern, to a small beach.

I watched as again Shadow transformed to a dolphin and then just as quickly regained her form as a girl once she and Charlotte walked onto the beach. I took a quick glance at the peculiar surroundings -- a cave hidden below the lake, away from the prying eyes of the Buraqs, Raven, and any of the others. It was a shame to leave when we finally had a moment of reprieve, but then again we couldn't stay forever, so gathering up my mental stamina, I dove under the water and swam through the claustrophobic cave toward the hidden beach paradise where Charlotte had followed Shadow.

There were various places to stop and catch our breath -- hidden ledges along the walls of the cave where we could sit before having to dive under the surface once more and swim to the next rest point. It was a matter of trusting Shadow, a challenge as far as I was concerned.

"Charlotte, I can't see that there's another rest point," I indicated the direction that Shadow had taken. "It's fine for her...she's a dolphin!"

"She's not a dolphin. Don't be so derivative. She's an Encantado...and she's my...my..." Charlotte shook her head, as if she couldn't bring herself to say what was on her mind. "Anyway, she saved your life. The least you can do is trust her, so come on!" Charlotte dove under the water and then popped up once more. "Come on, Suki, the water is even warmer when you get to the beach. It's amazing! You'll love it!" And with that last exclamation, she was off again, leaving me no choice but to follow.

Suki ... where are you? I need to know you're okay.

Maybe it was time to put this fight behind us. After all, it was James, the man who stole my heart, was a supernatural Shade, my protector. Shouldn't I trust him?

I'm fine. Samantha is safe and so is Charlotte. There's no need to worry. You can go home.

There. That should satisfy him. At least he wouldn't worry.

I'm not leaving you. Where are you?

I'm going for a swim.

His voice. How I missed the smooth, baritone sound. I remembered what it was like when he would whisper in my ear after...

"Suki, are you coming?" Charlotte interrupted her thoughts.

I looked around. The cave up ahead was even darker than the last. A narrow passage led to it in which we had to wade through waist-high water single-file. Something that looked very much like a sea eel slipped past and I caught my breath and jumped, grazing my head on the ceiling that rested just inches above us.

"By the way, Shadow says the sea snakes won't hurt you," Charlotte replied.

"Oh, if Shadow says..." I started, but Charlotte had already dove under the surface and was headed toward the mouth of the next cave.

I heard the sound of Charlotte's kicks as she dove into the water again, making her way farther into the cave to where ever it would end. I dove in after her, but as I plunged under, something wrapped around my ankle and pulled me backwards, under the surface and down into darkness.

Charlotte heard the sounds of what sounded like a struggle, and called out, "Suki?"

When no answer came, she began to panic. "I can't see her. I'm going back."

Shadow clung to her, throwing her arms around her waist. "But we're almost there. We can be together...forever."

A warning sounded in Charlotte's mind. "Shadow, I've done everything you've asked of me. But if this is going to work, you and I...you have to trust me."

Shadow nodded her head solemnly. "But you still can't help her. Look."

Charlotte turned, but saw nothing except the calm, smooth water. The passageway was completely dark and not a ripple could be seen on the surface. It was as if I had never been there.

"No, no, no..." Charlotte closed her eyes, and without thinking of the consequences to herself or Samantha, she did the one thing that I warned her against. Without a second thought for herself, she uttered a stream of words without thinking of the recourse and changed everything.

"Please, let Suki out of this watery hell. Don't let her drown. She's done so much for Samantha and myself. I beg of you to make it true..."

"Charlotte stop!" Shadow instinctively knew what was coming next, but it was too late.

"I *wish* it to be."

Chapter Eighteen

James and Phineas arrived with a splash. They found themselves in a crystal blue lagoon, just outside the mouth of the first cave.

"Something tells me that's the way in," Phineas said.

James swam easily to the opening and paused upon seeing the darkness that awaited them. "After you."

"Always the gentleman," Phineas replied glibly. "No biggie," he said and swam inside.

"What do you see?"

"Nothing. It's pitch dark."

James shouted into the cave. "Use the flair, Einstein."

Within a moment, the whistling sound of the flair gun could be heard and the opening became illuminated.

"Hey James, you coming or should I tell Suki you wimped out?"

James adjusted his dive belt, grabbed a waterproof flashlight and held it between his teeth before diving below the surface. When he got inside, Phineas was sitting comfortably on a rock shelf. "What took you so long?"

"You see how far in this goes?"

"Nope," Phineas accentuated his response by shaking his head, letting his wet hair spray James in the face.

"You're like a dog. Let's go."

"The extra torch?"

James rolled his eyes and threw another flashlight Phineas' way, which he easily caught behind his back.

"Hey hot shot, you up for this? According to Maebeline, her vision indicated that we would find a series of interlocking caves."

He recalled Maebeline's description of the caves...narrow passageways that fed into wider lakes like mouths, only to twist and turn into darkened caverns again.

"There's no telling how many we have to go through to find Charlotte and Suki."

"It's a walk in the park," Phineas answered, smoothing back his hair.

"No fear," James answered, serious for the first time, and held up his fist.

Phineas bumped his fist against James' and nodded his head. "No fear."

I had my eye on the next passageway and started to

wade through the water toward it. This part of the cave had given way to a claustrophobic tunnel like section with rock formations on either side as well as low hanging rocks above. One would think that having spent centuries confined to a bottle would make me impervious to small spaces, but this wasn't the case. My bottle was home, decorated in fine silks and pretty girlie colors with a light smell of perfume always wafting through the air. It embodied my favorite things.

This experience and space couldn't be more opposite, however. I shuddered to think about what lurked ahead, never mind under the surface of the water.

Keep your thoughts positive.

James' advice before I left for the Romani Realms came back to me as if he were speaking right now. Was he?

Your safety has been granted.

His voice was different. More like a hallucination....it didn't sound the way it usually did inside my head. He didn't speak to me in the way of my lover, but more like my Shade. I had never felt his protective quality over me so strongly, but I was troubled by it.

Instinctively, I knew that Charlotte had instigated this through a wish. I tried to ignore her request...I couldn't let her waste it.

"Okay, I can do this."

I readied myself and then after taking a deep breath, ducked below the surface to try and swim through the opening that wasn't much wider than my own torso. Whether I tried to do the crawl or the breast stroke, my arms kept hitting the sharp rocks around me.

As I gave it one more try, a sharp pinch sliced just above my elbow, telling me I had just broken skin. I brought my arm up to my mouth and gingerly licked where I felt pain. Blood. A new fear crept over me. It was ridiculous to think that anything that had the ability to eat me could dwell in such a small space, but the idea planted itself firmly in my mind, along with something else...what sounded like laughter.

I stopped and listened, but only heard the occasional drip from the stalagmite above me.

"It's just a little scrape. There's nothing that can hurt me," I told myself knowing that fear in the Romani Realms was something that would spread like a virus. Once it entered one's mind, it could easily fester. I guided my way through the water, this time trying to wade rather than swim. It was still slow going as the bottom was sandy, forcing my feet to sink into the sludge. The sensations caused my mind to betray me again as I wondered what lived in that muddy sand. Instantly, I felt something slither around my legs. Seconds later the long body of an eel glided past me, only to dive below the surface again.

I could have sworn I heard the caw of black birds, but that would have been impossible. I had only traveled a few miles since leaving Samantha in the safety of Daniel's hidden cottage. Certainly this hidden cavern was still off the map, hidden from

Raven. I would rather deal with an eel than Raven...at least she wouldn't have the satisfaction of bringing about my doom.

The thought gave me strength and I tried to make my way through the passage way to the exterior of the cave, but the area was too narrow to swim effectively and the water was too deep to wade through. I pressed myself against the rock sides of the cavern, hoping that by being in more shallow water, the eel wouldn't be able to reach me. But the rocks were slippery with moss and I slid easily back into the water only to have the massive eel wrap itself around my waist this time, squeezing the air out of me. I was plunged under the water and dragged a few feet, only to have the creature lift me above the surface for a momentary breath of air. It was toying with me, giving me only enough air to keep the life in me, but brutally weakening my body. With every time it lifted my body above the water, it would then counter by throwing me underneath, until finally, I was thrown against the rocks. The eel continually pummeled my body against the rocks, scraping my arms and torso. Blood appeared and with it, new threats.

Through hazy eyes, I saw the unmistakable outline of a dorsal fin. With nearly all the fight in me waning and no strength left, the eel threw me one final time, hitting my head against the rock. It was so easy to close my eyes. The sound of black birds rang in my ears. Laughing and mocking my plight.

I screamed in spite of myself.

It's your imagination! Don't give in. Let me help you.

This time I knew the voice in my head wasn't deceiving me. It was James!

The time to let go of our misgivings had come and I knew that if I were to survive, I would have to forgive. The darkness of the cave was suddenly juxtaposed with flashes of brightness, like strobe lights that sent my mind into a confusion of thoughts. Was it my destiny to be with James or Charlotte's wish that sent him back to me? The thought of what I was trying to forget, plagued my mind and I heard the laughter again. Beyond any doubt, it was Raven. She was watching.

He was fantastic, Suki. Raven mocked me.

Again, I felt something brush against my legs and only moments later, the eel surfaced and now, as its full length stretched across the surface level of the water, I could see that it was nearly six feet long. The sight struck absolute panic in me, and I released a scream that reverberated inside the small cavity where I was now paralyzed with fear. The eel dove deeper under the water and as it did, I jumped and tried to guess which way it would travel, pushing myself against the sharp rocks. The effort was useless as it immediately wrapped around me, gripping me tighter and tighter. And with my balance disrupted, it again pulled me underwater. In spite of the fact that I could feel part of it around me, the tail bobbed out of the water, giving me even more reason to panic -- the very idea of being in the water with something that

big made me light-headed, my nerves getting the best
of me.

Just one cave up ahead, Charlotte was making her
way through the interlocking water tunnels with
steady progress. Shadow led the way in her
Encantado form and Charlotte felt a sense of calm
swimming with her. She felt as if she were meant to
take care of her, even though now, there was no doubt
that Shadow looked after her. If Charlotte ever lagged,
Shadow would circle back and nudge Charlotte's back
onward. Sometimes the tunnels would twist into a
narrow darkness and Charlotte found herself
hesitating. That was when Shadow would dive under
the water, come up underneath Charlotte and literally
carry her forward on her back.

When they finally reached the last cave and the
beach was in sight, Shadow changed back into human
form and walked onto the sandy shore. The difference
in her appearance even as a human was dramatic as
her blonde hair now hung in soft ringlets around her
shoulders, its silky smoothness begging one to run
their fingers through it. Her face was wide-eyed and
innocent without any malice. There was no trace of
the snakes that previously plagued her hair or the
black voids that were her eyes. This was a little girl
whose beautiful features resembled Charlotte's.

She turned and looked over her shoulder and
then smiled broadly at the sight of Charlotte following

her. Shadow opened her arms, and Charlotte happily walked to her, wrapping her own arms around the little girl. She picked her up and twirled her until both released a sound that wasn't heard often in the Romani Realms -- laughter.

Just when I thought I would totally lose my self-control, I heard something swim through the passageway, approaching closer. For a moment it looked like the Encantado with its smooth body and panic struck me at the sight of two of them, until I saw that it was James and Phineas, wearing wet suits and looking better than I could ever imagine.

I threw myself in James' arms, and he held me tightly. "I'm so sorry," I said.

"Don't say that. You had a reason. I'm sorry."

"It's in the past. If Raven hadn't planted the image in my mind..."

"Errr, guys?" Phineas had been silent, but suddenly the body of the giant eel splashed out of the water momentarily, giving him an eyeful of what I had experienced. "We're not alone."

Its body bent above the water once more and I screamed as I felt something grab my legs from under the surface once again.

"Suki, just stay calm. You're safe now."

"Easy for you to say," Phineas added. The giant eel now wrapping itself around him, squeezing his torso. Its suction like mouth pulled at his skin, and he sucked in his breath in pain.

"Listen, it's a figment. It's been planted by Raven because she knows Suki would fear it." James splashed the water, trying to draw attention to himself, but in spite of his actions, no harm came to him. Phineas looked across the darkened cave to where I indeed seemed paralyzed by fear and in contrast, James was the picture of calm.

When the eel squeezed Phineas even tighter, he grimaced in spite of James' advice.

"Phineas, man up. It may be a figment, but if you believe it, it will burst your lung."

Phineas took a deep breath, closed his eyes and exhaled until he felt calmer. When he opened his eyes, he shrugged and smiled. The tight feeling around his chest was gone and there was no indication that anything had ever accosted his body. Nothing held him. There was nothing to fear. At least where James and Phineas were concerned.

But I screamed and was suddenly pulled under the water.

James grabbed a knife from his sheaf. "The only way we're going to get her out of here is by killing it."

"Are you kidding me?" Phineas shouted, above the sound of the rushing water. "How do you kill something that doesn't exist? You're likely to slice her in half!"

James dove under the water and searched for me. He came back to the surface, looking notably less calm. "She's gotten herself wrapped in kelp. I need help."

Without hesitation, Phineas and James both dove under again, pulling their bodies farther under the surface to where the water was colder and darker. As Phineas cut back the kelp, my eyes grew wide with fear and the more I feared, the more plentiful were my visions, making my imagination come to fruition. The kelp morphed into the slinky body of the eel, and the flowering leaves turned into a head whose teeth bit down upon Phineas' arm as he worked frantically to attack it with his knife.

I watched in horror, fighting against the eel, which they insisted was kelp, but it couldn't be. I was becoming more and more entangled in its hold and for some reason, James was doing his best to restrain my efforts as I tried to swim away from it. It was madness, especially since when I saw it continually bite Phineas, his blood forming dark pools all around us.

I lapsed into unconsciousness.

When I came to, James was carrying me in his arms through the water and toward a small bit of embankment inside the cave.

Phineas popped his head up seconds later and swam easily to join us. "You get the girl and I get bit by a fucking eel?"

"How can you get bit when it's all in Suki's imagination?" James retorted.

"I guess I have more empathy than you do."

"You saw it too?" I asked.

Phineas nodded. "I never liked snakes as a kid and I can't imagine anything worse than underwater snakes."

"I know, right?"

James smoothed my hair away from my face. He looked in my eyes, wearing the evidence of how pleased he was that we were together again. "You do have a vivid imagination."

I looked at him with all seriousness, knowing what he was referring to. "This place. It's Raven's playground. She loves getting inside people's heads."

"She's always been good at that. Suki, she did fool me once. But that was before I met you. It would never happen again."

I threw my arms around his neck, snuggling my head into his throat and breathing contentedly. He transferred me onto his lap and lowered his forehead onto mine. "There's something I want you to know..."

"Listen!" Phineas had no qualms about interrupting our reunion. "Black birds."

Indeed, the caw of thousands of birds sounded so loudly that they could be heard from inside the cavern. "Charlotte!"

"Where is she?" Phineas asked, his voice breaking with nerves.

"I'm sorry. She went ahead of me. I never meant to leave her alone, but she was with..."

Phineas was already peeling himself out of his wet suit. "Who? Suki? Who is she with?"

"What are you doing?" James asked.

"I'll meet you outside. I have to fight Raven on her own terms and that means shifting into bird form."

"But Charlotte...she's..."

"I know," Phineas answered. He never wanted Charlotte to see him in the form of a black bird, to view him in the form that demon gypsies took, but he had no choice as time was running out. He felt it. "Tell me, Suki. What brought you to these caverns."

"Shadow. But Phin, there's something you should know..."

"Nothing matters more than getting that creton away from her."

"But Phin!"

Before I could insist, he raised his head skyward, and transformed into a black bird, shinier and more majestic than those I had seen before -- somehow prouder. And although Raven's bird form always manifested itself with an air of danger, Phineas seemed equally ready for battle, but to avenge his love rather than harm her.

"Godspeed, Phineas," I whispered under my breath and held on even tighter to James.

Chapter Nineteen

Without warning James doubled over, his ears ringing in pain with a high-pitched sound caused by Raven's mind control.

"James! What's wrong?"

I realized only too late that Raven was the cause of whatever ailed him. Thousands of black birds swarmed the skies and dive bombed me. Their wings beat against me until I faltered and fell to the ground. From the corner of my eye I could see James still reeling from the sound waves that Raven accosted him with. But I was helpless to do anything as the beaks from the birds pecked me, cutting my face with their beaks and talons.

I cried out in pain, which made James react in spite of what was happening to himself. He focused his strength and mind and worked beyond his own discomfort. Focusing his mind on me, he sent a message: *"We can fight her -- together."* The effort to speak telepathically placed James at an even greater risk as his senses were focused on me. Blood dripped from his nose and ears.

I screamed aloud. "James!"

"Don't. Don't let her in. Don't let her see that she's affecting us."

I covered my face from the attack of the birds, rolling into a ball. They didn't relent, still biting the back of my arms, clawing at my head and neck, but at least my face was protected and in more ways than one. With my face hidden, Raven couldn't see the anguish on it over what was happening to James.

"A diversion!"

James held his hands over his ears, but responded to me, ignoring the pain. *"I know where you're going with it. On the count of three --- one, two, three!"*

Although I was hurt and James was suffering, between the two of us, we manifested our thoughts to conjure the image of peace I always carried with me throughout the ages -- butterflies. I reached for James' hand and as his fingers entwined with mine, a cloud of butterflies descended on the scene. Butterflies of every size and color fluttered around us, their wings gently tickling our faces and filling us with happiness.

Send them on their way. James instructed.

I nodded and the butterflies surrounded the black birds, throwing them off course and interfering with their flight patterns.

James' hearing improved nearly immediately, the high-pitched ringing dissipating with every new butterfly that emerged on the scene. When he could focus all of his powers properly again, he turned his attention to me.

Come here, but don't speak. He warned silently.

I glanced over at the butterflies ensuring that they would remain in place, and continuing to cause confusion in the birds. I tiptoed over to James and faced him.

Close your eyes and imagine my healing touch.

Whoa.

Not that sort of touch. He smiled.

He ran his hands along my face and as he did, the cuts miraculously started to close. And, as each one closed, he placed his lips gently to where the angry red lines once were, ensuring that not a scar would remain in their place. With each healing moment, he traveled his hands to the next area of my body that had been hurt -- my shoulders, arms, back. Repeating the process of his magical touch, paired with loving kisses until I was without any pain or trace of an attack.

I smiled at James when he had finished. *Too bad that had to end.*

Consider that a prelude. He answered wickedly. *For when I get you home...*

Looks like someone else is ready to get out of here.

Not caring for the assault, the birds started to scatter, first one and then the next until soon, all followed suit. The butterflies seemed to shimmer in response, their delicate wings glowing with beautiful shades of azure blue and lavender. Only one black bird remained and it suddenly shifted into the form of Raven, who stared at us with open hostility, her hands whisking away the butterflies with annoyance.

"Those *insects* are the bane of my existence."

I stood next to James, wrapping my arm around his back. "I know the feeling."

The move wasn't lost on Raven, who smiled her uneven grin, her eyes settling on the sight of the two of us standing as one. "Ahh, lookie. You're such a united front. That's always so endearing to me that even occasional lovers can pretend to experience...hmm, what is the word I'm searching for...oh, I know! Trust!" she said with a snap of her fingers.

"I do trust him. It's you who has proven to be manipulative. I know what you did." Despite my attempt to be strong, my voice still wavered with the effort of confronting Raven about my man.

James rubbed his hand over my back, trying to reassure me, to calm the brewing anger he sensed bubbling beneath the surface.

"You know what I did?" Raven repeated evenly. "But do you know just how much I enjoyed it? Fucking James was fucking amazing!"

"Suki, don't!" James tried to hold me back, knowing instinctively that I would have no qualms in starting a fight with Raven considering the verbal punch that was just thrown. But he was too late. I lunged at Raven, grabbing her hair and letting centuries of anger that I had contained within myself finally loose. Forget Southern gentility!

Holding Raven's hair by her ponytail, I pulled it backwards staring into eyes that didn't have the decency to show any remorse. "You are despicable."

"That I am," Raven sneered. "And you know what, in spite of what men say about wanting a girl they can bring home to *mama*," she said mocking my accent, "they sure as hell have a good time playing around with the bad girl." And to punctuate her thought Raven spat at me! My reaction was immediate as I released my hold on her.

"You disgust me," I said wiping my cheek. "I can't believe I was ever friends with you. You hide the real you from everyone."

"Mmm? James seemed to like it. Didn't you, *sugar*?" Again, she mocked me, and trailed her finger, displaying her black painted nails, down James' chest. He grabbed her hand firmly and whipped her arm behind her back, bending it at a precarious angle. "Oh James, you know I love the rough stuff."

"Stop it, Raven. This has gone on long enough. Let me make this clear under no uncertain terms. I *love* Suki. What happened with you occurred before I knew that she was my destiny. And when I learned about her -- about what she would mean to me...I *waited* for her."

I stared at James, my mouth dropping open. "You..."

He smiled and took me in his arms, totally ignoring Raven who stood fuming beside us. "I love you."

I beamed up at him and then turned and laid a sugary sweet smile in Raven's direction.

"Oh please. Don't look like the cat who ate the canary. Big whoop." And with that, Raven reverted back to bird form once again and flew off with an angry caw.

James reached for me, running his thumb over the back of my hand. I squeezed his hand in response, and although neither of us said anything, our eyes told a million tales. He brought me in closer, holding me against his strong chest. As he stroked my long, brown hair, gently letting his fingers weave into the waves, I released a sob.

Pulling himself back, but keeping a hold on my shoulders, he searched my face. "What is it?"

I shook my head, afraid to open my mouth for fear that one runaway tear would turn into a flood.

He held me close, petting my hair and letting me cry into his chest. "Suki, I'm so sorry." He closed his eyes and I suspected that he was trying to read my mind. I couldn't stand that humiliation too. I kept seeing images of himself and Raven that played over and over and continued to haunt me. For a moment, it seemed as if my anguish had subsided, but then another image came, which only set me off again. It was a vision of James smiling at the sight of Raven coming toward him.

"No!" James suddenly held me more forcefully against him. "Suki, I can't deny my past, but what you're seeing now isn't all the truth."

"You're in my head? Now? God James, why now when I'm at my most vulnerable?"

"Listen to me, Suki," he said, turning my head up to face him. "She's distorting the images. Like I said, I was with her...long ago. But that last image, the one with me smiling as she approached..."

I interrupted, "It's the worst. It's as if the very sight of her made you swoon. As if you...you love..."

"Stop. Don't even go there. You don't realize what she did. Yes, she showed you a time when I was with her, but she also made you see me at other times -- times when I wasn't even around her. The look on my face? That was how I looked when I first saw you walk into the bar at Maison 360. The first time that we met face to face.

"That's how you reacted when you looked at me? But you didn't know me?"

"I knew you," he said smiling. "I just hadn't met you," he said, kissing my cheeks and wiping away the tears at the same time. I lifted my head tentatively at first and then met James' glance. He bent his head and kissed me so softly as if worried that he would scare me off, but when he felt me give into him, accept his kiss, well...then, he pulled me in so close that I could feel my heart keeping time with his own. We had been through so much, heartache, loss, danger, but in this moment, it was just the two of us and regardless of the perils that still faced us, we were both damned if we weren't going to stay in each other's arms for just a bit longer.

He stared into my eyes without saying a word. Shaking his head in disbelief he said, "How can you be so beautiful even here? After trudging through mud, swimming with eels, and dodging the soulless beings that exist at every turn...how do you radiate such purity?"

I felt a blush rise up my cheeks. I turned my eyes downward, but James was having none of that. He placed his hand under my chin, lifted my face to him and this time, the kiss wasn't tentative. He kissed me like I hadn't been kissed in a very long time.

"You deserve to be kissed like that every day."

"And you're just the man to do it?" I teased.

"And then some," he said, taking my hand and leading me to where the rocks jutted out from the mountain, forming a natural canopy to keep us hidden from view. Our mouths never left each other as he pressed my back against the smooth rock. We poured all of our emotions into that kiss -- the sorrow of our recent loss, the hope of our reunion, and the need to always be together. My senses were heightened and every touch of his hand that lightly ran down the length of my body sent desire through me.

It might have been that the air was thinner where we were, but I suspected it was James and the power he wielded over me -- knowing my mind and body intimately -- that made me feel a dizzying rush. I wrapped my leg around his and he pressed against me. The feel of him matched the hard surface of the stone that I rested against.

"I don't want this to end."

"It doesn't have to," he answered, his voice husky from passion.

"I meant us...not this."

For the briefest of moments, he pulled back and stopped to stare in my eyes. "That's what I'm talking about."

Although it wasn't the most comfortable of surroundings, romance was never lacking with James. After we made love, I slept, and when I opened my eyes half an hour later, I found even more evidence of his love. Daisies and wild flowers surrounded me. Their petals had been strewn over the rocks where we lay, creating a fragrant blanket. He picked up one petal and tickled the tip of my nose with it.

"Wow, what is all this?"

"This is me saying that I love you."

"You didn't have to do all of this. You must have had to walk for miles to find this many flowers here."

"It didn't take that long. You forget that I'm graced with special abilities."

"After that performance I could never forget about your *abilities*."

He brushed a hair out of my eyes. "Seriously now, I just didn't like the fact that Raven was present when

I first said it to you. It's not what I would have wanted."

"It's okay." I rolled onto my back and stared up at the sky. It was dark except for one patch of brightness behind the clouds. Somewhere, the light was trying to free itself from darkness. "Do you think Phineas has found Charlotte?"

"You said she was just ahead of you. Of course he has. He would have come back and found us if he had gotten into any trouble."

"That's...that's not what I meant. Do you think he found her...the way she was before coming here?"

"I don't know," he said shaking his head and sighing. "You never told me...how did you get Charlotte away from the Reckoning ceremony?"

"That's what I tried to say earlier...to Phin...it was Shadow."

"What was Shadow? What do you mean?"

"All of this," she said, letting her arms expand wide, emphasizing her point. "The Romani Realms...while horrible and built on fear...there's something else here too. It's not all bad."

James looked at me with a questioning glance.

"Don't you see? One can't know friendship if you've never had a foe. Without hatred, we wouldn't know love...and without fear, we would never recognize the serenity of our thoughts. Shadow is a dichotomy. She's everything that is wrong and right with this place."

James lay down next to me, sharing my view of the sky. We were quiet for a moment, watching the clouds move quickly across the darkening sky, which was changing to a dark purple as the sun set over the mountains.

He remained silent for awhile as if trying to sort through the nonsensical ways of this Realm. "I'm not sure I understand why she is so important to Charlotte."

"Charlotte may have come here to avenge Samantha's death and bring her back. But that wasn't what fate had planned. She's been through a lot here; we all have. But, it was always for Shadow, she just didn't know it."

"I'm not following...what was?"

"It was Shadow, not Samantha, who presented the real reason for Charlotte to come here. She came for Shadow."

Chapter Twenty

When Phineas finally made his way through the water caves and emerged onto the beach, he thought he would be prepared for anything. But the sight in front of him was like nothing he had ever expected.

On the beach were at least a dozen seal sleeping in a circle and in the midst of that circle, equally at peace, was Charlotte. As the water lapped gently onto their backs and retreated, the seal would shapeshift from their current form into that of other girls -- Selkies...seals when in water and women on land. Keeping watch over the scene was a lone dolphin that bobbed on the surface of the water, just a few feet from where it met the shore.

He approached quietly from the side, hoping to get to Charlotte and help her out of the circle unnoticed, but as if sensing his intention, the dolphin whistled and to his surprise, it immediately shifted into the form of Shadow. Her eyes narrowed as Phineas continued to come closer.

"Stay back!" she ordered, waking Charlotte.

Charlotte lifted her head, her eyes opening wide in surprise to the scene in front of her. Phineas was approaching slowly, his hand on a sheaf by his hip. Charlotte could see a knife encased in it. Instinctively, she placed a protective arm around Shadow, who clung to her and started to whimper in spite of her earlier show of bravado.

"Phineas, do what she says."

Phineas kept his eyes on Shadow, but his heart melted at the sound of Charlotte's voice. It had been too long since he heard her say his name and he wished it wasn't in the context of telling him to stay away.

"Charlotte, I want to help you."

"Then, put the knife down and you can come over here."

There was no question that he was going to listen. He reached for his knife and threw it to the ground before moving toward Charlotte slowly for fear of Shadow trying something that might harm her.

"Why don't you sit down?" Charlotte suggested when he was beside them. With Charlotte sandwiched between Shadow and Phineas, the trio sat in awkward silence for a moment.

"We have a plan," Phineas said under his breath. "A plan to get you home."

"I don't want to talk about that until you hear what I have to tell you."

Phineas shook his head in frustration. Unless all of them were in the same mind frame they couldn't risk time traveling out of the Romani Realms. It was too dangerous and likely that one would get left behind.

Phineas took Charlotte's hand, he couldn't help himself being so close to her. "I've missed you so much, Charlotte. I've been so worried. Please, listen to me."

Charlotte smiled at him and turned to Shadow. She smoothed down the girl's hair that had once again turned to snakes, a reaction that occurred when she was nervous or feeling protective of Charlotte. "Will you give us minute alone?" she asked of Shadow.

"You won't leave me?"

"Of course not," Charlotte said and held her close. The snakes disappeared showing only Shadow's beautiful, blonde curls. Charlotte leaned closer so that only Shadow could hear her. "You and I are always going to be together. We just may have to wait for that special time I told you about."

"Will it be soon?"

Charlotte looked at the little girl and then she snuck a glance at Phineas, who looked nervous and edgy that she was holding Shadow in her lap. "I think it will be real soon."

Shadow nodded and then walked to the water. She called over her shoulder, "I'll be back after my swim," and then dove in and immediately shifted into the form of a dolphin.

Phineas stood up and watched her swim farther from the shore, his mouth agape. Pulling Charlotte up by the hand, he urged, "Let's hurry. The others are waiting."

"No Phin, we need to talk," Charlotte insisted and patted the ground beside her, indicating he should sit down again.

Without hesitation, Phineas sat down. Hell, he would face off against the Buraqs if it meant keeping Charlotte safe. "Is everything alright?" In spite of the time that had lapsed, Phineas reached for her as if they had always been together, and to his relief, she melted into his arms.

Charlotte rested her head on his shoulder. "It is now...now that you're here and I know the others are waiting. Tell me about Samantha. How will we get to her?"

"James and I worked out a signal system. We let him know that we're safe and he'll meet us with Suki. Then, we wait until it's dark to travel back to Samantha and get the hell out of Dodge."

Charlotte smiled at his silly reference. "I miss her. I can't believe this is all going to be over soon. What do you think she's doing right now?"

"She's probably bored out of her mind. I would be if I weren't here with you."

If they weren't in the Romani Realms, one would think Samantha and Daniel were an old married couple, enjoying the day and each other's company. Samantha watched Daniel tend the crops that lined the fence at the edge of his property. He had ensured that his small slice of heaven in the midst of so much chaos provided well for him.

"This should be enough to can for next winter," he said referring to his bounty that included beets, carrots, and even cherries.

Earlier they had feasted on roast pheasant along with the runner beans and a tomato salad that came from the garden, and for dessert, Daniel had surprised Samantha with a sweet potato pie.

"You work hard," she noted. "That was just about the best meal I've had here. It sure beats the beetles that I ate the first few nights.

"Yeah, but you probably enjoyed the food served in the glass gazebo dining area."

"Once I got past the mute girls who served it."

"They had me totally freaked out when I first got here...so did the Nephilim. They're pretty, but totally creepy," Daniel smiled, happy to have someone to talk to. He grew quiet...knowing that it couldn't last.

Sensing the shift in his mood, Samantha looked up at him and wrinkled her nose, a habit that Daniel had grown to love. "What's wrong?"

He put his bushel down and crossed to her, sitting down beside her on the blanket that she had spread out next to the lavender bushes whose fragrance filled the air -- a welcome respite from the dark side of the Romani Realms that smelled like stagnant water and death.

"What could be wrong?" he said, sitting behind her. He wrapped his arms around her waist, pulling her back against his chest and holding her closely. He inhaled the sweet smell of her wild, red mane, and closed his eyes as he leaned his head against hers.

The sun was just level with the horizon, casting glorious colors of pink and orange across the sky.

"Your hair against the sky would make for a beautiful picture," he said, pulling it back in his hands and with her neck exposed, he leaned forward and kissed the back of it. Samantha's breath caught.

"I'm sorry. I...it just felt right."

"You should've done that a long time ago," she said turning her head over her shoulder and sending a mischievous gaze in his direction. Within a second, she felt his reaction as his hardness pressed against her back.

"I'm sorry," he repeated.

"You have to stop saying that," she teased, and then shifted her body so that she could feel him even more so.

"Sam...would you like more pie?"

"Uh uh," she said reaching her hand behind her and purposefully letting it rest on his upper thigh, nearly touching him where he most wanted her to.

"Do you want me to read to you?"

"Uh uh." Growing bolder, Samantha shifted her body so that she was facing Daniel and leaned forward so that she could gently press her lips to his cheek. He naturally wrapped his arms around her, and she hopped onto his lap, throwing her legs around his waist.

"Oh god."

She could feel him straining in his jeans.

"Samantha, there's something you should know."

"I know everything I need to about you."

"Well, you don't know that I've never done this."

Samantha stopped, and stared up at him.

"How?"

He smiled and chuckled. "You never mince words. Well, the technical 'how' is that I've never been with a woman."

"No, I mean how is that possible? You're a guy; you're way hot; and you're 22."

"When you mess around with black magic when you're 17, and end up in a place like this, you don't exactly want to give it up to a demon or one of the other lost souls who did unspeakable things to end up here. You're the only thing that is right about this place. It makes me happy that I waited...for you."

"I haven't done it either. But...," she leaned in and kissed him, this time on the mouth and he responded tenderly, letting his lips gently mold against hers, his hands lightly caressing her back.

"But?" he asked, coming up for a breath.

"But I want to...with you."

Daniel smiled and leaned into her again, gently laying her down on her back as he kissed her. His hand reached for her breast and when he heard a soft moan escape her mouth, his fingers deftly undid the buttons on her blouse, letting it flow open. He bent his head and kissed her collarbone, making his way down her stomach.

When he stopped to whip off his own shirt, Samantha admired his toned chest muscled arms and chiseled abs. She sat up and removed her bra, pulling her long hair in front of her chest modestly. Daniel leaned over her, bringing his lips to hers once more.

"Are you sure?"

"More than sure."

He helped her shimmy out of her jeans and as he tugged them down, he planted little kisses along her stomach, working his way down, kissing her hip bone and then letting his mouth rest over her panties. With his thumb laced inside the light fabric, he gently removed them and continued to allow his mouth to explore her. Her body responded to him immediately, feeling his tender kisses, the way he held her hips and the undeniable fact that she wanted this to go on forever.

"Daniel...you better stop that or...

"Or..." he teased and looked up at her. Her eyes met his and she smiled, a smile that warmed his heart and filled him with hope that he once thought was completely lost. Samantha crooked her finger at him and he didn't hesitate to fill her silent request. He trailed his mouth up her neck until he found her lips. With his arms planted firmly on either side of her, he straddled her body and leaned into her. His knee gently nudged against her inner thigh, letting his desire be known. Their kisses grew more passionate and with it, so did their desire, until Samantha welcomed him inside and they became one.

"Samantha owes you her life," Phineas said in amazement, holding Charlotte against his chest. "You two were truly meant to find Suki's bottle. Only those with great potential do so."

Charlotte looked down, appearing momentarily uncomfortable with his observation. "I don't know about that," she said modestly and changed the subject. "You're sure she's alright? You've seen her?"

"She's fine. She told us how you found her first, but her memory was gone. How did you do it?"

"I believed in her...in us and our friendship. I knew that she would come back to me."

Phineas nodded, now completely understanding, for it was how he felt about Charlotte. "She had you, but she got lucky as well in finding Daniel." Phineas shook his head, not quite believing the situation himself. "Imagine finding the one good guy in this entire Realm."

Charlotte took his hand. "It's her gift...spotting a true soul. If anyone could do that here, it's Samantha. But, you're wrong about one thing. Daniel isn't the only good guy here."

Phineas looked at Charlotte and his heart soared with the meaning behind her words. He ran his thumb along her porcelain cheek, and when she bit her lower lip, he just couldn't restrain himself any longer. He leaned in and kissed her, gently and slowly, willing the moment to last. He felt her arms go around his neck, pulling him in closer and he knew that Charlotte had missed him as much as he felt empty without her.

His hand ran down her back, holding her closely. The kiss wasn't like any he shared with Raven. It wasn't based on lust, but of love. True, he still felt a need with Charlotte, but it wasn't strictly a need of passion as much as it was to feel close to her and to show her comfort and tenderness. The reality struck him that with Raven he was wrapped up in his own desires, but with Charlotte her every whim and pleasure was at the forefront of his mind.

As they kissed, she leaned back letting her body lay down upon the ground and pulling Phineas on top of her as she went. He wrapped his arm underneath her, not wanting to lose one inch of their contact. It had been too long and he knew how closely he had come to losing her. The thought of being without her made him bury his head into her neck, inhaling her scent as he let his lips travel over her.

He stopped to press himself up, hovering over her. "I want a future with you. Please Charlotte, tell me you want it too?"

"I do, Phin. More than anything."

His lips met hers again, tentatively and gently. He smiled and spoke directly into her mouth, not wanting to release from her kisses, but unable to stop his words. "You are so...amazing," was punctuated by a kiss. "I am never going to let anything happen to you," followed another.

Finally, Charlotte laughed and placed her hands on Phineas' cheeks, holding him in place. "If you don't kiss me properly, I might just bite those irresistible lips of yours."

"Really?" Phineas leered, liking where this was going. He was used to a demure Charlotte, but her bold words made him realize how much a person could change particularly when faced with death. Admiration filled his mind when he thought of how much Charlotte had risked unselfishly for those around her. She was everything that Raven wasn't and he knew that what he was feeling was something new, something he had never experienced before. Raven had restored his life and given him an everlasting life when he wasn't even twenty. She had been his only lover and while Raven was exciting and experienced, he craved what he was feeling for Charlotte.

Although he had lived for over 130 years, he had never felt this before. This is what it was like to be human, to be in touch with his own lost humanity. "You've made me feel again," he said in amazement. "I thought that Raven had stripped me of every human emotion, but..." he let his words trail off, knowing that he could never fully express his appreciation for Charlotte. Instead, new found passion stirred within him and he couldn't help the desire to press his hips forward, letting them rest against Charlotte. And to his amazement, she responded.

They kissed again, the passion growing as Charlotte wrapped her legs around his waist. He groaned feeling her pull himself toward her even closer, but in spite of how much he wanted her, there was something he wanted more. Her love.

"Phineas?"

He stopped suddenly, worried that he had somehow hurt her or she had changed her mind about him. "What is it?"

She shook her head, but a single tear fell from her eye. Phineas wiped it away immediately. "Charlotte, please tell me."

"I'm just happy. It's crazy and I'm acting like such a girl," she said wiping another runaway tear away.

Phineas sat up and pulled her up as well. "It's not crazy. Listen to me...Your necklace...the Amulet of Pollox...with it you can see all of the secrets from every Releasor that Suki has been beholden to."

Charlotte nodded. "Scientists, politicians, artists..."

"All that knowledge is yours for the taking, and is what Raven so desperately wants," he added gravely. "But there's one piece of information that you don't have."

Phineas got down on one knee, and stared up at Charlotte. Her hair shone like spun gold in the sunlight, her ice blue eyes smiled down at him and he knew beyond any doubt that he was capable of real love, that Raven could never take away what remained of his humanity.

"Charlotte Bloom, would you marry me?"

A little squeal escaped her as she clapped her hands in joy.

"You so know I will...yes. Yes!"

Phineas stood up and wrapped his arms around Charlotte, twirling her until her feet lifted from the ground. When he finally put her back down, he kissed her once more. "I wasn't sure you would say 'yes,' you know, given the situation. I really must be the happiest man alive."

Charlotte laughed in spite of the situation. "You're not just any man and as a demon, I'm not sure you qualify for 'alive' status, but yes, I would be with you even if this didn't happen." She indicated where they stood. Although the lake was placid and calm and the sun was shining, they had been through harrowing terrain and situations. Charlotte looked out to the water where Shadow still bounded in the form of a dolphin. Upon seeing her, she waved and Shadow splashed the water in response.

"About...Shadow," Phineas said gently, unsure how to broach the subject. He was thrilled that Charlotte was back in his life and he didn't want to rock the boat by pointing out that she was hanging out with an Encantado.

"Charlotte, I'm sorry that I brought this upon your life -- what happened with Samantha, Suki...all of it. But we'll get out of here and you need to put this place behind you."

Charlotte hesitated oddly as if that were the last thing she would want. She simply said, "Things happen for a reason."

Phineas watched her carefully, noting how she was staring out at Shadow's dolphin form as if she were keeping a protective eye on her. But she reached for his hand and suddenly all of his worry about her mental well-being melted away. "I know we belong together. Otherwise, you wouldn't have been drawn to me when Raven ordered you..." her words drifted off and Phineas winced. He knew she was recalling how Raven had wanted him to kill her and Samantha. But he couldn't have even back then. He loved her from the moment he saw her.

Taking her in his arms, he pressed his mouth to hers once more, willing her never to change her mind about him and also not wanting to hear or accept the truth of how they met.

"Are you okay?" she asked.

"Yeah. I just...it's unrealistic to think that Raven is going to simply give up. The Buraqs will tell her you're alive, and she'll want to get rid of you so she can form the Triad with me." He let his finger drape down her neck and then he gently held the Amulet of Pollox around her neck. "She's not going to stop trying to get this beauty."

"Let her try. This whole place made me realize...we have a purpose together. So what do you say?"

She looked at him seductively, narrowing her eyes and biting her lip. She moved into him slowly, one side of her mouth curling up into a sly smile. Phin reached for her and pulled her closer, narrowing any gap or daylight between their bodies, holding her against himself so that he could press his mouth upon hers. His tongue intertwined with hers, his hands roamed down her back and settled upon her hips. His mouth left hers only to trail more kisses down her neck and when he felt her knees buckle slightly from her arousal, he easily held her steady.

"I love you, Charlotte."

"I love you, too."

They were the most intoxicating words he had ever heard. He bent his head and touched his forehead to hers. "When I think of what you've been through..." he shook his head.

"Shh, I'm okay now."

"Charlotte, I want to take you back to my home where you would never experience discomfort again. I would carry you into my bedroom, lie you down on a beautiful, four-poster bed and cover you in a down comforter. You would never be cold for I would light a fire both in the hearth and in your heart."

"There's one more need that you haven't mentioned..." she said coyly.

He smiled, relishing where her mind was going. "The idea that I am worthy of making love to you is more than I ever could have hoped for in my life."

"So, do we still have time before James and Suki get back?"

"Charlotte, I want your first time to be special -- not here. Not with memories of why we're here. I want you to know what love feels like and it's not something to hurry...at least it's not going to be with me."

Charlotte giggled and held onto Phineas tightly. Her laugh was intoxicating and he wanted to hear that sound for the rest of his life. He tickled her mercilessly, relishing the sounds of happiness, until they were interrupted.

"What's so funny?"

At the sound of Shadow's voice, Charlotte jumped back as if caught doing something she shouldn't be doing.

"Come here, sweetie," she called and held her hand out to Shadow. The little girl eyed Phineas cautiously, her hair shifting back and forth between curls and snakes, her eyes doing the same -- one minute appearing like dark, empty caverns and the next, icy light blue, just like Charlotte's.

Phineas looked completely baffled as Charlotte welcomed what he could only imagine was some sort of demon into her arms. It was one thing for him to hold Charlotte because for all intents and purposes, he appeared human, but Shadow? "Charlotte, she's not human. You should be..."

"Phin, there's no reason to worry," she said speaking in a soothing voice and gently smoothing down Shadow's snakes until only curls and ringlets remained. The little girl visibly relaxed and held onto Charlotte, wrapping her arms around her waist and burying her head into Charlotte's stomach.

She leaned down and whispered something in Shadow's ear and the little girl stepped aside, now looking at Phineas with open curiosity.

"Phin, there's someone I'd like you to meet," Charlotte said properly.

Shadow stepped forward and did a little curtsy. If Phineas hadn't seen what she could shift into, he would have to admit that it was rather cute. He waited expectantly for whatever Charlotte had to say, but nothing could have prepared him for her words.

"Phineas, I'd like you to meet our daughter."

Chapter Twenty-One

Just moments later, when James and I emerged from the caves, we found the scene in front of us quite curious. Charlotte was encouraging Shadow to approach Phineas, and when she did, he gingerly stroked her hair, looking up at Charlotte with an expression that was a definite mixture of apprehension and amazement.

"James, I'm a dad!"

We turned to each other, our eyes wide with a *has-he-lost-it* look on their faces.

"Errr Phineas, am I supposed to congratulate you?" James asked, looking disgusted at the sight of Shadow's hair and how the snakes were trying to nip at Phineas' hands and arms, which he would quickly move when one got too close.

Charlotte immediately went to Shadow and placed a hand on her shoulder, calming the small girl and settling her fears about the new arrivals. Instantly, the girl's image shifted into one of a sweet, blonde nine-year-old. It made it easier for Phineas to accept her closer into his arms and for the first time, he saw her the way Charlotte did. He looked down into her face and as she met his gaze, he saw himself in her features.

He smiled and reached out to touch her chin. "You really are the spitting image of your mom and me."

"Are you really my dad?"

Her voice was so small and innocent without a trace of malice. Only hope that she would find love and acceptance came through, and Phineas had no choice but to fall in love with her as Charlotte had done. Perhaps it was the instantaneous bond that happens between parent and child, or maybe it was the mysticism of the Romani Realms, but at that moment Phineas felt the Celtic Knot he wore around his neck heat with undeniable strength.

He leaned down and opened his arms wide. No words were necessary. Shadow walked into his arms, placed her small head on Phineas' shoulder and he squeezed her in close. Charlotte stood behind Phineas and wrapped her arms over his shoulders. She looked up and smiled happily.

"Charlotte, your Amulet!" I pointed to the necklace and Phineas turned to look over his shoulder at what drew my attention. He also drew his breath in at the sight...the Amulet glowed a vivid hue that shifted from blue to green and then settled on purple.

"You've formed the Triad," I stated excitedly.

"So, we can leave?" Phineas looked at Charlotte expectantly. "You hear that? We're going home."

"But what about..."

Charlotte didn't have to finish her thought. Instantly, Phineas realized what he had said. "I'm sorry, guys...I didn't mean that we would leave you," he said to us. "I guess it's just new father jitters," he laughed nervously, although the reality was still painfully serious.

"Don't worry about it," James answered with raised eyebrows. "Congratulations, by the way."

I moved to Charlotte and took her into my arms. "Thank you for what you did for me. You shouldn't have, you know."

"Suki, you mean everything to me. You came here...I owed you."

"No more of that sort of talk."

The sentimentality of the moment was affecting us all. Phineas shook James' hand only to have him pull him in for an unexpected, but manly hug. "There's just one problem," he said after giving Phineas a strong, pat on the back. He lowered his voice, speaking directly into Phineas' ear. "She's an Encantado and tied to her own kind and the Selkies here -- all the souls who are trapped as dolphins and seals."

"And?" Phineas asked.

Charlotte placed a hand on her Amulet, already knowing the answer. She looked at James, and instantly, he also knew that she was aware of the problem. "Phineas..." she said softly, placing a hand on his arm. "The Encantado are tied to these Realms by dark magic. The only way to fully separate Shadow is to also perform a dark magic rite."

"How do you know this?"

Charlotte turned to me, before answering. "Aleister Crowley."

"Please don't say his name," I implored. "He's the only dark person in my past, someone who should never have been granted wishes, nor one who I would want you to access his mind."

Charlotte nodded, understanding. "Your Releasors are said to have great potential." She turned to Phineas and added, "And sometimes that potential is not for greatness, but for despair and wrong doing."

"Charlotte, it's my past and I want to leave it there. Just because you've been privy to it, doesn't mean you have to respond to it."

"I'm so sorry, Suki," Charlotte answered. "But you've given me a gift and with this Amulet I can see into the minds of all of your Releasors -- the good...and the bad."

Phineas turned to both of us. "What did he do that was so terrible?"

"The press called him 'the wickedest man in the world' and for good reason," James answered, this time surprising me.

"You knew about him?"

"I was watching over you even then. How could I not? He was a drug-user, followed the occult, and was even vain enough to start his own religion."

"Thelema," Charlotte said knowingly. "It spawned other modern day religious sects who prey on the unsuspecting and those in need of guidance."

I stepped up and took Charlotte's hand. "Whatever you're thinking of doing, please know that you can't perform dark magic without it affecting you."

"Perhaps..." Phineas started.

"Don't...don't justify this," I scolded. "We all want to get out of here, but this isn't the way. What will she be like when she's on the other side?"

Phineas took Charlotte in his arms and kissed her gently on the forehead. Shadow squeezed in between them, not wanting to be left out. "She'll be fine, Suki. You have to trust that."

He spoke aloud, but stared directly into Charlotte's eyes. "She'll be fine because of who she is - - pure and good. Hey, if someone like me can separate from Raven, even when she is influencing me, then this will be a snap for Charlotte."

James took my hand. "There is no choice here. Charlotte needs to separate Shadow from the Realms...or they won't form the Triad."

We stood silent for a moment until Charlotte got down to business. "Come on. We're all here. Let's do this."

She leaned down and found a grey flint stone, sharp and perfect for her intended use. Charlotte met Phineas' eyes and then, when he nodded his support, she sliced her wrist with one fast motion. Instantly, her blood appeared and she repeated the words used by Aleister Crowley to attract his many followers. "Do what thou wilt shall be the whole of the law."

Instantly, the wind started to stir and Shadow shivered in response. She looked at Charlotte and smiled, feeling the bond to the Romani Realms shrink away, and her connection to Charlotte grow simultaneously.

"It's working," Phineas encouraged. "Keep going."

But the clouds opened up as if daring her to do as he said. The rain poured down and coinciding with the arrival of the threatening weather was Raven.

She swooped down in bird form and materialized in front of them, her eyes as angry as the weather. "Quoting my dear friend Aleister?" she asked with raised eyebrows. "Bring it on, Charlotte. You aren't coming out of this alive, at least not with a happy family to boot."

Raven turned to me and her animosity was palpable. "It was bad enough that you thought the Triad was meant for you and two teenage girls, but now to encourage Charlotte to form it with my intended," she said pointedly looking at Phineas, "that's just plain stupid."

"Ignore her, Charlotte," Phineas guided her. "Focus your mind on Shadow and we'll still get out of here."

Charlotte continued her incantation, but was momentarily halted when she saw Shadow's eyes return to their hollow black form and then shift back to their clear blue again. Practicing dark magic to separate the bond was an alien endeavor for someone as pure as Charlotte and as a result, Shadow's form kept shifting between human and Encantado, weakening Charlotte in the process.

James instinctively wrapped an arm around me. Although Phineas tried to do the same for Charlotte, it was too little, too late. Raven threw her arms skyward and turned her head upwards toward the clouds. Thunder sounded and blood rain poured down upon her face. "You wanted to summon the mind of Aleister Crowley? Then, you shall have him because Suki wasn't the only one to have met him."

"I was Released by him and suffered with him against my will. For you to seek him out is evidence of your evil nature," I shouted above the sound of the horrific storm.

Raven laughed and smiled as if she had a secret that the crowd didn't want to hear...but they would. As Charlotte tried to repeat her phrasing, Raven threw another Aleister incantation into the wind.

"Paganism is wholesome because it faces the facts of life!" Raven screamed. "Aleister's greatest moments were his ability to bring about the darkness and convert innocents to his thinking. Paganism is wholesome..." she repeated, and as she did the darkness that Charlotte was carefully controlling for her own purposes -- for the greater good of her friends -- spun out of control. Blackbirds descended on the scene from every direction. They surrounded us and moved closer, unafraid of contact and in fact, bold enough to peck at Charlotte's feet.

All the while, Raven continued to conjure the spirit of Aleister Crowley, the man who had influenced so many to act against others.

I tried to reach for Charlotte, but James held me back. "She's throwing the darkness at Charlotte faster than she can control it. It will take over."

"She'll never be like Raven," James soothed, the shelter of his Shade hovering over me like an umbrella. "If you want to help her, you need to repel the darkness. Work with Phineas."

I nodded at Phineas, who also watched in horror as blood poured down on Charlotte and indeed, she looked as if the darkness was being absorbed into her body. In spite of Phineas doing his best to hold her and force an aura of light and love into her, she was using all her strength and will to escape Phineas' grip. Shadow also seemed to be moving closer to darkness with half of the hair on her head now emerging as snakes.

All the while, Charlotte continued the incantation, and I worried with despair, "The darkness is too strong; she'll be just like Raven."

"We wouldn't want that," Raven chided.

Instinctively, Phineas and I struck simultaneously, taking advantage of Raven's bravado to get a foothold. Thunder sounded and a lightening bolt struck within inches of where she was standing, but it wasn't enough.

"Impressive...not!" Raven glared at both of us, particularly Phineas, whom she was most angry at his rejection. I saw the pain in her eyes and immediately twisted the knife.

"They say that stressful situations bring about a person's true nature. Look, Raven." I pointed to Phineas, whose arms wrapped protectively around Charlotte. "They belong together. They're meant for each other."

"*That's it,*" James whispered into my mind. "*Use her weakness against her.*"

"*If only I could speak with Phineas without her hearing.*"

James looked uncomfortable as if he had new knowledge that he didn't want to share. Like a cat who ate the canary, he tried his best to swallow his secret, but his connection to me had grown incrementally since our fight and reconciliation, as if we had overcome a mountain in our relationship. It made keeping secrets more of an impossibility.

"*You can reach him?*" Hope sounded in my voice.

Raven interrupted our silent communication. "Enough of this," she shouted and unleashed hundreds of blackbirds to dive bomb us. "Enjoy yourselves. I'll be circling with the others...waiting to feast on the carrion."

Raven returned to bird form and true to her word, the other birds became aggressive, drawing blood from us.

"*James, can you do it?*" my arms were being bit while birds on the ground sickeningly moved around my ankles, their wings fluttering against my legs, their beaks taking bites whenever they pleased and all along, I was helpless to stop them.

"It will mean bonding to him." James sounded as if he were going to be sick.

"Suck it up and do the bromance thing."

Whether it was because he so dearly loved me or to prove his manhood to himself, James grabbed the back of my head and pulled me in for a kiss that was as strong and powerful as his capabilities as a Shade. After releasing his hold on me, I was breathless. The blood rain still pounded down upon us, but I hadn't noticed while in James' embrace. Then, with a you-owe-me look, he nodded and focused on Phineas.

I kept an eye on Charlotte, who was now shaking, either from the cold, the darkness pummeling her body, or both. *"Hurry,"* I encouraged, speaking softly into James' mind.

He looked at Phineas, who still had his arms wrapped around Charlotte, trying desperately to stop her shakes. Taking a deep breath as if to steady his own thoughts, James focused his attention on the task at hand. His eyes narrowed on Phineas and I saw with amazement that Phineas suddenly shook his head as if a fly were settling on his face and the sensation was too much to handle.

"Can you hear me?" James concentrated his thoughts into Phineas.

Although Phineas closed his eyes momentarily, he didn't respond and James knew that he believed himself to be hallucinating from the effects of trying to repel Raven's dark orbs from taking over Charlotte.

"*Listen to me,*" James concentrated.

Phineas swatted his arm in response, as if something had tickled him.

"*Don't let go of her,*" James scolded.

And that's when it sunk in. It wasn't his imagination. The electric tingling that went up and down his body. The voice in his head. "*What the hell, dude?*" Phineas' thoughts were loud and clear, sounding in James' head in response to the effort of his Shading over Phineas.

"*I said to keep your arms around Charlotte. I know the sound of my voice can be pretty intoxicating, but do your best to think of your girl.*"

"*Holy fuck, what are you doing in my head?*" Although Phineas was clearly freaked out, he did as James had instructed and in fact, held onto Charlotte even tighter, nearly keeping her completely steady in spite of Raven's continual onslaught of darkness.

"*Don't get too excited. It's just a means to an end. Are you ready?*"

Phineas wrapped his arms around Charlotte and saw that she was still clinging to Shadow, although both looked like they were weakening. The rain was pouring down on them and the blackbirds were becoming more agitated and bold, taking occasional pecks now at their necks and fluttering toward their faces. They were forced to accept any attack for shooing them away would mean releasing their grip on each other and they needed to be connected in body, mind and spirit in order to escape.

When Phineas ensured that he, Charlotte, and Shadow were all interconnected he answered James, testing their new found bond. *"Ready, but please...be gentle. It's my first time."*

"You are disgusting. You know that, right?"

"And here I thought you liked my kinky side."

In spite of the gravity of the situation, I snickered, only to have James tighten his hold on me in warning. *"Suki, this isn't a laughing matter. You need to focus as well."*

"Sorry."

Neither Phineas nor I were privy to any conversation not directly aimed at ourselves and so the break in conversation from James, regardless of how temporary, affected Phineas' concentration. The blackbirds started biting his face and the temptation to swat them was becoming overwhelming.

James came back and directed him. *"Just think about the end game. We get Charlotte and Suki back to Samantha, and get out of here."*

"Ah, there you are. When I didn't hear you, I started to think you were one of those one-night-stand types. You know, get inside my head, have your way with me, and then cast me aside."

"No such luck. This is sort of a permanent deal."

"No shit?"

"Jeez Phineas, you don't have to sound quite so pleased with that knowledge."

"Well James, you are quite the catch..."

Not one to be teased, especially by Phineas, he narrowed his eyes in warning. *"Yeah get over it, I'm taken."*

"I'm just saying...if you're going to help save our ass this time, who knows, my ass might require you again in the future." Phineas smirked, loving that if he had to be bonded to James, he could have some fun at his expense.

"Okay, that's enough."

James held my hand and brought me closer into his body. Upon feeling me relax against him -- trusting him -- he squeezed my hand in signal. He kicked at the blackbirds that still swarmed around our ankles like rats, and braced himself for what we had to do. "Ready?"

Phineas gave the thumb's up signal and held onto Charlotte. Although weak, she nodded her head as well and wrapped her arms around Shadow.

"To Samantha," I affirmed.

James nodded. For the first time since we had been in the Romani Realms we were all of the same mindset and held the same goal in mind. "Something's odd about this," James said shaking his head.

"Let's just do this," I urged.

We closed our eyes, held tightly to each other and listened for the sound that would be most welcome -- the grinding of the gears indicating the passage of time. The wind buffered us from the rain and soon all sight and sound left us as a we transported to where we had left Samantha safely with Daniel.

Chapter Twenty-Two

Bypassing the trek over the ravine to Daniel's cottage was one benefit of time travel; the second was that we arrived in time for dinner. Samantha threw her arms around Charlotte, holding her in a warm embrace like none she had been able to experience with her best friend since their arrival in the Romani Realms.

The two girls stared at each other for a moment making sure that their memories of each other were as they should be.

"I can't believe I didn't recognize you," Samantha said, shaking her head in disbelief at her own shortcoming just a few days earlier.

Charlotte smoothed down one of Samantha's runaway red curls. "But you did...deep down you did. And what do I do? I go daydreaming and start eating slugs. Gross!"

Samantha smiled at the memory, but her eye caught Shadow watching her every move. "Well, it looks like you had a very good reason to be...distracted. Are you going to introduce us?"

Samantha bent down and formally extended her hand to Shadow.

"Shadow, this is my very best friend, Samantha. Samantha, meet Shadow...our daughter."

Samantha smiled at the little girl and then cast her eyes up toward Phineas, who watched her interaction. A hush fell over the gathered crowd, even Charlotte was too afraid to interrupt. She had experienced first hand the warnings of Samantha's gift to see into a person's true nature when she first fell for Phineas and he wasn't of pure heart. Fortunately, he had redeemed himself, not only in her eyes, but in Samantha's as well. She wouldn't be able to carry on with him had Samantha not given him the stamp of approval -- not with everything they had gone through. Samantha nodded at Phineas, a silent statement of her acknowledgment that he was part of Charlotte's life.

Whether Shadow had inherited more of his demon qualities or those carried over from when he was human remained to be seen. The little girl had remained quiet, her eyes cast downward when Samantha approached. But now, as Samantha showed her patience and waited for her response, she beamed at Samantha and Charlotte released an audible sigh of relief. Shadow's smile was a toothy grin, not a black gaping hole in sight. Her long, blonde curls blew in the wind and remained touchably soft. And when she accepted Samantha's outstretched hand and held it in her own, Samantha closed her eyes momentarily and when she opened them, she smiled back as well.

"It's a pleasure to meet you Miss Shadow. I hope we can be friends too."

"I'd like that Miss Samantha."

Phineas took Charlotte's hand and gave it a squeeze. He was well aware that her friend, although a mere human, held a gift just as Charlotte did, and her approval was important to him. He moved Charlotte's straight blonde hair aside and kissed the back of her neck. She turned her head over her shoulder, inviting a kiss on her cheek as well, which Phineas happily obliged.

Samantha rose still holding Shadow's hand. "Daniel built a swing set behind the house, if you want to try it out." She turned to Charlotte and I, "And for us, there's sweet tea already prepared."

"After what we've experienced, I think I've died and gone to heaven," I declared. "You'll be okay without me?" I said casting my eyes on James.

"I thought James and Phineas could help me with the barbecue," Daniel offered.

"We're there," James answered and Phineas followed Daniel to the back of the house as well.

While Samantha and Charlotte sipped their tea and watched Shadow play, I took in our surroundings. A little house in the midst of green meadows, a spring running along the side of the property, plenty of fruit trees to provide shade, and the smell of wild flowers greeted me. "Grass, flowers...a barbecue! I must say, this is weird."

"You get used to it. And it's obvious why Daniel tries to spend as much time as possible at home,"

Samantha commented. "Aside from the ballroom and the area where we all first landed in the Romani Realms, it's pretty horrific out there."

"I forgot about that first green meadow," I mused. "It's been so long since I've seen beauty here."

"That's where I first met Shadow," Charlotte replied wistfully.

"All things happen for a reason," I added. "Sometimes, it's hard to recognize that reason while you're in the moment."

As the girls chatted, the guys talked around the barbecue where an array of meats cooked, the delectable smell wafting through the air. Samantha had earlier harvested vegetables from Daniel's garden and although she wasn't a cook, she had learned from his expert guidance and had in fact, prepared them well, perfectly grilling them and then adding a light, french vinaigrette.

A long, carved oak table, another example of Daniel's handiwork, was set for the party of seven. Charlotte called for Shadow to join us and before we took our seats, she walked around the length of the massive table, carefully placing a daisy by each place setting.

"Where did you find those sweetie?" Charlotte asked, bringing one to her nose. The sight of them reminded Charlotte of when she first arrived and cast her eyes upon Shadow.

"They're just like the ones I gave to you."

"That's just what I was thinking," Charlotte replied by tickling Shadow's nose with one of the flowers.

"I found them growing on the other side of the fence at the end of the meadow," she said pointing.

"Gosh Daniel, this place is like a small slice of heaven in the midst of so much chaos," Charlotte beamed, lifting her glass to her lips.

"Thanks. It makes being here...bearable. Why don't we take our seats?"

His words were a reminder to all of us that he would remain even after we returned to our permanent world. Shadow broke the tension of his comment. "I would have gotten more, but a lady scared me and my hair went...well, you know. I ran away before it got too ugly."

As James held a chair out for me, he turned his head over his shoulder as if suddenly aware of a presence that shouldn't be there. "What lady?"

There was no need for an answer.

Before we could even take a sip of wine, the shutters on the cottage's windows clamored loudly with a sudden gust of wind that also sent the silverware flying and the flowers scattering. The tranquility of the earlier scene was all but forgotten as the wind announced a change occurring...and Raven's arrival.

Chapter Twenty-Three

Raven slowly and methodically moved around the table, much like an animal circling its prey.

"Charlotte, you always were such a perceptive girl... 'a slice of heaven amidst the chaos.' Hmm, charming statement. It kind of reinforces my own philosophy that appearances can be deceiving. Isn't that right, Phineas?"

Phineas wouldn't take the bait. He whispered in a nearly imperceptible manner to Charlotte. "We're fine."

"Fine? Did I hear you say?" Raven goaded. "I suppose you're right...if you like dining with those who are dead," she said looking pointedly at Daniel and then to my horror, directly at Samantha.

Raven's voice was like acid burning away any trace of happiness that lingered around the table. "So why wasn't I invited?"

Her rhetorical question was only met by the stares of those around the table until Daniel spoke up. "This is my home and no, you were not invited."

"I understand...you're enjoying, as Charlotte said, your own private Heaven...or is this Hell?"

Her comment was met with our annoyed sighs and rolls of the eyes. Only Daniel met Raven's gaze head on and seemed uncomfortable...nervous even, about where her dialogue was going. And in spite of himself, he couldn't react to ask her to leave again.

Raven showed off a sinister, tight lipped smile and twirled her shiny, black hair around one finger coyly as her eyes traveled over each one us, seemingly deciding which one to rest on.

"Heaven and Hell..." she said with a flourish, "both attract humanity and often times there's little difference between the two. Each person has the potential for good and bad. Isn't that right?" she asked us.

"Raven, what do you want?" Phineas finally addressed her.

"Ah Phineas, you of all people should know what I'm getting at. I gave you second life, but when someone gives you a gift like that, there's always a price. You were aligned with me, my partner in so...many....ways," she said boring her eyes into Charlotte, who took a deep breath, trying not to become agitated. "I suppose, Phineas, that you think risking yourself for the lives of Charlotte and Samantha is your redemption?"

Raven moved down the table, stopping directly behind me. "What a sweet little genie. Everyone loves you. You serve so selflessly. Or do you?"

"Remember this? 'Power tends to corrupt, and absolute power corrupts absolutely.' That catchy phrase was spoken by one of your Releasors, historian Lord Acton, who get this...also called himself a moralist. Typical..." she added with a tsk.

I met Raven's stare and even I was taken aback by the sheer hostility and hatred she spewed at me.

"Suzette," she spat, using my formal name to emphasize her point, "Your Releasors are not perfect. None of them have been. That Lord Acton was a stuck-up, stodgy old man... who *you*," she said staring at me, "for whatever reason thought was a bloody genius. He also said, 'Great men are almost always bad men,' and yet, even after him, you continue to grant wishes to anyone who releases you without a second thought as to what they want."

"What's your point, Raven?"

"You don't know what to do with absolute power. You say wishes have to be made in the name of selflessness, but you are smart enough to know that a clever man can twist his words. You, who have served the likes of Aleister Crowley...selflessness my ass."

"That's enough, Raven," James spoke up.

"James, my heart be still," Raven mocked, placing a hand on her chest. "Always the protector, you just can't help yourself...misguided loyalty even to those who don't deserve it."

"Are you referring to yourself?" he spat out.

"Perhaps I'm referring to any number of women? It seems that often times, your baby brain...you know, the one that resides in your Southern regions," she said mocking my origins again while her eyes boldly traveled down to James' lap, "does the thinking for you."

James turned toward me, either to reassure me or gauge my reaction to Raven's diatribe. The pain of realizing that James and Raven had once been lovers was still too fresh and raw to revisit. I lowered my head in spite of not wanting Raven to see she had hit a nerve.

"And dear, innocent Charlotte and Samantha," Raven continued. She moved behind the two girls who were seated side-by-side, and ran her hand down Charlotte's straight hair and continued to stroke it with one hand as if she were a pet. With the other, she turned to Samantha and placed it under her chin, forcing her eyes to look directly at her. "You two think you're innocent of all evil? You've *both* dallied in selfish behavior, which is what landed you here.

This time I spoke up, outraged. "Their behavior was never selfish. It was their thoughts and concern for each other that got them into trouble. That is evidence of their goodness."

"But that goodness that you speak of was laced in a desire to act on each other's behalf because they didn't want to be alone. They brought all of this upon each of you. Have you enjoyed your little vacation here?"

Raven watched the truth spread across each of our faces. "Of course not. I didn't think so."

"Why are you here?!" Phineas exploded, the frustration at having nearly been free of his partner only to be reminded that he was bound to her...that she would always know where he was and what he was thinking...thrown back in his face.

Raven simply smiled at him, knowing that his outburst was only a sign of his demon youth in comparison to Raven's extended life.

"Careful." James words echoed in his head and Phineas bit his tongue, but his Celtic Knot no sooner started to burn and he involuntarily jumped at the shock of the sudden heat.

Raven narrowed her eyes and looked at him curiously. Instinctively, Phineas grit his teeth to deal with the pain. But something else attracted her eye. Like a magpie attracted to bright, shiny objects, Raven immediately spied the Amulet of Pollox, which was also glowing around Charlotte's neck, again radiating different colors like it has never done before.

She reached for it, but her outstretched hand was greeted by a bolt of lightening. Any yet, not a cloud was in the sky. Raven turned to Phineas and then over to me, trying to determine which one of us could have so boldly struck her. Upon seeing the fire burning in my eyes, she had her answer.

"Don't be stupid," she spoke to me.

Feeling more brazen than ever, along with a deep instinct to protect my Releasors, I commanded her, "Leave."

"I'm not a dog to be ordered about. I'll do as I want."

She circled to the other side of the table, keeping her eyes on me all along. James placed his hand on my knee under the table, ready to help if I required it. My powers over the elements were strong again, now that I was used to the atmosphere in the Romani Realms, but James knew better than anyone how Raven could get under one's skin and make them do something they regretted.

She was also incredibly perceptive.

She bypassed me and came to stand right next to James. "You know, if there's one thing I've learned...once you have a man, it's hard to go back to a boy...although with the right training," she said smiling at Phineas and sending Charlotte's confidence into the ground, "a boy can grow into an incredible lover as well. I guess, when one thinks about it, it's men who are dogs." Her comments were meant to backhand everyone seated: James for having made the mistake of sleeping with Raven in the name of protection; Phineas for allowing himself to act on evil simply because his lover commanded it. Charlotte and I were both slapped again with the knowledge that we would never be able to forget the fact that such a hateful woman had compromised the men we had fallen for.

Only Samantha and Daniel seemed to escape her words.

An eerie silence fell over the group seated around the table as if the curious nature of her omission crossed each person's mind simultaneously.

Phineas put a hand to his Celtic Knot, and then trying his new found trick that James had taught, he tried to communicate, although initiating mind conversation was harder than responding to it. When no words entered James' mind, Phineas simply kicked him under the table, meeting James' glare head on and then with his eyes, indicated he had something important to say.

"Yes?" James asked silently, his tone annoyed.

"The Triad." Phineas responded, not able to say more than a few words given his recency over learning this new skill.

"Yeah, you're one of the lucky ones at this table. What about it?"

"There's more," was all Phineas could muster.

"For heaven's sake," James rolled his eyes, and noticed Raven now pouring herself a glass of wine, relishing how uncomfortable everyone at the table was growing. *"Suki..."* James spoke to me, his voice silent, but strong in my mind. *"Phin has something to say and can't quite spit it out. Something about the Triad and 'there's more'...just can't tell me what that is,"* he gave a false smile to Phineas.

I immediately answered in James' head. *"There's more...more to the prophecy...more Triads?"*

James sent the question to Phineas. *"Phin...your Celtic Knot, Charlotte's Amulet...they bind you and together you have Shadow. So, do you mean that another Triad is available?"*

Raven watched all of us. Phineas gave one nod in James' direction and he knew that they had figured it out...as had Raven.

Chapter Twenty-Four

Suddenly, it all made sense. Raven would never have allowed this party to convene unless she knew about the possibility of forming a second Triad. With the countless number of soulless people, the Nephilim, the Buraqs...certainly she would have been able to direct a search party to intercept them...had she really wanted to. But now it became obvious that having them all gathered in one place was her next tactic.

"She's willing to risk our escape in order to bring us together so that she can take one of our places," James silently warned.

"I see the wheels turning in your minds," Raven addressed me, while stabbing a piece of meat. The others ate in uncomfortable silence.

"Enjoy your food...*our* food, Raven," I spoke up. "Because then we're leaving and you're not coming with us."

"That's no way to speak to an old friend."

"Don't wind her up," James reminded me. But it was so hard to ignore her.

Raven held her empty glass toward Phineas. "Can you give me refill...Darling?"

Phineas rolled his eyes, but filled her glass up. And then waited. Waited for the inevitable shoe to drop. Raven had something planned and we were helpless to endure her company until she decided to tell us.

"So, who's going on a trip?" she finally asked.

"We all are," Phineas declared. "Well, all of us except you."

Raven shook her head in mock confusion. "Math was never your strong suit. Let's do a counting lesson, shall we?" Holding up one fist, she counted off her fingers. "One, two, three...the definition of a Triad. And I see..." she pointed her red-polished nail at each person, "...seven. Why, that's not even divisible by three."

"This is my home. I stay," Daniel spoke up, but no sooner stared down into his plate and continued eating. His words may have been neutral, but his tone gave away his sorrow.

"Wow Samantha, you found a very chivalrous young man here. Couldn't be all bad, huh? But, his gallantry is for nothing because you'll be right by his side...indefinitely."

The pain on Samantha's face was palatable, and I rose to be by her side. With a hand on her back, soothing Samantha's tension, I worked to set Raven straight. "Samantha will be coming with us."

"I see...somehow you think it's possible to enlist two Triads." Raven's eyes blazed with the knowledge.

I met James and Phineas' gaze with worried eyes. They would have to make their move quickly, although now it was impossible to get word to Charlotte or Samantha. Unless we were all of like mind, and Raven's reminder about Daniel remaining was certain to upset Samantha, we would not be successful in riding the gears of time out of the Realms.

Raven enjoyed mocking our pain and despair. "It's really so much fun watching your brains twist and turn with so much effort. Do you need a little more help with the math? Here..." she said pushing up her sleeves as if preparing for a difficult job. "So, we take away Daniel and we're left with six. I'm still not convinced you can handle two Triads, but it doesn't matter..." she said casually pacing around the table... "the way I figure it, there will only be four of you remaining anyway. And that simply won't work."

Although we pretended to ignore Raven's interruption by continuing to eat the delicious meal that Samantha and Daniel had prepared, our efforts were reduced to merely picking at an occasional bite and shifting the food around our plates. But even that minuscule effort ceased with Raven's declaration. We stared at her, willing her to continue although hating her for the information.

"Goodie, I've got your attention again." The sarcasm dripped from her voice. "Okay, so we've gone from seven to six. That was easy. Now, who do we take away?"

Raven pointed a finger at each person and below her breath whispered acerbically, "eenie-meenie-minie-mo." She paused on Samantha, and raised her eyebrows to the group. "Here's one." And then she continued her childish show with another countdown until she stopped and pointed to Shadow, who had been sheltered to the threat of knowledge by Charlotte, who had kept her busy up until that point with colored pencils and paper.

With a deep sense of maternal instinct, Charlotte involuntarily shouted out, "No!" "I'm sorry dear Charlotte, today you will lose your friend once again and your...child...if that's how you want to refer to this..."

"Stop it!" Charlotte yelled again, now standing up in full protective mode.

Raven pretended to back down, placing her hands up even though everyone was well aware that she could easily strike if she wanted. "I see I've upset you. Let me clear things up. You see, neither Samantha nor Shadow are really in human form. Shadow is an Encantado and did you forget that Samantha went over a cliff? She's dead."

"Samantha is fine," I said, but the gravity of the situation had indeed been forgotten by all of us. Although we could interact with Samantha, she was only hovering in this Realm, unreal and dead to the other worlds. To leave with her would mean having to resurrect her soul and retrieve her spirit. As for Shadow, it remained to be seen whether she could stay in the form of a little girl or not. Raven's words unfortunately carried a degree of truth.

Raven started to laugh. "Don't you see the irony of this gathering?"

A stream of bright blue butterflies filled the sky as I looked skyward, trying to figure out a solution. But Raven looked at them and merely raised her arms, sending blackbirds that had been perched among the trees, silent and unmoving until this point, flying into their midst. The two species intermingled, each trying to distract the other, until finally they both flew away -- a standstill.

I shook my head in anger. "Nothing is remotely funny about this situation."

"Oh, but it is," Raven retorted. "You came here -- all of you -- to bring Samantha back and yet, she will remain."

Samantha met Raven's stare head on. "I'm safe here," she said and linked her arm within Daniel's, but she no sooner also gazed at Charlotte and saw a single tear escape her friend's eye. She knew how much Charlotte had risked to find her.

It wasn't unlike the time when Charlotte kept a vigil by her hospital bed after Raven caused a tree branch to fall in front of a car, which then swerved to avoid it and instead, hit Samantha. Charlotte's prayers catapulted me out of my bottle and when Samantha awoke, the two friends discovered me ready to serve them. Naturally, they used up their first wish to have me prove myself.

Now, they found themselves here because each had risked everything to rescue the other. "I would do it again," Samantha said to Charlotte, who immediately knew of what she referred. The incident that made her plummet over the bluffs of Malibu for fear of Charlotte being in danger. And simultaneously, Charlotte prayed for Samantha's safety. Neither had even enlisted a wish, but rather, worked on their own accord to benefit the other.

To my chagrin, Charlotte wished for my own safety. I would have done anything to stop it from being so, but as my Shade, James had other ideas and came to my aid when her pleas were uttered.

And now only one wish remained.

"You could wish your way out of this situation." Raven waited for the response of her suggestion. But both Charlotte and Samantha, in spite of Raven's declaration that they were selfish, were not. Another wish brought me that much closer to being back in my bottle, imprisoned for who knows how long until another Releasor stumbled upon me.

Charlotte shook her head and Samantha acknowledged her desire. "Suki also risked her life to come to the Romani Realms...we won't do that to her," Samantha said defiantly.

One could say I came here out of duty, but everyone at the table knew that no wish had been cast, no request was asked. When Charlotte entered the Romani Realms in search of Samantha, I couldn't help but follow.

Raven was jubilant. "Well, my work here is done. There's a lovely ball occurring tonight. Phineas...you've been so quiet. Shall I save you a dance?"

Phineas refused to meet Raven's eyes, instead turning toward Charlotte and gently kissing her forehead.

"I'm off now." And Raven transformed into a blackbird and flew to the nearby trees where the others were perched, watching and waiting.

Chapter Twenty-Five

"Mommy, what was that lady talking about?" Shadow stared up at Charlotte sweetly, only now taking a break from her drawing.

Charlotte turned to Phineas and smiled broadly. Amidst the despair that Raven flung onto their lives, she couldn't remove the love that Charlotte had in her heart for Phineas or the daughter that they had found, and had they been in the real world, would have created together.

"Did you hear that?" she asked Phineas.

Knowing what had pleased her, he took Charlotte in his arms. She looked over his shoulder and smiled at Shadow. "You called me Mommy."

"That's because you are my Mommy. Do you want to see my picture now?"

Phineas released Charlotte and took the paper from Shadow. It wasn't a child's crude drawing, but an elaborate picture of fine art with detailed pencil shadings that perfectly depicted the features of the three people portrayed: Phineas, Charlotte, and

Shadow. What's more, they stood outside a palatial home that was a ringer for Phineas' Malibu property.

"That's eerie," Phineas noted, albeit with admiration for Shadow's obvious supernatural power of seeing the images inside a person's mind. "How did you know?"

"I saw you thinking of it when that lady was here. Only you wanted me and Mommy to live there. So, I drew it for you. Here..." she handed Phineas the drawing.

"Thank you. But, I can only accept such a wonderful gift if you let me do something for you," he said lifting Shadow onto his lap. For the first time, he did as he had seen Charlotte do, smooth down her unruly hair until the emerging snakes turned back into their golden curls. She relaxed against his chest and sighed deeply. "Can I be your Daddy?"

Shadow threw her arms around Phineas' neck in response. "You *are* my Daddy, silly."

And as they embraced and the declaration was made, again Phineas' Celtic Knot grew warm and glowed, sending a signal to Charlotte's Amulet of Pollox. They were united and not just as a couple, but as a family.

Samantha watched the scene and knew she couldn't let Charlotte's risk be in vein. "Daniel..." she beckoned, leading him away from the table.

They walked along the side of the house where Daniel's flowering bushes grew.

"Roses?" Samantha asked, pausing to smell one, although they didn't release a scent.

"No, they look similar, but they're Camellias. Too many thorns here already," Daniel said wistfully. "I didn't want to add to the assortment. What did you want to talk about?" he asked, although instinctively, he knew the answer.

"It's just that Charlotte is my best friend. And, she risked her life for me. She has a child and she deserves a life with her family. She won't leave here unless I..."

Daniel nodded. "Then you should go."

Tears immediately dripped down Samantha's cheeks, and she buried her face into Daniel's broad shoulder. "I don't even know if I can go, but what about you?"

"Me? I'll be fine...because I've known you."

Samantha gave him a wistful smile. "I love you."

"And you are my first love. Don't worry about me, Samantha. The memories I have of our night...that'll keep me."

They walked hand in hand back around the house to where the rest of our group was deep in discussion. My voice carried on the wind. "Unless you request a third wish, Charlotte, there is no guarantee."

"There is another way...if everyone is in agreement."

Charlotte knew what James was referring to -- if they all were in a similar mindset, they could time travel, instigating a second Triad, but only if they were together.

"That depends on Samantha. I'm not leaving her," she replied.

Samantha came into their view as Charlotte's words were spoken. The three of them looked at her expectantly. "I'm coming with you." Samantha offered them a small smile. Her news carried mixed emotions for they knew who she was leaving behind.

But Charlotte ran to her, throwing her friend into a bear hug. "I think I know what to do," she said with a glimmer of hope in her eyes. "James...Suki...you think it can be done too?"

"We managed it to come here," I answered.

"But we were separate and you had Raven," James explained. "What Charlotte is considering is a lot riskier -- taking six people into not only another time, but another Realm."

"But it's a risk we have to take," Phineas pointed out.

Charlotte grasped her Amulet. "I know the mathematical equation used by Charles Babbage for time travel. I know of Aleister Crowley and his pension for conjuring the other side. Using the knowledge of both, all we have to do is harness our minds together."

"It can work," I confirmed. "We have a chance of creating another Triad."

Charlotte grabbed Phineas' hand with excitement. "You, me, and Shadow."

And I looked at Samantha and James. "And the three of us."

Daniel stood to the side, and everyone turned to him in the uncomfortable silence that ensued. "Don't look at me like that," he said firmly. "You need to want this. It's the only way. Don't you dare worry about me. Look at what I've created here," he said spreading his arms to show off the little paradise he had built.

Charlotte offered him a thankful smile and Samantha nodded her head bravely. "Charlotte, you came here for me. I'm going back for you."

"Okay then, let's get started," Charlotte said, her eyes scanning each of us who stood before her. We moved into a circle and clasped hands. "Alright, let's do a warm up," Charlotte instructed, before closing her eyes. We took her lead and did the same, waiting for her to continue. "Those of us who can communicate silently, please start. All others, try to tune into their energies."

"I'm with you," I spoke in her mind.

"And I'm with you," James answered.

"Right here with you," Phineas responded.

Once we confirmed our status, we squeezed the hand of the person standing to our right until the circle was complete...James and myself, followed by Shadow who stood next to Phineas and then Charlotte, ending with Samantha and back around in a continuous bond. We grew quiet and concentrated on our end goal that now was the same for each of us. Using Superluminal Communication, the process of sending information at faster-than-light speeds, our thoughts of home and leaving the horrors of the Romani Realms behind were at the forefront of our minds. We employed the methods of Charles Babbage's time travel theories that Charlotte had prepped us on, and the knowledge filled our minds. Our eyelids flickered with the images that passed and our breathing slowed so that inhalations and exhalations were steady and as one.

Our thoughts transferred to a form of group velocity in which each person's thought waves took shape and propagated through space. Like throwing a stone into a lake and watching the circle of water ripple off its impact, so did our ideas. One person's thoughts attached to the next person's. We formed a quiescent center and each image propagated the next, traveling at different speeds in time we were caught up in the velocity and floated away on the wind -- saying goodbye to the Romani Realms forever.

We were home.

Chapter Twenty-Six

Left behind to clean up the mess of the party was Daniel, who slowly stacked the plates and then turned his attention to moving the extra chairs back into storage. They wouldn't be needed for a long time...if ever. The only time he had guests was when the Romani Realms magistrates insisted that he take part in quarterly Reckoning reporting meetings, which kept tabs on the status of everyone's minds.

He had taken to inviting them to his place for a meal, which appeased them enough so that he didn't have to be involved in the Hunting Committee. This had been going on for so long that they allowed Daniel to live his quiet existence, staying to himself and never upsetting the balance of the Romani Realms.

In his five years here, he had never met another woman who didn't somehow deserve this horrific existence...until Samantha, whose arrival was as much a mistake as his own.

It wasn't as if no woman had ever approached or propositioned him. Sure, he had felt desire toward them, but he was smart enough to know that any beautiful woman could just as easily be ugly and dark on the inside. They were as deceptive as the Arrival Meadows. One minute beautiful only to morph into the swamps and dark forests. Yes, the last thing he had wanted was to lose his virginity to someone and then wake up having found that he had been with a person who wasn't what he had been led to believe. In the real world he may have been ridiculed for remaining a virgin for so long, but here, he was proud that he had resisted and waited so that his first time was with Samantha.

But now an internal burning of desire pulsated through his body like never before. This was most definitely his own private hell...even if he had done his best to disguise it.

Few ever got to leave and Daniel had been here long enough to see how those who spent their days planning and plotting their departure only succumbed to madness. He picked up a hoe and mechanically started to tend to his land, drawing it back in the dirt to create rows of straight lines for his next crop. He whipped off his shirt and kept pulling the hoe through the land, working hard to break up the soil and rid it of any rocks that would interfere with the crop. The sun beat down on his shoulders, but he didn't mind. The rhythmical work had always done wonders to ease his mind in the past, and he longed to return himself to a state of not caring, just subsiding, as soon as possible. Otherwise, the memory of Samantha would certainly consume him.

The trees rustled with the movement of the blackbirds that were still perched above his house. He hated the audience. Seeing them reminded him of Samantha and the way it ended. He glanced skyward and one in particular seemed to meet his gaze head on and no sooner, swooped down to land by his feet.

He kicked at it, but it easily fluttered out of reach and yet remained nearby.

"Just go already," he said with irritation and then picked up his hoe again, and pointedly turned his back on the bird. They wouldn't invade his quiet place. He had worked out a deal with the magistrates. He agreed to live out his days here, but they would allow him certain liberties and freedoms. After all, his punishment of being here certainly didn't fit his crime. He should have been dead. That would have been kinder, but they needed at least one person of pure heart and intention in the Romani Realms.

The birds up above had now taken off, he noted with relief. He looked over his shoulder to check on the large remaining one, to see if it had given up on him as well. It was no where in sight and he turned back around to return to his garden when he was surprised by someone standing right in front of him. Raven.

Her hair was different from earlier that evening. No longer did it hang straight down her back. Now, a gentle wave graced her shiny locks. She wore a dress of all black as well, and although it appeared to be the same one as earlier, as he looked at her, the dress shifted imperceptibly. One minute it had a high rounded neck and the next, his eye was drawn to her cleavage placed upon attention due to a plunging neckline. Her skin looked nearly translucent, glistening with a glittery body powder.

"Alone again, eh Daniel?"

"It's fine. It is what it is."

"Is it?" she asked, and shamelessly allowed her eyes to wash over him, taking in his strong arms and broad chest. His toned abs glistened with a bit of sweat from the effort of his gardening...or from his proximity to Raven.

"I thought I would check in on you....You seem distracted."

Daniel turned his back to her and picked up his hoe again. "I'm fine."

Raven gently placed a hand on his back. He stopped his work and for a moment, just stood still, feeling the coolness of her touch. She reached around him and took his hoe from his hands before letting it drop to the ground. She placed her other hand on his back and slowly, moved both of them over his shoulders, rubbing away any tension and easing his troubled mind. Finally, he turned around to face her and she ran her hands over his chest. His breath hitched and his eyes once again went to her breasts, rising gently over the top of her dress.

"Do you see something you like?"

He shook his mind back to reality. "I just noticed the...that little red part of your dress..." he said referring to the handkerchief that was tucked into her cleavage. "It reminded me of the dress Samantha wore when I met her," he said trying to give Raven a message while refocusing his own thoughts. And yet, doing so only saddened him with the memories.

There was no doubt that being with Samantha had awoken something in him. Daniel swallowed as he looked at Raven, her eyes full of desire, staring at him hungrily. She reached between her breasts and pulled free the handkerchief. "It's actually not part of the dress."

Daniel swallowed hard. With the fabric removed, her neckline was exposed even more. "On second thought, it doesn't look like Samantha's dress after all."

"It's a shame that you're left behind. How will you cope?" She said moving even closer, placing one foot between his legs.

"I'm happier to have loved Samantha for a short time than never to have experienced a moment with her. I'm content because I know the one I love is safe."

Raven nodded as if accepting his explanation, but then with the handkerchief, she gently ran the silky fabric over his chest, drying away the signs of exertion, and relishing in the reaction that she knew she was causing. He closed his eyes and took in a deep breath.

"Well, now that you finally know the ways of love..." her voice trailed off, her intention clear.

Epilogue

They had been back in Los Angeles for a week, easily falling back into the casual lifestyle of Malibu where Charlotte joined Phineas in his home. Initially, Charlotte didn't like the idea of moving into the home that he had shared with Raven, but he assured her that it was only temporary and the view of the Pacific Ocean out his back window was unparalleled. At least they could live in luxury. Memories of Raven made it not ideal, but the truth of the matter was that one couldn't hide from Raven. If she wanted to find them, she would, but it seemed that she had remained in the Romani Realms.

With still one more wish beholden to Charlotte and Samantha, I was happy to have more time with the girls. I secretly hoped to be with them for the length of their lives, and they had no objection to that either. Both girls were wiser now, aware of how easily a wish could escape their thoughts especially if they believed someone to be in danger. For now, they relished in their companionship and took solace in being together so that no misunderstandings could arise.

They hadn't left each other's side since returning to the Realm of reality except in the evenings when Phineas held Charlotte close to him. Shadow had made it safely out of the Romani Realms, but in this Realm she was not yet born. As Phineas liked to joke, her presence was something of the future. For now, she was simply a mass of water and hydrogen--her human form yet to be realized.

Although Phineas had bonded with Shadow in the Romani Realms and considered himself lucky to be a father, he secretly hoped that he and Charlotte would have plenty of time to practice making a baby before they were actually blessed with the inevitable news that would befall them.

The morning sun was just coming through the curtains when Charlotte stretched awake. She turned over to smile at Phineas, who was already on his side waiting for her to stir. He kissed the tip of her nose.

"It's about time, sleepy head."

"You should've woken me," she said, suppressing a yawn and rolling into his arms. He felt so good. Strong and safe. Everything she wanted and craved. Almost.

She and Phineas had now been with each other at least half a dozen times, but Charlotte didn't think she would ever grow used to the knowledge that she held some power over him. She felt his excitement as she rolled on top of him, pressing her mouth into his neck.

"You're insatiable," he said in mock complaint.

"You love it."

"That I do," he said easily flipping her over, so that he was poised above her. She stared up at him, her eyes shining, her hair fanning over the pillow. "Charlotte, you are so beautiful. You're gentle and kind, and never did I think I would be so blessed to have you in my life."

"Well, you better get used to it. We've got a baby to make."

And with that, Phineas lowered his lips to hers, at first softly and then soon growing with a need that matched Charlotte's. He could kiss her forever and only allowed his lips to leave her in order to explore the rest of her body. He ran his mouth lightly over her neck and collarbone. As he let his tongue trail down her torso and stomach, she shuddered and dug her fingers into his hair, relishing what he was doing to her.

Their bodies intertwined and his knee gently edged Charlotte's leg aside and when he entered her, a soft moan escaped her mouth which he caught with his own. They moved like a waltz, slowly in rhythm until the crescendo of their dance took them to new heights. And when they had finished, again they relaxed in a gentle slumber, holding each other closely.

Charlotte was still getting dressed and Phineas had

just emerged from the shower when the doorbell sounded.

"It's probably them. Can you grab it?" Charlotte called from their room.

"Yeah, I've got it," he said wrapping a towel around his waist.

Phineas was always toned and strong, but since being in the Romani Realms where he navigated the treacherous terrain, not to mention fighting creatures at every turn, his physique had experienced considerable muscle development. His torso was beyond buff and when he answered the door, Samantha and I were momentarily silenced at the sight of him standing before us shirtless and wearing just a small towel.

"Jeez, put some clothes on, will you?" James complained.

"Good morning to you too," Phineas smiled, knowing that he had gained James' respect and friendship during their time together. "Welcome ladies," he said stepping aside to let us in. "Charlotte will be out in a second."

"Brought some beers for later," James said holding up the six-pack. "I'll put them in the refrigerator for you. I wouldn't want you to strain yourself."

"You know the way." Phineas smirked and went to turn on the television. They were looking forward to watching USC beat Stanford while the girls caught up with some shopping.

Charlotte emerged from the bedroom and immediately kissed Phineas. "Have fun. We'll be back after lunch."

He held onto her tightly, wrapping his arms completely around her small waist.

"Come on, you two...we've got shops to hit," Samantha said lightly.

I caught James' eye and blew him a kiss. "Play nicely."

He grumbled a reply under his breath before we left, and I laughed at his mock annoyance over Phineas. The five of us had been inseparable since our return and it was obvious that Samantha and Charlotte's BFF status had now spread to James and Phineas, although James would deny that to the end.

Yet, as we shopped, Samantha wasn't her usual jovial self. While Charlotte and I nattered on about where to have lunch, debating whether Sweet Lady Jane on Melrose had better desserts than La Conversation on Doheny, she remained uninvolved.

"What's wrong, Sweets?" I asked.

"I feel like a third wheel."

Charlotte and I looked at each other, truly confused by the comment. "We didn't mean to leave you out. Where would you like to go?"

"No, it's not with us. It's when you guys are with James and Phineas. I'm...alone. I know you wanted me home, but I'm beginning to think that my home is with Daniel."

A hush fell between us until Samantha verbalized what I already knew to be in her mind.

"Suki...Charlotte...I need him in my life...even if that means returning to the Romani Realms."

The Romani Realms

Released

Resurrected

Returned

About the Author

Mia Fox is a Los Angeles-based novelist who writes across varied genres including Young Adult/New Adult Paranormal Romance and Chick Lit. She received her Bachelor of Arts Degree in Communications from U.S.C. followed by a Masters Degree in Professional Writing also from U.S.C.

A lifelong reader and history lover, Mia loves infusing her own writing with details of the past. Her other interests include cooking and baking. Fortunately, she is also a yoga enthusiast, which proves useful in keeping her other passion -- eating -- in check.

Mia is happily married to her best-friend, a Brit who has inspired her with annual visits to England, an appreciation for dark chocolate, and the blessing of their three children.

Mia's books are available from Amazon, Barnes and Noble, iBooks, and Kobo.

Stay tuned for "Returned," the final installment of the Romani Realms series.

Keep in touch with Mia...

Website:
www.miafox.net

Facebook
www.facebook.com/MiaFoxBooks

Twitter
@MiaFoxBooks

www.ingramcontent.com/pod-product-compliance
Lightning Source LLC
Chambersburg PA
CBHW020242200626
46816CB00001BA/82